BURNED

PERFECTLY IMPERFECT SERIES

dreams

NEVA ALTAJ

For my readers who wanted to read Az's story (and asked for a "reunion" scene with Sergei to be included).
I hope you'll like it.

TRIGGER WARNING

Please be aware that this book contains content some readers may find disturbing, such as mentions of a deceased spouse, domestic violence and abuse, graphic descriptions of violence and torture, and gore.

BURNED

dreams

PERFECTLY IMPERFECT SERIES

Tabs

Romance

Spice

Sad

Quotes

Quotes

Love

Real Life

prologue

━━•━•━•━🂠Alessandro🂠•━•━•━━

Nineteen years ago (Alessandro—eighteen years old)

THERE ARE TWO RULES WHEN IT COMES TO PICKING locks.

One—all locks have weak points.

Two—some weak points are more exploitable than others.

That's the first thing my old man taught me when he took me along to do a job. Too bad that was almost ten years ago, and some of his teachings don't apply anymore.

I put the flashlight into my mouth and take the lock pick and the tension wrench, focusing the light on the lock in front of me. The damn thing doesn't have any apparent exploitable weak points, so the only way to crack it will be by disassembling it with skill and sheer determination.

A dog barks somewhere down the street. I pause and listen. The frigid autumn wind blows around me, swirling the dry leaves through the air, and the cold seeps through the thin hoodie into my bones. I left my jacket with Natalie at the house because the heating isn't working, and it's been too chilly inside. She caught pneumonia last month, and I didn't want to risk her getting sick again.

Another round of barking from a dog, but moments later, silence descends over the neighborhood. I cast a glance around me to make sure there aren't any nosy neighbors close by, then focus back on the lock. Fucking pins and their pressure system. As if disarming the alarm system wasn't enough, I now need to handle this sophisticated shit, as well.

I'm nearly finished when I feel the touch of cold metal on the back of my neck.

"Hands where I can see them," a male voice says behind me, "and turn around, slowly."

Fuck.

I let my tools fall to the ground and raise my hands in the air as I straighten up and turn. A man dressed in jeans and a leather jacket stands in front of me with his gun pointed at my face. What the fuck? I spent three nights casing the joint and the neighborhood and hadn't noticed any security patrols. This guy is holding the gun as if he knows what he's doing. An off-duty cop?

"You're coming with me," he says.

Yeah. Not happening.

The guy seems fit, and the weapon does give him an advantage. I'd rather risk death than end up in jail like my old man, who's serving a thirteen-year sentence. I relax my jaw, allowing the flashlight to fall from my mouth. The motion distracts the guy, allowing me to quickly shift my position and get the leverage I'm after. Grabbing the asshole's wrist with both hands, I twist his arm to one side and slam my knee into his stomach. The guy bends over, coughing. I knee him again, this time to his face, while I try to pry his fingers off the gun.

It fires, a gunshot piercing the still air, and the bullet hits the door behind me.

I'm still trying to wrestle his gun away when I hear approaching steps behind me. I glance over my shoulder just in time to see a fist coming at my face.

"Your name, kid?"

I spit blood and meet the gaze of a middle-aged man in tactical clothing looming over me. The dim light from the bare bulb hanging from the ceiling behind him makes the shadows on his face more profound, emphasizing the line of his tightly clenched jaw.

"Az," I bite out and take a quick look around the room.

When the motherfuckers hauled me over here, I thought they were taking me to the police station, but now it's clear that's not the case. I have no idea where exactly they dragged me or what this facility is, but it most certainly isn't a police station. The walls are bare, there are no windows, and the air seems stale, almost as if we're underground. From my kneeling position in the center of the room, the only point of exit I can see is the door on the opposite wall.

The man in the tactical gear curses, obviously not happy with my answer. He appears to be the one in charge.

"I want your full name, not a stupid street name!" he yells.

There's no way I'm giving him my name. I've put in a lot of effort to make sure I'm not on the cops' radar and there isn't a record of me in the system. Even if anyone runs my prints, they won't get anything. And I never carry ID when I'm on a job.

When I don't respond, he nods to the man on my right.

Another blow hits my chin, snapping my head to the side, nearly making me lose my balance as I kneel on the concrete floor. This guy seems hell-bent on dislocating my jaw. I shake my head to clear the fog out of my brain a bit.

A pair of black polished shoes enters my vision. I tilt my head up and observe an older man with glasses who's now standing next to the boss guy. I noticed him the moment he entered the room, which was shortly after the motherfuckers started beating the shit out of me. He was standing at the side up until now. The man's unassuming tweed jacket, complete with elbow patches, and checked shirt seem entirely out of place. He reminds me of my history teacher.

"He won't cooperate, Kruger," the tweed jacket guy says. "The boy is too old for your project, anyway. And too stubborn. Why don't we just put him back where you found him?"

"Are you telling me how to run my unit, Felix?" the boss guy barks. "You need to remember your fucking place."

"The kid is just a small-time thief. Why bother?"

"Because during the two months my men have been following him, he managed to break into eleven houses with top-notch security, without setting off the alarms, a skill that would be extremely valuable to us," Kruger says and turns to face me. "Where did you learn to bypass the security systems like that, boy?"

I spit out another mouthful of blood. "Suck my dick."

"Tsk, tsk, tsk . . ." He shakes his head. "Looks like you need an incentive to cooperate. How about I have one of my men go grab that girl of yours and bring her here? I'm pretty sure she won't take the beating as well as you do."

My body goes stone-still. How the fuck does he know about Natalie?

"Oh, I see that got your attention." He smiles. "I always

4

make sure I get to know the person I'm considering recruiting. Their strong points. And their weaknesses."

"You won't touch her," I sneer.

"No? Well, it depends on you, Az. If you do what I say, no one will touch your girl. In fact, you'll soon be making good money. More than enough to get her out of that dump the two of you have been living in."

Blood from the cut on my forehead drips into my eyes, making it hard to see. My hands are tied behind my back so I try blinking it away, but it doesn't help much.

"Do what?" I ask.

"Work for the government. Or, more specifically, me."

I let my eyes glide around the room one more time, trying to figure out a possible way to escape. To reach the door on the opposite wall, I would need to overpower the men holding me down, as well as this Kruger guy. All of them are armed, but it's not impossible. The old man in the tweed jacket shouldn't pose a problem. He looks more like an accountant or something. What's he gonna do, throw a calculator at me?

"And if I say no?" I ask.

Kruger's lips curve into an evil sneer. Reaching into a pocket of his tactical pants, he takes out a photo and throws it on the floor in front of me. The picture flips twice in the air before it lands face up. I stare at the slightly blurry face of my girlfriend. The shot was taken while Natalie was exiting the grocery store where she works.

"Let me demonstrate what's going to happen if you don't cooperate." He takes out a knife from a sheath strapped to his belt, crouches in front of me, and thrusts the tip of the blade right into the middle of Natalie's face. "Do I make myself clear?"

I don't have the slightest idea who these dickheads are

or what their plan for me is. Government, my ass. What interest would they have in someone like me? But the fucker knows where we live. I won't risk them hurting my girl. So, moving my eyes off the photo, I meet the sinister gaze of the boss guy. "Yes."

A smirk pulls at his lips. "See, Felix? He's not stubborn at all. Trained properly, he'll make a perfect soldier." The son of a bitch laughs. "Won't you, Az?"

CHAPTER
one

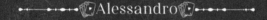

Alessandro

Eight years ago

"**A**z."

I remove the last of my guns and look up at Felix, who's standing by my locker.

"Kruger wants to talk with you," he says. "It's urgent."

I nod and remove the bulletproof vest, wincing as the pain from the hit I took spreads through my chest. It was supposed to be a simple recon mission, but we were ambushed by the security team twenty minutes in. Belov caught a blade across his arm, but considering it was just the two of us against fourteen guards, we did well. I close the locker and peer at the blond man sitting on the bench by the wall. Sergei Belov is staring ahead with vacant eyes, and if his chest wasn't moving, I would think he's dead. Of all the guys who were dragged into this fucking program, he always seemed like the most normal one. Until he started going nuts a few years ago. He probably never hurt anyone before Kruger inducted him and shaped him into a cold-blooded killer. Just as he did with the rest of the boys who ended up in the Z.E.R.O. unit.

"You need to get Belov out," I say.

"I know." Felix sighs and squeezes the bridge of his nose. "I'm working on it."

I give the old man a once-over. The relationship between the operatives and their handlers in our unit is supposed to be strictly businesslike. Typically, handlers provide support from a base of operations—mostly data collection and surveillance during the mission—but the relationship between Felix and Sergei has always been different. I doubt anyone besides me has ever noticed, the old man is too careful to never show favoritism, but Felix cares about him, and not just as an asset. He looks after Sergei as if he is his own kid, making sure Belov doesn't snap and start killing people left, right, and center whenever he gets into one of his fucked-up moods.

"Work harder." I grab my jacket and leave the changing room.

Flickering lights cast long shadows on the bare concrete walls as I walk down the hallway leading to Captain Kruger's office. You'd expect the headquarters of a secret military base—one that has been in operation for over a decade now—to be a bit more polished, but instead, it's just concrete walls, electrical wires fixed to the walls with plastic hooks, and the pervasive smell of mold. It's better on the upper levels. These were used as sleeping quarters for the new recruits when the program first came into existence, but they haven't been occupied in years.

The Z.E.R.O. unit is a highly classified project, kept off the books, that has a single purpose—to dispose of people deemed unwanted by the government or by Captain

Kruger. Quickly, efficiently, and without a paper trail. It started as an eleven-man unit—five operatives, five handlers, and the captain. Now, we're down to six. Three operatives, two handlers, and Kruger. It doesn't appear like they're planning on taking on any new recruits, so the program will probably be shut down when Sergei, Kai, and I end up dead.

I'm halfway to Kruger's office when the elevator doors down the hall open, and a man steps out. The coat he's wearing is unbuttoned, revealing a white shirt covered in blood stains. Kai Mazur. The last in our trio of operatives.

He turns left and heads toward Kruger's office as well, his long jet-black braid swinging like a tail across his back. I always wondered why Kruger allowed him to keep his hair that length. The success of our missions relies on being covert, and it's really hard not to notice a six-foot-five guy with a braid hanging down to nearly his waist.

As he walks down the corridor, blood drips onto the floor from the brown paper bag in Kai's right hand, leaving red splotches on the concrete. Looks like the captain wanted a souvenir again, and judging from the size of the bag, it's probably someone's hand. When Kai reaches the office door, he drops the bag, and it makes a disgusting grotesque sound as it hits the floor. It might not be a hand after all.

Kai nods at me as we pass each other, and I notice a badly stitched cut on his chin that still oozes blood. He probably sewed himself up again. Since he killed his handler, medical personnel refuse to treat him unless he's sedated.

I grab the doorknob and step over the bloody bag on the floor, entering the captain's office. Kruger is seated behind the desk, watching the monitor in front of him and reviewing the mission reports. I wonder what he'll do when he finds me unreachable tomorrow.

He'll likely send someone to dispose of me. Probably Kai. Natalie and I will be long gone by the time that happens, though. I'd already decided this would be my last mission and, before I left, instructed my wife to pack and be ready to go the moment I get home. I tried calling her twice on my way back to the base, but the call went to voice mail.

"Have a seat, Az." Kruger motions at the chair on the other side of his desk.

"I'll stand."

"Suit yourself." He reaches for his coffee and takes a sip. "Your wife was in a traffic accident this morning."

My vision blurs as I process his words. I grab the back of the chair. "What?"

"The hospital staff mentioned that she may not make it through the night, so I guess you should head over there," he says nonchalantly, looking back toward the screen, as if discussing weather.

I turn around and storm out, while my heart climbs into my throat.

I stare at the doctor's lips as he speaks as if that will help his words penetrate into my brain.

". . . multiple fractures that resulted in massive internal bleeding . . ."

I can't make sense of what he's saying. It's like my mind won't accept it.

". . . resuscitated her twice . . ."

I grab the front of his white coat and press him to the wall. The words keep pouring from his mouth, and, with every syllable, rage and despair brew inside my chest. I need the motherfucker to stop speaking!

"... we tried. I'm so sorry."

My hold on the man's coat wanes. I want to smash his head into that wall until he takes back everything he said, but I seem to have lost the feeling in my hands.

"I want to see her," I bark into his face. "Now."

The doctor nods and steps out of my reach. My ears are ringing as I follow him down the hall until he stops at the door on the right.

"Leave," I say, gripping the knob.

I can hear the footsteps retreating, but I only stare at the door in front of me. It's a plain, pale-blue piece of wood, but for me, it feels like I'm standing at the gate of doom. The rage that consumed me earlier has evaporated, and the only thing left in my chest is soul-shattering pain. I grip the knob harder but can't make myself go inside. There's still a sliver of hope, a desperate thought at the back of my mind that this is some big mistake. It's someone else's wife in there. My Natalie is at home, sitting in her favorite chair in our living room, waiting for me to come back so we can finally leave.

I can still remember the day we met like it happened yesterday. She was trying to steal a wallet from a man in the snack aisle of a gas station in full view of the security camera. I dragged her outside and gave her an earful about how terrible of a pickpocket she was. We were both seventeen at the time and living on the streets, but it was as plain as day that she wasn't cut out for that life. I usually didn't give a fuck about other people, but I guess I saw a part of myself

in her that day. So, I took her to the abandoned house I
used to crash at after my old man ended up in jail two years
earlier. She was only supposed to stay a few days but never
ended up leaving.

I taught her how to pickpocket with finesse and even
took her with me to some smaller jobs. It was good to have
someone to come home to. To share the good and the bad.
And considering the conditions in which we lived in those
times, there was more bad than good. I'm not sure how our
comradery transformed into love. It crept up on me without my noticing, like a stream wearing away stone grain by
tiny grain. We were both young, neither one of us had any
family or anyone else left in the world, so we had to fend for
ourselves. It was the two of us against everyone else in this
fucked-up city. Friendship became affection, then reshaped
into something deeper. She became the only good thing in
my miserable life.

When Kruger nabbed me and made me join his
fucked-up team of killers, I promised myself I would dance
to his tune until I got enough money to move Natalie and
me far away, somewhere he wouldn't be able to find us.
I figured it would take me a year or two to save enough
money so we could disappear.

I was wrong.

In order to get off Kruger's radar, I couldn't use any
of the IDs I already had because he could track those. I
needed new documents for me and Natalie, and Kruger
had connections everywhere—the government, the police,
the underground, every fucking place. Getting new identities without him finding out was close to impossible. I
knew way too much to be let off the hook easily, so I had to
make sure I didn't raise any red flags. If I did, both Natalie

and I would end up dead. It took me years, several hundred thousand, and four dead bodies to find channels Kruger couldn't trace. I got the damn papers a week before I went on this mission.

And now she's gone. Some asshole has taken away the only family I had.

Closing my eyes, I open the door and step inside the room.

I throw the last of the empty jerry cans to the side and observe my reflection in the front picture window, the setting sun at my back. The panels on either side of the large pane are open, and the gasoline fumes permeate the air. I bought this house three years after I joined the Z.E.R.O. unit because I hated living in a rental. I purchased it right before I asked Natalie to marry me. It was just a dull brick-and-mortar thing, but it was the only place that felt like home to me after a very long time. And now, it's returned to being nothing more than a pile of brick and mortar again.

Pulling the lighter out of my pocket, I flick the wheel, sparking the flame, and throw it through the open window. The lighter lands on the gasoline-saturated furniture, igniting the fire, and by the time I reach my car, the blaze is already consuming the curtains.

Once I'm behind the wheel, I reach for the old metal box on the passenger seat. Atop the pile of passports and other IDs lies a silver bracelet charm of a teddy bear with a pink bow that I bought for Natalie years ago with the money I stole during one of my jobs. She was obsessed with bears of any kind, probably because they reminded her of the carefree childhood she had before she ended up on the streets. I don't think I ever saw her without that silly charm. The hospital staff removed the bracelet when they took her to surgery, and the chain got lost along the way. Only the teddy bear charm was included with her belongings when they were returned to me.

My eyes shift to the key chain hanging on the rearview mirror. A shiny pendant of a poker hand—a royal flush no less. The metal clasp attaching the pendant to the ring broke long ago, so now it's just secured with a leather string. My dad gave me that thing after I beat him at poker the very first time, and I've kept it all these years to remind me of him and one of his other lessons: Don't just accept the hand you've been dealt in life. Sometimes, you need to be the dealer.

I take the key chain off the mirror and remove the pendant from the string, throwing it into the metal box. Holding the teddy bear charm in one hand, I thread the leather through the loop at the top, then tie the string around my wrist.

When I look up toward the house, the fire is already eating at its sides. I lean back in the driver's seat and watch the flames annihilate what was once my home, as well as the last fragments of my soul.

I was never a good man. The first time I took a life, I was barely sixteen. It was in self-defense, but it doesn't change the fact. When you live on the streets, in the worst part of the city, it's either kill or be killed. Survival.

Not much humanity was left in me by the time I met Natalie, but having her by my side helped save those pitiful remnants. She became my purpose. The only thing that kept my heart from becoming an unbreachable cold rock.

I never told her the truth about my "work," fearing that she'd get scared of me. Natalie believed I was a security guard at a military installation and never knew she was living with a killer. Sometimes, I wanted to confide in her, to tell her about some of my missions, but I didn't think she would be able to handle it, so I kept my mouth shut. Having her with me was enough.

But she's gone now, and she took everything good with her. Hope. Dreams. Love. The only things left are agony and rage. From this fury within, a bloodthirsty, feral beast rises, asking for retribution. Blood. Death. The pices we give die with other is.

I don't give a fuck if what happened to my wife was an accident. Don't care if it was a high-as-kite kid or someone's grandfather with failing eyesight who was driving the car that hit her. I'm going to find them. And they will pay.

I take the stack of documents from the metal box and start leafing through them, looking at different names on each. Multiple identities are a necessity when your job description includes killing people for a living. My hand stops on the last ID, a name I haven't used for almost a decade. Alessandro Zanetti. Kruger kept pestering me about my real name for months, but I never caved, even after he had his men break my arm, and he finally dropped the subject. He had no use for a soldier who couldn't go on missions because he was too roughed up, and all recruits used fake names and IDs anyway. I'm not sure why I was so stubborn about it. Maybe because my name was the only thing I truly owned at that time. Or it could have been because I simply enjoyed pissing Kruger off.

Grabbing the stack of fake IDs and passports, including the documents I got last week, I throw them out of the window. It seems fitting to use my real name when I kill the bastard responsible for my wife's death.

By the time I put the car in reverse and pull out of the driveway, the flames have already reached the roof, turning my home into ash.

 **Ravenna**

Four months ago

The rain is relentless, drenching my already wet jacket and plastering my hair to my face. I forgot my umbrella at work, too shocked by the news that the diner where I work will be closing next week. That leaves me with only my part-time job at an accounting firm, which isn't enough, and I'll need to start looking for something else right away.

I'm trying to move one of the wet strands out of my eyes when a truck zooms by me on my left, racing down the empty but puddle-covered street and splashing me with the dirty curb water. A sigh of defeat leaves my lips as I stop in the middle of the deserted sidewalk and look at my new white sneakers which are now soaked and stained in muck.

Even though I'm still being pelted by the torrential rain, I can't look away from my shoes. Yesterday, I felt a little guilty because money is tight this month, but I was so excited when I left the store after purchasing my runners. If I knew that I'd be losing my job today, I never would have bought them.

The blaring of a car horn pulls me away from my thoughts, and I look up to see Melania, my best friend since high school, waving at me from the driver's window of her car.

"Jesus, Ravi!" she yells. "Get in!"

I rush toward her vehicle and open the passenger door, but when my eyes fall on the nice interior and the dry seat I just shake my head. "I'm all muddy."

"Oh, for God's sake. Just get in, Ravenna." Melania leans toward me and grabs my hand, pulling me inside.

"Late shift?" I ask as I put on the seat belt. Melania works at a pharmacy just down the street.

"Yeah. I should have been done by midnight, but we had some deliveries that came in late, so I had to sort that out. We got that pain balm you asked about for Mamma Lola."

I nod. Considering the situation, I'm not sure we can afford it at the moment.

"I saw Vitto when I was heading to work this afternoon," she continues as she pulls back onto the street. "He was with Ugo."

"I told him that I don't want him hanging out with that kid, but he won't listen. That dude is a bad influence."

"Are they stealing again?"

I lean back on the headrest and close my eyes. My brother has been extremely difficult over the past year. "I hope not. The grocery store manager said he'll file a police report if he catches them again."

"Maybe you could try to find him a job for the summer. I can ask around if you want?"

"Yeah, that would be great," I say even though I know nothing will come of it.

Since our father died a year ago, Vitto started hanging out at places where Cosa Nostra members gather, doing small errands for them from time to time, hoping he'll get offered to take over a soldier position that our father held. Both my mom and I have been doing our best to get that idiotic idea out of his head, but to no avail. I forbade him from going to any of those places, but I'm sure he's still doing it in secret.

"He's going to come around, Ravi. You'll see." Melania parks the car in front of my building and reaches over to squeeze my hand.

"I hope so." I squeeze hers in return and open the door. "It was only one block. You didn't need to drive me."

"I still owe you for all the math homework you did for me back in high school." She laughs. "Say hi to Mamma Lola for me."

"I will."

My wet sneakers make squishy sounds as I run toward the building and then up the four flights of stairs. Trying to be as quiet as possible, I let myself inside the apartment and head straight to the bathroom to change when my mother's trembling voice comes from behind me.

"Vitto isn't home, yet."

I turn around and stare at my mother with dread. It's almost three in the morning. My brother might be problematic, but he's never stayed out all night without letting me or my mom know. "What do you mean?"

"He went out with his friends and said he'll be back by eleven," my mom chokes out. "His phone is off."

"Why didn't you call me?"

"You were working. I thought he was just late, so I laid down on the couch to wait for him. I fell asleep." She bursts out crying. "I tried calling his friends, but no one has seen him."

"Shit. I'm so sorry, Mamma." I wrap my arms around her and try to make my voice steady. "He probably went to sleep over at Ugo's and forgot to call you."

"Maybe we should call the police, Ravi."

I close my eyes. "You know we can't."

We might not be active members of Cosa Nostra, but my father was. We can't risk attracting the attention of the police unless it's absolutely necessary.

"What if something happened to him?"

"He's okay. I'm going to call Ugo, and we'll find him." I'm reaching for my phone when a hard, loud knock sounds at the door.

My mother's eyes widen in fear, and a tear rolls down her cheek. When someone knocks on your door at three in the morning, it can't be anything good. I dash across the room, throwing the door open.

A man in a dark suit is standing on the other side of the threshold. I've never seen him before, but one look at his stance and the holster visible under his unbuttoned jacket says enough. Cosa Nostra.

"Ravenna Cattaneo?" he asks, staring me down.

"Yes," I choke out.

"You need to come with me."

"Is this about my brother? Is he okay?"

"For now." The Cosa Nostra soldier grabs me by the arm and ushers me down the hallway. He doesn't even wait for me to take my purse or jacket.

"Everything is going to be okay, Mamma," I call over my shoulder as I try to keep pace. My mother is standing in the doorway, one of her hands gripping the frame and the other pressed over her mouth as she watches me leave.

When we exit the building, and the man approaches a black car with tinted windows, I get inside without asking questions. I squeeze my hands in my lap while we drive, trying to keep myself together. Vitto must have fucked up terribly this time for Cosa Nostra to come to our apartment in the middle of the night. Was my brother caught stealing again? Or maybe he said something he shouldn't have? Oh God, if he ratted on someone, he's as good as dead.

The car turns into a narrow alley and stops in front of a restaurant with red and white checkered curtains. I don't recognize the place right away because I'd only been here once when I had to bring my father his wallet after he forgot it at home. He was on guard duty in the back room.

I step out of the car and look up at the wooden sign above the door. Luigi's. The place where Cosa Nostra soldiers come to play cards.

The driver wordlessly guides me among the empty tables toward the doorway at the far end of the room. A woman with a stained white apron is washing dishes and stares as we pass through the kitchen. When we reach the door hidden behind a curtain next to the wine crates, the man opens it and pushes me into the concealed room. The door closes behind me.

Inside, the air is filled with heavy cigar smoke, making it hard to breathe. The light from the fixture above the big round table illuminates the forms of four men seated around it, playing poker. I take a few steps into the room, and the one facing me looks up from his cards and leans back while a smug smile pulls at his lips. I take an involuntary step back. It's one of the capos. Rocco Pisano.

"We're done for tonight," he says and throws his cards in the middle of the table.

The other three men stand up, their chairs scraping against the floor as they rise, and collect their belongings. None of them meet my gaze as they pass me and leave the room. The door closes behind them with a soft click, but I flinch from how ominous that small sound feels.

"You sent for me, Mr. Pisano," I choke out, trying to

maintain eye contact without cowering. I don't like the way he looks at me—like a cat who just got an unexpected treat.

"I did." Rocco reaches for his drink and leans back in his chair, observing my drenched clothes. "There's a debt that needs to be settled."

A sinking feeling takes hold in the pit of my stomach. "A debt?"

"Yes." He smiles and shifts his gaze to something behind me. "Isn't that right, Vitto?"

I swivel around, and a strangled cry leaves my lips when my eyes fall on the curled body in the corner. My brother looks up, his face is smeared with blood, and one of his eyes is swollen shut.

"Oh my God." I take a step toward him but the sound of a palm hitting the table stops me midstep.

"Come here, or I'm going to finish what I started!" Rocco roars.

I swallow the bile and make myself turn around to face the capo. Rocco nods toward the chair across from him and watches as I approach on shaky legs.

"Sit," he snaps.

I drop down onto the chair and clasp my hands on my lap. I don't know what's going on or what the hell my brother is doing here, but I know it's bad.

Rocco takes a drag of his cigar and blows the smoke in my face. "Vitto here thought he could play poker with the big fish. He came in earlier tonight, waving a stack of money, asking to be allowed into the game."

I close my eyes for a moment, trying to stop the tears from falling. My father's death hit my brother hard, and Vitto's been causing problems ever since. Bad company. Stealing.

Even selling marijuana. But I never expected he'd be crazy enough to come to a Cosa Nostra place to gamble.

"He's only fifteen," I whisper.

"The boy needs a lesson. He's old enough to be held responsible for his words and actions." Rocco smirks. "And old enough to pay."

"How much does he owe you?"

"The four grand he brought was just enough for the initial deposit."

Four grand. I wring my fingers. There is only one place where my brother could have gotten that money. The old cookie tin that's under my bed. I've been working since high school to save money for college. Most of it went to cover the medicine when my father got sick, but I managed to save up about four grand in the last year.

"I'll visit the bank and see if I can get a loan," I say. "We'll return every cent Vitto owes you, but please let my brother go."

"I doubt any bank would give you a loan big enough to cover the amount your brother owes me. So, Vitto and I came to an agreement, one that will benefit us both. I will forget about the money and won't kill him." He blows the smoke into my face again. "And I will take you as repayment."

CHAPTER
Two

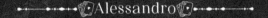

🂠Alessandro🂠

Present day

THE SNOW CRUNCHES UNDER THE TIRES AS I PARK MY
car in the driveway of a huge gray stone mansion. It's
almost six in the evening, but that's the time I was
ordered to report for duty. I turn off the ignition and lean
back in my seat, regarding the house through the windshield.
Given the location and the size of the surrounding property,
it's probably worth five or six million, but it's smaller than I
expected. Only two floors.

It's a beautiful home.

And it'll burn magnificently.

I exit the car and head toward the wide stone steps leading to the stained wood double front doors. Earlier, as I drove
in, I noticed two guards at the gate. At least three more are
positioned on the outside of the high perimeter wall that surrounds the property, but there are none at the front entrance
or anywhere around the house. From what I've gathered, my
new employer doesn't allow anyone from his security team

close to the house. That's most likely the reason why every inch of the estate grounds surrounding the house is monitored by cameras.

As I set my foot on the first stone step, the front door opens, revealing a man in a light-gray three-piece suit. The yellowish light from the hall beyond illuminates his tall, lanky form as he stands before me with a smug expression on his face. Rocco Pisano. A capo in the New York crime family.

"Zanetti," he says as he motions for me to follow him. "I'll brief you in my office. It'll have to be quick. We have to be at the theater in two hours."

I walk a few paces behind him as he turns left and leads me across the spacious marble foyer toward the sliding wooden door on the far side. The interior screams opulence, and my steps echo off the walls and the high ceiling adorned with stucco decorations. Fresco paintings on the ceiling show angels in vibrant colors, looking down on us. Pieces of baroque dark wood furniture that's been polished to a shine are positioned in the corners. A wide stairwell leads to the upper floor, and the elaborate wooden banister has flowers, vines and other decorative shit carved into it.

Pisano's office is equally large. A massive wooden desk in a deep cherry finish takes up the central spot. On its surface, close to the edge, is a thick, carved nameplate that matches the desk veneer.

The rest of the room displays similar examples of gaudy. There's an enormous crystal chandelier, which is more suitable for a dining room than an office. Two life-size gold sculptures of crouching lions as if they're on guard are set on either side of his desk, and massive bookshelves line the wall behind it. The books are protected by gold-en-framed glass doors.

Rocco takes a seat behind his desk and reaches for the wooden box containing high-end cigars. As he picks up one of the *puros*, the light from the chandelier overhead reflects off a thick gold ring with a massive ruby stone on his bony index finger.

Eight years. Eight fucking years I've been searching for this man and here he is, finally sitting before me. I can barely manage to control the urge to wrap my hands around his throat, snapping his neck on the spot. But I haven't waited this long to let him off with a simple, swift death. No. I will destroy him, piece by little piece, and he's going to watch. Only when there is nothing left of his gilded life will he be allowed to meet his maker. And I'll make sure the path we take to his final destination will be very, very lengthy. And extremely excruciating.

Rocco's eyes don't leave me as he cuts the tip and places the cigar in his mouth as if he's trying to make an impression. He also doesn't offer me a seat in one of the chairs positioned in front of his desk.

"So, I heard you don't like women," he says as he lights the cigar. "Is that true?"

I've been expecting the question. The boss told me Rocco was pathologically jealous, and that he killed the last three bodyguards assigned to his wife. The only reason I'm taking over the role is because Rocco believes I'm gay. I'm not entirely sure where the idea had come from, but Ajello mentioned that's exactly what Rocco thinks of me. Perhaps he heard that I never go to the strip club frequented by the other Cosa Nostra soldiers every Thursday night. Or maybe he figures I'm gay because I turned away the girls that idiot Carmelo sent to my place as a gift for my fifth anniversary of joining the Family. It doesn't really matter to me what gave him that impression. I hold his gaze and nod.

"Your secret is safe with me." Rocco's lips curve upward. "Let's get down to business. You will be in charge of my wife's safety, twenty-four seven. As you've probably noticed, guards aren't allowed inside the house. That only changes when we have guests over. Otherwise, the only people in this house are me and my wife. We also have a housekeeper and two maids. They come at eight and leave at seven."

"Security systems?" I ask.

"Alarms on front and back doors, as well as ground floor windows. Cameras outside the house and along the perimeter wall. They're monitored from the guardhouse at the gate. Three shifts of security guards, five men on each."

"My tasks?"

"You have only one. My wife," he says and leans back in his chair. "Ravenna is not allowed to leave the house without supervision. She likes to go for walks around the property, so when she does, you're to go with her. Also, she often heads out shopping and to do other female shit. Hairdresser. Manicure. You'll be with her wherever she needs to venture out."

"Any exceptions?"

"No exceptions. If she needs to go to a fucking gynecologist, you're going with her." He gets up off his chair and comes to stand in front of me. "Your job isn't to simply act as Ravenna's security detail. That's secondary. What I need you to do is follow her every step and report anything suspicious to me."

"What's considered suspicious?"

"Talking to other men. Or strangers in general, women included. She's not allowed to make calls from your phone or anyone else's, either. She has a cell with the only numbers she's permitted to call programmed into it, and she's to use that phone only. Her daily agenda is to be confirmed with me every morning. No deviations are permissible."

control freak

I keep my face expressionless as I mull over what he said. The woman must either be a ditz or a pushover if she's okay with being controlled in this manner, but that's not my problem.

"Understood."

"You'll keep this with you." He reaches into his pocket and pulls out his wallet, handing me a credit card. "Let her use it when she needs to purchase something, then take it back."

Maybe Mrs. Pisano likes to indulge herself too much? I take the card and nod.

Rocco tilts his head to the side. "You don't talk much, do you?"

"No."

"Perfect." He heads toward the door. "Ravenna should be down at any moment."

As I follow him out of the room, I wonder what the woman I'm going to kill looks like in person.

♥ Ravenna ♥

I tilt my chin up, looking at my reflection in the mirror. Three layers of foundation did their thing. The bruise on my neck isn't visible, and the wide diamond choker necklace covers what the makeup couldn't. It's been four days, so hopefully, it'll fade soon.

Picking up my coat off the back of the chair, I exit my bedroom. My husband's room is just across from mine, and I can't suppress a shudder as my eyes fall on his door before I head down the hall to the main staircase. *Soon,* I tell myself. I just need a few months more.

Rocco is standing at the foot of the stairs, watching me descend. His eyes do a quick pass over the dress I'm wearing, and his lips widen into a satisfied smile. When he came to my room earlier, he threw the dress and necklace at me, ordering me to wear it tonight. I waited for him to leave before I took a look at the red gown. It's worse than the previous dress he bought me, and the idea of going out, especially to the theater in that thing, makes me feel so ashamed, but that's nothing new.

I'm so engrossed in calculating how much money I still need until there's enough for my escape and what would be the fastest way to earn more, that I don't notice the man standing by the door until I reach the landing. When I do, my steps falter for a moment, but somehow, I manage to cover up my near trip. My husband is a tall man, but the person behind him is almost a head taller.

"Ravenna, bellissima, you look stunning." Rocco smiles as I approach and takes my hand. "This is Alessandro Zanetti, your new bodyguard."

Trying my best to keep my face blank, I throw another look at the man standing with his hands behind his back. The stance emphasizes his broad frame as the muscles in his arms strain against the material of his black suit jacket. He's probably the largest man I've ever met. My gaze travels up his wide chest and stops on his face. Sinister. That's the first word that comes to mind. He's cleanly shaven, with a strong jaw and sharp cheekbones, but it's not his face or his enormous bulk that makes me want to step back. It's the things I see in his dark eyes. Hate. Loathing. And barely contained rage. I want to look away, but I can't. It's as if his eyes ensnare me and keep me prisoner. If looks could kill, I'm pretty sure I would be dead on the spot.

I make myself nod and finally glance away, focusing my eyes on the front entrance. As we pass through the door Alessandro is holding open for us, I can feel his eyes on me the entire time, all the way to my husband's car. Only once I've slid onto the passenger seat and Rocco has closed the car door do I let myself exhale.

In the side-view mirror, I spot my new bodyguard walking to a black SUV, his steps slow and calculated. Just before he gets in, he looks up toward our car. There is no way he can tell I'm watching him, but somehow, I know he does. The vibe of hostility he's giving off is like a living thing. I don't remember the last time someone made such a strong impression on me at the first meeting, without even uttering a word. Is he angry about being assigned to this job? He's probably heard the stories about how the last three of my bodyguards ended up—with a bullet hole from Rocco's gun in their foreheads.

The driver's door opens, and I quickly avert my eyes from the mirror.

"Well, it looks like I've found the perfect security detail for you," Rocco says as he takes a seat behind the wheel. "This one won't fall for your charms."

I squeeze the clutch I'm holding in my hands and bite at the inside of my cheek, trying to subdue the need to look at him and yell in his face.

"Yes, Rocco," I mumble, keeping my gaze fixed on my lap.

Alessandro

I lean back against the wall and regard the Pisano couple who are sitting on velvet-covered chairs a few feet in front of me. There are eight seats in this private balcony booth, but the others are empty.

Rocco seems bored. His left arm is resting on the back of his wife's chair, and he has his phone in his free hand. He's been fumbling with his device since the woman on the stage started wailing, so, clearly, he's not an opera fan.

His wife is a hard one to read. Something feels off between these two. Mrs. Pisano sits ramrod straight and avoids looking at her husband. From the moment she took her seat, her gaze has been focused on the stage. She hasn't moved a muscle for almost an hour, and I can't determine if it's because she's immersed in the performance or if there's another reason for her stoic posture.

When Rocco listed the parameters of my assignment earlier, I was surprised. The motherfucker had to be crazy in love with his wife, but I didn't understand why a man in his position would be so insecure that he would resort to such controlling measures. When I saw Ravenna Pisano descending the stairs, however, I barely managed to keep my jaw from hitting the floor. I've seen several pictures of her, but they didn't do her justice.

There are beautiful women. And then . . . there's her.

The skintight red dress she's wearing has a deep V-neck,

showcasing her firm breasts. It's also scandalously short, reaching just below her ass. The vibrant color contrasts with her raven-black hair, which she has tied into a tight bun at the top of her head. I don't think I've ever laid my eyes on a more perfect face, despite the excess makeup she's wearing. Heavy shading around her big green eyes. Blood-red lips, the same shade as her dress. Long, thick eyelashes, probably fake. It's hard to guess her age with all that crap on her face, but I estimate she's in her late twenties.

As she was descending the stairs at the house, I noticed her shiny sky-high black stiletto heels and how they complemented her hourglass figure. It was only when she came to a stop next to Rocco did I realize she was much shorter than I initially thought. Even in heels, the top of her head barely reached his nose. Standing barefoot, she would probably only come up to the middle of my chest.

Ravenna Pisano is a pixie of a woman, one who shouldn't be too difficult to smudge out of existence. And I plan to do it right under her husband's arrogant nose. Fitting, it seems.

The performer on the stage finally stops howling and a huge round of applause ensues. Rocco stands up from his chair and offers a hand to his wife. Mrs. Pisano rises slowly, the act so regal it's like watching a queen appear before her subjects. An ice queen, to be more exact. As they pass by me, she holds her head high, looking straight ahead, ignoring my presence completely. I guess she feels I'm beneath her, as "help" usually is for their kind.

I follow the Pisanos down the wide hallway toward the open space at the end where refreshments are awaiting the privileged patrons. Rocco tilts his head to whisper something in his wife's ear, then joins a group of men at the center of the room as they laugh boisterously while nursing their drinks.

Mrs. Pisano moves off to the side, coming to stand in a relatively people-free spot. Her stance is even more stiff than it was inside the theater hall, and her eyes seem to focus on something on the opposite wall. I follow her gaze, wondering what has attracted her attention, but there is nothing there. Just a pristine white wall. Not even an art piece or a light fixture in view.

I take a couple of steps and position myself on Ravenna Pisano's left. The moment she feels my presence, she freezes, every muscle pulled tight in recoil.

"Please, move back," she says, and, for a second, I'm taken aback by how young she sounds. But then her words sink in and disgust overwhelms me. I take a step back. Of course, she can't have her regal sight tainted by the likes of me. It's pathetic how entitled people sometimes forget that they are not so different from the rest of us. Especially as they bleed.

I wonder if she'll feel the same when her blood runs down her slender neck after I cut it open.

 Ravenna

I take a deep breath and keep my eyes fixated on the wall across from me. It's a technique I've adopted recently to keep my eyes from wandering and meeting a man's stare by accident. I can see Rocco in my peripheral vision. He's talking with another capo, Cosimo Longo, and pretending to be immersed in the conversation, but I know very well that he's watching me. Waiting for me to slip. I won't. I've had plenty of practice to prevail in this twisted game of his, and I've taken a slew of hits and sported enough bruises to motivate me to keep my gaze glued to that wall. But there is nothing I can do to prevent men from looking at me. Or worse, from approaching me. Rocco knows it and he finds great satisfaction in seeing it happen because it means he can punish me when we get home without his consciousness taking a blow.

My husband has a unique outlook on the world. In his mind, he is a good, just man who never does anything without a cause. If I'm on my best behavior, nothing will happen. Well, most of the time, at least. But if I do something wrong, like look at another male or do something to attract their eyes, he feels the need to punish me. Rocco likes to call it "martial education methods." So, I stand apart, hoping that no one will pay any attention to me and that Rocco will get bored soon so we can head back to the mansion.

"Ravenna," a male voice says from my right. "Why are you standing alone? Do you want me to bring you a drink?"

I squeeze the clutch purse in my hand harder. "I'm fine, Pietro. Thank you."

Go away. Please, please, go away. I repeat the mantra in my head. Maybe if he leaves right away, Rocco won't notice him.

"You sure you don't want anything to drink?" He places his hand on my shoulder.

I close my eyes for a second, trying to suppress the panic rising inside me, and make myself smile. Pietro worked alongside my father for a couple of years and he even came to our house a few times. He was always nice to me, and at one point, I considered asking him for help, but I never worked up the courage.

"I'm fine, just deep in thought. Thank you."

Pietro nods and heads toward the group of people on the other side of the room. When he's out of sight, I chance a look over to where Rocco was standing and find him looking at me

33

over the rim of his glass. He's smiling. Shit. I take a step back, bumping into a wall of hard muscle. A huge male hand lands on the side of my waist, steadying me. My blood goes cold.

Since I married Rocco, three men have died because of me. The first one was barely twenty-six. Only two years older than me. I still have nightmares about that day. I'd just come home from my manicure appointment, and Gaetano reached out to help me with my coat, brushing my shoulder with his hand by accident. A minute later, Rocco stormed out of the library with a gun in his hand and shot my bodyguard in the head. At first, I didn't realize what had happened and just stared at Gaetano's body sprawled on the floor while blood oozed from the hole in the center of his forehead. Rocco started yelling, ordering me to go to my room, but I couldn't make my legs move.

I learned my lesson after that and made sure I never, even accidentally, touched my bodyguards when Rocco or his cameras were in the vicinity. It didn't matter, eventually. The other two ended up dead because my husband concluded they were looking at me inappropriately.

"Remove your hand," I choke out, staring at Rocco as panic rises from the pit of my stomach.

Nothing happens.

"Right the fuck now, Alessandro."

The hand vanishes from my waist. As I watch, Rocco leaves his drink on the nearest waiter's tray and heads in our direction. Oh my God. He's going to kill Alessandro, too. Rocco wouldn't do anything to Pietro because he's part of the don's inner circle. *I* will be the one paying for that encounter. But my husband won't hesitate to execute a bodyguard as soon as we're back home. I can't live with another innocent man's death on my conscience. I can't.

"Leave," I whisper. "Please. Leave."

I don't think Alessandro hears me, because I can still feel him at my back when Rocco halts in front of me. He's still wearing a sinister smile.

"Next time, when a man approaches my wife," Rocco says looking over my head, "you'll remove him from her sight. With force, if necessary. Is that clear?"

I don't hear an answer, but I assume Alessandro nods. Rocco places his hand on the small of my back and ushers me into the hallway. We're leaving, thank God.

The bedroom door closes with a soft click behind me. I leave my clutch on the vanity table on my right and turn around. Rocco's palm connects with my cheek before I'm fully facing him.

"Pietro? Really?" he hisses as he pushes me toward the wall. "You need a cock? I'll give you a cock, you slut."

My chest collides with the hard surface. Taking a deep breath, I close my eyes and press my palms to the wall. Rocco grabs the hem of my dress, pulling it up, then tears at my panties. I can hear him undoing his belt, and I plaster myself to the wall, making sure to move as little as possible. It excites him more when I fight. A moment later I feel his flaccid dick pressing to my backside. He grinds against me a few times, his breathing fast.

"Fuck! Where are my pills?"

I hear him walking away, probably to get the Viagra he makes me keep in the drawer of my nightstand. A minute passes. I don't move from my spot. His hand comes to my ass, squeezing. I shut my eyes tighter.

Grunting. Rapid breaths as he pumps his cock behind me.

"You fucking slut." Rocco lets go of my ass and grabs my hair instead. "I can't get my cock up for you even with the fucking Viagra."

I almost stumble as he pushes me toward the bed and throws me down.

"You are not allowed to leave your room until morning. Do you hear me?"

"Yes, Rocco," I choke out.

The bedroom door slams shut but I keep lying on the bed, staring at the ceiling, and return to calculating how much money I need to get myself out of this horror show. Mulling over the details has become a coping mechanism. Whenever Rocco manhandles me, I detach myself from the situation by planning my escape.

My mind unintentionally drifts to the big silent man who's going to become my ever-present shadow. Will my husband do something to him? Maybe Rocco was too focused on Pietro and didn't notice as Alessandro touched me at the theater. If he had, there would have been another death tonight. I move my hand to my hip and brush the spot where Alessandro's hand briefly landed on me.

I'll have to be very careful around him, at least until I get to know him better. Hopefully, he's not an overly attentive person. Maybe I should put my . . . extracurricular activities on hold for a few days. No, I can't afford that. Every second I spend in this house with Rocco is a living hell. The situation started badly and has only become exponentially worse. I guess the bloodshed that happened on our wedding day was just a precursor of things to come. A foreshadowing of the nightmare that pulls me deeper daily. Drenching me in misery and drowning me in hurt.

I knew from the start that my husband is a troubled man. No sane person would obtain a wife as a payment for a gambling debt. At the time, I didn't understand why he needed to resort to such measures. Rocco has always been popular and well respected, and since he was a capo, he was even feared. Many women would have jumped with excitement at the possibility of marrying him, but Rocco stayed single. I couldn't understand why he suddenly felt the need to get married, to me nonetheless—a daughter of a lowly Cosa Nostra soldier. That question was answered quickly, on our wedding night.

Rocco Pisano is impotent. And he is ready to slaughter anyone who may dare to reveal his secret. The only person who knows is the doctor Rocco visits covertly. And now me. I'm not sure if his problem is congenital or a recent development, but I have a feeling he's been dealing with it for quite some time. His impotency is most likely the reason he stayed away from marrying a woman from a higher-ranking family. He probably feared that she would tell her parents or siblings, and, soon after, everyone would know. But Rocco would never allow his secret to be exposed. And he couldn't risk raising his hand against such a woman to keep her quiet. If her family were ever to find out, so would the don.

Maybe if my father was still alive, my life would've been different. Or maybe it wouldn't have. Marriage has always been considered sacred by my family. For years, I heard my father say how a woman should invariably respect her husband, no matter what. She should be docile and know her place, never contradict her man. It was so ingrained in me that the first time Rocco hit me, I was convinced it was my fault. After it started happening on a regular basis, I wanted to tell someone, ask for help, but I couldn't bring myself to defy him.

When we are in public, Rocco always acts as a doting,

loving husband. No one would believe me. And Rocco has made it very clear what will happen to my mother and brother if I ever say a word. So, I keep my mouth shut and endure it until I can stash enough money for all three of us to get as far away as possible.

Soon.

CHAPTER
Three

•───•───•❧Alessandro❧•───•───•

I CLICK ON THE GRAY ICON IN THE CORNER OF MY LAPTOP
screen. A box reading "Connecting . . ." pops up. Ten
seconds later, the computer desktop fills with a mosaic of
a dozen small windows, each one showing a different camera
feed from the Pisano mansion.

"Is it working?" Felix asks from the other end of the
phone line.

"Yes. I'm in. If I run into problems, I'll call you."

"Don't you fucking hang up on me!" he barks. "I want to
know what you're planning."

"Nothing that should concern you."

"We had a deal, Az. I help you get off Kurger's radar, and
you stay low."

"I am staying low, Felix." I click on the window showing
the front gate and observe the guards amid shift change. "I'll
need you to get me a body."

"A body? What kind of body?"

"The dead kind. Male. Late thirties. Caucasian. Black hair.

Six foot seven. Around 250 pounds," I say. I haven't measured myself lately, but it's a good guess.

"Absolutely. When do you need it delivered?"

How much time is needed to destroy a man's life?

"Two months," I answer.

"Sure. And what about eye color? Do you have a preferred hairstyle, maybe?" he sneers through the line. "Do you think I'm running a fucking 'dead people to order' service? Where the fuck would I get you a body?"

"You know people, Felix. Find a way." A smirk pulls at my lips. "As long as it's close enough so it can pass for me, it'll work."

"You're going to fake your own death?"

"Yes. As soon as I'm done here."

"Done? Done with what?" Felix snaps. "If you—"

I cut the call, throw the phone on the bed next to me, and focus on the laptop screen. There are more than ten cameras installed around the exterior of the house and six more on the property's perimeter walls. But there is only one on the inside, mounted above the front door. It'll be a helluva lot of work overriding them all when the time comes, but not impossible.

My phone pings with an incoming message. It's Mrs. Pisano's schedule for today. Shopping, three hours. Lunch at a restaurant, one hour. Visit with her mother, one hour. There is an address next to each listed activity. The message ends with a note in bold.

I expect a detailed report tomorrow.

Surveillance of the guard shifts will have to wait until another day, apparently. I take my holster off the nightstand, put it on, and, with my jacket in hand, leave my place.

I arrive at the Pisano mansion half an hour earlier than I need to and use that time to walk around the property, observing the layout and camera placements.

Two over the front entrance—one pointed at the door, another aimed at the driveway. Three more—one on each side—covering the flanks of the house. Pretending I'm taking a casual stroll, I follow the narrow path between the trees scattered around the grounds and continue my inspection. I spot cameras on each corner of the perimeter wall and a couple at the guardhouse and gate. Returning to the main house, I find more overlooking the patio and the nearby lawn.

There is only one other building on the property, fifty or so yards from the mansion. It looks like a garage but it's too large. I step off the path and walk across the grass, getting closer to the entrance so I can have a look inside through a raised bay door. It *is* a garage, and five cars are parked inside. The Cosa Nostra men love to gossip among themselves, and I've often heard them talking about Rocco's obsession with expensive cars. The rumors seem to be true because, by my quick assessment, the vehicles here are worth at least two million. He probably won't take well to losing these. I head left and circle the garage. Only one camera, just above the bay door. Good. Turning around, I stride back to the mansion.

I reach the foyer just in time to see Mrs. Pisano descending the stairs. She's wearing an elegant outfit of brown pants and a silk shirt in the same color, with a long white coat over it. Her hair is in a high bun again, and big brown sunglasses are covering half of her face.

The door to Rocco's office opens, and he steps out, hurrying across the foyer to meet his wife at the foot of the stairs. My hands clench, itching with the need to wrap around his neck and slowly choke the life out of him. I hoped it would be easier to control myself in his proximity, knowing that his demise is coming soon. Last night, I dreamed that he was suspended upside down from the ceiling while blood trailed down his body and dripped into the puddle on the floor, each drop making a wet splashing sound as it landed. It was the best fucking dream I had in ages.

"Slept well, bellissima?" Pisano smiles and lowers his head to place a kiss on his wife's cheek.

"Yes, thank you."

"Good. Enjoy your day and don't forget to buy that gold bracelet we liked. Giancarlo's wife has a similar one, but smaller, and we can't have Elisabetta wearing better jewelry than you."

"Of course not." Mrs. Pisano smiles. "Thank you, Rocco."

I head back to the front door and hold it open for her. As she passes me, a faint powdery scent invades my nostrils. For someone like her, I would have expected something pungent and musky. Something that draws attention and lingers long after she's disappeared from sight.

Mrs. Pisano walks down the stone steps ahead of me and toward the silver sedan on the driveway that I assume to be hers. With my height, there is no way I'm going to fit into that fancy shitbox.

"We're taking my car," I say.

Mrs. Pisano stops and turns around, watching me. It's impossible to decipher the look on her face behind those ridiculous glasses. I nod toward my SUV parked further to the left.

Heading over, I open the back door for her and wait. She approaches the car and stares at the seat. With non-stock tires, my vehicle sits significantly higher than standard cars. No use being an asshole just because I'm planning to kill her, so I extend my arm, offering to help her up.

As strange as it may seem, my hatred toward Ravenna Pisano is not personal. <u>She had nothing to do with my wife's death, but she represents everything that her husband had stolen from me.</u> People say that time heals all wounds, but in my case, it's been the opposite. With every passing day, my anger and the need for retaliation have only grown stronger. Revenge against Rocco Pisano has become my life's purpose, the sole reason for my existence, and the driving force behind why I spend every breath seeking to spill his blood. Before, I might have cared about an innocent becoming collateral damage. Not anymore.

Mrs. Pisano tilts down her face, looking, presumably, at my outstretched hand for a couple of seconds. Then, she grabs the back of the seat and hoists herself up, ignoring my offer of assistance completely. I close the door behind her and walk around the car with my jaw tightly clenched. She might not like me, but it doesn't come even close to what I feel for her or anyone else connected to Rocco Pisano.

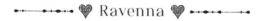 ❤ Ravenna ❤

My bodyguard doesn't utter a word during the whole one-hour drive. I wish he would because he has a very nice voice. Deep and hoarse. It suits him. He doesn't even look at me while we're headed to our destination, not even a passing glance in the rearview mirror. I, on the other hand, spend the entire time watching him. Good thing I'm wearing sunglasses, or he would probably think I'm some kind of a creep for staring at him nonstop.

I move my eyes to his hand as it rests on the stick shift. He tried to help me, offering me that same hand when I was getting into the car. When Rocco does it, I have to swallow the bile before making myself touch him. Not taking my husband's hand would be out of the question. He is obsessed with portraying our marriage as perfect and loving, especially when there is someone around. Rocco only shows his true self when we're alone.

When I saw Alessandro's outstretched hand, I didn't dare to touch him. There's a camera that monitors the driveway, and Rocco checks the recordings often. I don't want my husband to hurt Alessandro just because I allowed my bodyguard to touch me. I don't know what the deal is between him and my husband, but Rocco doesn't seem to be concerned about Alessandro. That's unusual. With all my previous bodyguards, Rocco would go ballistic when he thought that they looked at me a certain way or, God forbid, touched me.

I wish we were somewhere else when Alessandro held out his hand, anywhere where cameras aren't present. I wanted to take it, maybe because his animosity toward me isn't hidden behind a fake smile. I'm so sick of this farce my life has become, that I began to believe there isn't a single sincere person left around me. My bodyguard doesn't like me, and he's not inclined to pretend otherwise. I respect that.

My eyes shift up Alessandro's thick arm and stop on

his profile. He's very handsome—in a harsh, unconventional way—and he's definitely bigger and brawnier than any man I've met before. Rocco is tall, but he's rather lanky. Alessandro towers over my husband and outweighs him by more than seventy pounds. He certainly looks like a professional bodyguard, but I have a feeling he's not just a regular muscle for hire. There was something in his eyes when our gazes met yesterday, something under that deep loathing that I initially thought was directed solely toward me. But he had the same vehemence in his stare when he looked at my husband earlier. It was almost as if he was barely restraining himself from killing Rocco on the spot. I don't think Rocco even noticed it. Or maybe he just didn't pay him any attention. My husband rarely looks the staff in the eyes even when he talks to them since he considers laborers beneath him.

Alessandro parks the car in the mall's underground garage and comes to open the vehicle door for me. He doesn't offer his hand this time. I exit the car and head toward the elevator, and he follows a few paces behind. When I enter the elevator cab, I hit the button on the control panel for the third floor and plaster my back to the wall, keeping my eyes fixed on the row of numbers over the threshold with the lit one indicating the level we're on. Alessandro steps inside, his huge frame barring my view. The elevator cabin is not that small, but with him inside, it feels tiny. As the door closes, I squeeze my purse to my chest and swallow.

"Can you please move to the side?" I mumble, hating myself for having to ask. My body is not the only part of me that my husband has battered.

Alessandro takes a half step sideways. I can see the right part of the door, but it's not enough. The walls of the elevator seem to be closing in on me, threatening to squash me. I need to see that door unobstructed! My eyes flit over the numbers again. Just one more floor. A moment later, there is a ding announcing we've reached our destination. I take a deep breath and wait for the door to open. Nothing happens. There is a button on the panel to open the door and I hit it, twice. Another ding sounds, but the door remains shut. A strangled sound leaves my lips. No. No. No. I hit the button again.

"That's enough." Alessandro's fingers wrap around my wrist, pulling my hand away from the controls.

"I need to get out," I whisper.

"You will." He presses the emergency button. It didn't even occur to me to do that.

Another ding. Then, one more. The door stays closed. I look up at my bodyguard, ready to ask him to open the door by force, just as the light inside the elevator flickers out. The words die on my lips. I have my phone in my purse, but I can't make myself move to take it out and turn on the flashlight. The only thing I can manage is quick, shallow breaths. Alessandro's palm is still wrapped around my wrist, and I anchor myself to his touch.

A strange clicking sounds a moment later, and orange light spurts to life in front of my eyes. I stare at a small flame coming from the Zippo lighter in Alessandro's other hand. It flutters lightly from our combined breaths. Slowly, I glance up, and our gazes lock. The reflection of the glow makes his eyes look like they are on fire, as well.

"Let's count," his deep voice says.

"What?"

"Odd numbers only. Backward. Start at seventy-one."

I blink in confusion.

"Sixty-nine," he says. "You're next."

I take a deep breath. "Sixty-seven."

Alessandro nods and releases my wrist. "Sixty-five."

No! I reach out and grab the sleeve of his suit jacket and, keeping my sight fixed on his, move my hand down until I can feel his hand in mine again. The skin of his palm is rough as if he's spent years doing manual work.

I hook my pinkie with his. "Sixty-three."

He narrows his eyes at me. Is he going to ask why I'm freaking out? Will he laugh at me? Or remove his hand from mine? My breathing escalates.

"Fifty-nine," his voice fills the space around us.

"Fift—" I shake my head. "You skipped sixty-one."

"No."

"Yes. Mine was sixty-three."

"It wasn't."

The flame flickers again, its movement rearranging the play of light and shadow on Alessandro's face. His jaw is tightly pressed, and there is that malevolence in his eyes again, clearly visible even in the dim illumination. This man hates me, and I don't understand why. What I do understand even less, is the fact he's still holding my finger with his and, obviously, is trying to ease my panic by distracting me. Because I'm sure he missed that number on purpose.

There is a barely audible click, followed by a sudden brightness as the overhead light comes back on. A ding rings out and the elevator door opens, revealing a man in a maintenance uniform on the other side. He's saying something about a circuit glitch and apologizing for needing to turn off the light while overriding it, but I keep staring at my bodyguard. He's still holding his lighter in front of me.

"You skipped sixty-one on purpose," I say.

Alessandro tilts his head to the side. "And why would I do that, Mrs. Pisano?"

I can hear a subtle hostile undertone in his voice. He closes the Zippo, extinguishing the flame, and pulls his hand from mine before he steps out of the elevator.

Alessandro

You can learn a lot about a person by simply watching them, especially when they don't know you're doing so. Mrs. Pisano has been perusing the shelves in various boutiques for almost two hours, and I've noticed a very unusual thing. Every time she enters a shop, she walks amid the racks, pulls off a thing or two from each, then continues to the next one. She doesn't try any of the items on, and she barely even looks at the stuff she picks. And then, just before going to the checkout counter, she approaches the exclusive section.

All the clothes in these shops are pricey, but the apparel in the exclusive sections is a different level of crazy. In the first shop we went to, she purchased boots that cost six grand. In the next one, she bought an extremely ugly purse for twice that amount.

Now, I watch as she approaches a rack with coats and starts looking at the labels. She never does that when she's browsing the rest of the shop, but for the higher-end items, she checks every single price tag.

She pulls off a long coat with faux fur trim over the collar, checks the size label, and then heads to the cash register. She didn't even try it on, but even from a distance, I'm sure that it's at least two sizes too big. I focus on her feet. Now that

I think about it, the boots she bought earlier seemed rather large, as well.

Mrs. Pisano places the heap of clothes on the counter next to the cash register and looks at me. I take out the credit card Rocco gave me yesterday. As I'm passing her the plastic, our fingers touch, and it's as if a hot iron sears my skin. Just like when she hooked her pinkie with mine in the elevator. I don't like it, but at the same time, I can't make myself move my hand. Mrs. Pisano looks up, but I can't see her eyes. Those dreadful sunglasses are still hiding most of her face.

I let go of the card and collect the bags after the attendant packs up her purchases, but the feeling of her skin against mine still lingers, tingling the tips of my fingers.

When we leave the boutique, Mrs. Pisano heads right toward the jewelry store at the other end of the mall, walking a few steps in front of me. She left her coat in my car, so I'm gifted with an undisrupted view of her perfect round derriere. I've never understood the fascination some men have with female asses, but as I watch her buttocks shift under the soft fabric of her brown pants, I have the urge to place my palm on her behind and check if it's as firm as it looks. Disgusted with myself for my thoughts, I quickly look up and focus my gaze on the back of her head.

She looks so regal as she walks down the promenade with her focus fixed in front of her, while her four-inch heels make a distinct tapping sound on the tile floor. Every man who passes her, no matter their age, stares at her with wide eyes. Even those accompanied by their girlfriends or wives. It's as if they can't help but be drawn to her.

And it seems I'm one of them, as well. I should be paying attention to our surroundings, but I find myself unable to move my eyes off her. Ravenna Pisano doesn't appear to notice the uproar she's creating. Majestic and controlled, she keeps strolling with her head held high, absolutely unperturbed by what's going on around her.

It's such a difference in her behavior compared to how she acted in the elevator earlier. At first, I thought she freaked out from having me so near in the small space. Most women tend to be intimidated by my size. But then, she grabbed my hand, holding onto it as if for dear life. That's when I realized that it was the enclosed space that triggered her. I should have exploited that fear.

But I couldn't make myself do it.

Just as Mrs. Pisano reaches the entrance of the jewelry store, a man exiting stops at the threshold. His lips curve upward as he gives her an undisguised once-over.

"Well, hello there." He smirks as he stands there, barring her entry.

He's one of those hipster types—expensive suit with too-short pant legs, a neatly trimmed beard, and blond hair slicked back in some moronic style. I set the shopping bags on the floor and take a step forward until I'm standing right behind my charge. Wrapping my arm around her waist, I move her to the side. She lets out a small yelp of surprise, which quickly transforms into a muffled cry when I grab the fancy idiot by the knot of his yellow silk tie.

The man's eyes flare in shock as I pull him out of the way and nod toward the escalator on the left. "Get lost."

I let go of him and keep his retreating form in sight as he hurries away, then collect the shopping bags and stretch out my arm in the go-ahead gesture. Ravenna Pisano blinks at me, then quickly looks away and enters the shop.

How is it possible to want to kill a person, and feel the urge to protect them at the same time?

We've nearly reached our next destination, Mrs. Pisano's mother's house, when I feel a light touch on my shoulder.

"Can you make a stop here? I need to get something from the pharmacy."

I pull over and park, and then walk around the car to open the back door. The sidewalk is in bad condition, and there's a puddle and half-frozen mud where the mess has collected near a curb drainage grate under the car. As my charge starts to exit the vehicle, my eyes fall to her shiny white heels. Without a thought, I lean forward, grasp her waist and lift her out, setting her onto dry ground. The moment her feet touch down, I release her and close the car door.

Why the fuck did I just do that? Why would it matter to me if she got her fancy shoes wet? I turn and head toward the pharmacy. Mrs. Pisano's heels click on the pavement as she tries to keep up, but I maintain my steady pace, mad as hell at myself.

I hold the pharmacy door open for her, making sure my gaze is focused straight ahead and over the top of her.

When she passes me, I post myself by the door and clasp my hands behind my back. I won't be looking at that woman again unless it's absolutely necessary. Forming any kind of connection with a person you intend to eliminate is never a good thing.

My resolve falters barely a minute later when I hear her voice. She is speaking in an even, casual tone, but there is a faint note of distress in it. I turn my head to the side to see her standing at the counter, speaking with the pharmacy employee.

"I'd really prefer to have Melania help me. Please."

"Ma'am. I already told you. She went to the back room to take a private call," the male on the other side of the counter says in a condescending tone. "If it's just a prescription, I'm completely capable of handling that for you."

"I . . . I'll come back later. Thank you," Mrs. Pisano says and turns to leave.

"Ravi?" A woman in her early twenties comes out and then turns toward her colleague. "I've got this, Charles. Go take your lunch break."

When the guy disappears out of sight, Mrs. Pisano places a paper on the counter. "How are you, Melania?"

The girl takes the prescription but instead of checking what's written on it, she glances in my direction, then quickly looks away. "I'm great." She smiles, but it seems artificial. "And how are you? Everything okay at home?"

"Of course," Mrs. Pisano says.

The girl nods, reaches into the drawer under the cash register, then places a white paper bag on the counter. She hadn't even looked at the prescription note.

Mrs. Pisano takes the package, but instead of saying goodbye, she remains in place. Nervous energy seems to radiate off her, matched by the pharmacy girl on the other side of the counter. The moment is brief, barely a few seconds, but it feels like the two are having a wordless exchange. And I doubt it has anything to do with settling the payment, either.

"Thank you."

There is an unusual tone to Mrs. Pisano's words when she finally says them. It doesn't sound like a simple courtesy.

"Any time, Ravi," the pharmacy girl whispers and places her hand over Mrs. Pisano's. Her eyes once again dart toward me before she quickly slides the prescription note off the counter and stuffs it into the pocket of her lab coat.

My charge walks past me on her way out, and I can't help but wonder what she just received in that package. Because I'm willing to bet it sure as fuck wasn't what was written on her prescription.

I don't know what I expected when I parked the car in front of the building where Mrs. Pisano's mother lives, but it wasn't a place that looks like it's barely holding together. The elevator is out of order, so we climb the four flights of stairs and head down the narrow hallway with cracked and peeling paint and a scuffed linoleum floor. Some of the bulbs are out or missing entirely from their fixtures, the dim light only accentuates the derelict conditions. The stench of body odor and piss that hangs in the air is hardly a selling point here, either.

Mrs. Pisano stops at the last door and reaches to take the bags I'm holding. She insisted on bringing all twenty of them inside, saying that she wanted to show her mother the new clothes she bought.

I look around the place and feel disgusted. Instead of spending the thirty grand on the clothes she seemed to care little about in the first place, Mrs. Pisano could have moved her mother out of this shithole and paid rent on a new place for an entire year with that money. Is she really this selfish? What the fuck is wrong with her? Why would she let her mom live here and also feels the need to brag about the crap she's just purchased? I wish I can see her eyes to get a sense of what's happening in her head right now, but she still has those fucking sunglasses on. She hasn't bothered taking them off even in this murky hallway.

"You can stay here," she says, tugging on the bags. "I won't be long."

I keep a tight hold on the bags and knock at the door.

The woman who opens it is a spitting image of Mrs. Pisano, only older. Black hair speckled with grays, the same green eyes, and an identical small nose. There's a twinkle in her brilliant depths as they land on her daughter, but as soon as she notices me, that glint disappears.

"Mamma. This is Alessandro," Mrs. Pisano says. "May we come in?"

The older woman nods and steps aside. When we enter, I let Mrs. Pisano take the bags and shift to stand by the wall, right next to the door, focusing my gaze on the window across the room. Even without looking around, I can see that the inside of the apartment, although clean and tidy, isn't much better than the building itself.

The mother and daughter sit down on the beat-up sofa and start looking at the clothes. Every few moments, the mother throws a quick look in my direction.

"This one is beautiful, Ravi," she says but her tone doesn't seem to match the sentiment. "Oh, and look at that skirt, you'll look stunning in that."

Mrs. Pisano doesn't say a word, just keeps taking out the clothes. In fact, the whole scene feels off. Staged somehow, as if they are acting for my benefit. I turn my head to the side so I can see them better but pretend that I'm still looking at something beyond the window. I school my expression to appear vacant, bored even, so they'll stop paying me any attention.

Mrs. Pisano reaches for the largest bag, the one that holds the faux fur coat, and quickly pushes it behind the sofa, out of view. Then, she takes out a few of the blouses and passes them to her mother, but when she comes to the expensive purse, that ends up tucked behind the sofa, as well. When they finish perusing her purchases, she puts everything back into the bags. The boots, however, are nowhere in sight.

"How are you doing?" her mother asks offhandedly as she takes a small folded piece of paper off the coffee table and leans toward her daughter as if to straighten the collar of her blouse. The folded paper changes hands in a split second.

"I'm fine, Mamma." Mrs. Pisano smiles. "How's work?"

"The same. I'm going to clean Mrs. Natello's house tomorrow, and again on Friday."

"I'll drop by before Friday, then."

Mrs. Pisano adjusts her sunglasses, which she still hasn't taken off, and glances over her shoulder. "Where's Vitto?"

"You know your brother. He stayed at Ugo's last night." The older woman shrugs.

"They still hang out?"

"Yes. At least he stopped playing cards after . . . you know."

"Good. Do you need help with anything?"

"I'm fine, Ravi."

"What about your back? Still hurts?"

"It's good, but I think I pinched a nerve this morning when I tried to wash the windows."

"Geez, Mamma." Mrs. Pisano shakes her head as she stands up and retreats into a small kitchen on my right.

She takes out an old rag from a drawer and grabs a spray bottle from beneath the sink before depositing both on the counter nearby. Then, she rolls up the sleeves of her silk blouse and climbs onto a rickety old chair she's pulled away from the small kitchen table nudged against one of the walls. As I watch, Ravenna Pisano, the wife of a Cosa Nostra capo, picks up the cleaning items and starts washing her mother's windows. I stare at her, stunned, for almost an hour while she finishes the glass, then wipes all the kitchen counters and cabinets, and, finally, mops the floor.

When I get home that evening, I spend an hour going over the Pisanos' garage blueprint Felix had sent me. It looks like it was a small service building at one point that was later expanded and renovated into a garage. It has an alarm installed, but it's nothing complicated enough to present an issue. The electrical panel is located inside by the side door, making the wires heading toward it easily accessible. Perfect.

Picking up the blueprint off the table, I walk into my bedroom and pin the paper to the wall, next to the printout of Rocco's bank account. Then, I step back and take a long look at the sight before me. The entire surface of the wall is covered in a mosaic of papers, photos, and notes.

I know every single detail pinned to this wall. Over the years, I've collected countless tidbits of information—some with Felix's help, and some I extracted either through bribery or by force. Many were dead-ends or false leads, but I kept them anyway. I don't like staying in one place for too long just in case Kruger may still be looking for me, so I've moved frequently over the last eight years to make sure he doesn't pick up my trail. Each time, I've removed the items off my revenge wall and meticulously repined them—in the exact same pattern—at a new location. Every action in that process reopened the wound in my chest, but the pain is good. The ritual helps me maintain my focus.

The first item I always place at the center of the wall is a photo of Natalie. In it, she's wearing an orange dress that has white polka dots all over. I thought that thing was atrocious. But the bright pattern made her whole face light up when she saw it, and we ended up buying the dress. Pinning her smiling face to my revenge board is always the hardest part. With each relocation, it feels like a sledgehammer hits me right in the chest, reminding me of what was taken from me. Every. Single. Time.

After that, I add the doctor's report detailing what they tried to do to keep her alive at the hospital, and the police report on the traffic incident which was labeled as a hit-and-run. The next items to go up, surrounding the focal point, are the scantly written witness statements claiming that they didn't see anything, not even the color of the car. It took Felix several months to obtain these for me because someone conveniently forgot to input the info into the system, and he had to pay off the clerk to find the paper statements made by the two people who were present during the collision.

When I finally got the chance to speak with the two witnesses directly, both admitted that they saw a red sports car but couldn't remember the make or model.

It took me almost a year to find the mechanic who worked on the banged-up red sports car around the time Natalie was killed. Seems he ran a custom body shop in Jersey but was paid generously to fix up a busted front end and windshield of an Audi R8 at his private garage. He didn't seem interested in sharing much info at first but changed his mind after I broke his legs. We had a rather productive chat after. I left his place with a couple of important details.

The man who showed up with a smashed car was in his late twenties, clearly intoxicated, and seemed a bit shaken up. An hour later, an older man arrived, and they argued in Italian.

The mechanic didn't speak Italian, but he remembered the older man saying *famiglia* several times which he recognized by being a big fan of *The Sopranos*. The old guy then put a gun to the mechanic's temple and instructed him to fix the car and to keep his mouth shut. Although the shit-for-brains couldn't provide the men's names, I got enough. The guy responsible for my wife's death was a member of the Italian Mafia.

My father was Italian, so I thought it would be easy to get into Cosa Nostra, especially for someone with my skills and the background Felix fixed up for me. I was wrong. The establishment changed less than a year before, and the new don was very strict on who was allowed inside the organization. It took me nine months to get in. Four more years passed before I worked my way into the inner circle and got the opportunity to dig deeper. Time didn't matter, though. I was hell-bent on finding the man responsible for my wife's death no matter how long it took.

I knew I was looking for someone from the higher-ups, a lowly soldier wouldn't have had money or influence to cover up Natalie's death. As years passed, I still couldn't find out who it was. But I stayed. And I listened. When you don't talk much, people tend to forget you're in the room or believe you're not interested in their conversations. I don't say much. Never have. But I hear everything.

A month ago, I was playing poker with some of the men—mostly lieutenants working under a couple of different capos. I always make sure to lose more often than I win. People like that. They get excited. And when they're excited, they talk. Carmelo won the last hand that night, and he was yapping about smashing into a store window when he was drunk and tried to park his car a couple of nights prior.

"Maybe I should ask Elio to fix that for me," he said, *"like*

he did with Rocco's run-in with that woman at a crosswalk. God, remember that? Rocco was so shitfaced, too."

I still don't know how I managed to keep my ass in that chair instead of storming out to slaughter both of those motherfuckers. But I made myself stay there the whole evening, feigning calm and disinterest, while the rage brewed inside me. When I got home that night, I added more photos to my wall.

Rocco Pisano—my wife's killer. I pinned his photo above Natalie's and drew a red X over his face.

Elio Pisano—Rocco's father, who helped him cover up the crime. Another X.

Those two weren't enough, though. I needed to hammer it home. <u>An eye for an eye.</u>

So, I added the third photo.

Ravenna Pisano. Rocco's wife.

<u>My payback.</u>

CHAPTER
four

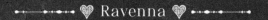

♥ Ravenna ♥

THE FAINT MORNING SUNRAYS FALL ONTO THE
surface of the vanity table before me, illuminating
the multitude of scattered makeup bottles and cases.
I tilt my head to the side and start applying the second layer
of concealer over the bruise near my left eye. It's not that
bad since Rocco slapped me with his open palm. The mark
is almost gone, but I don't want to take any chances. It'll be
cloudy today, and I'll look ridiculous wearing sunglasses.

When I'm satisfied with my work, I retrieve the paper I've
hidden in my eyeshadow compact and unfold it.

Nude heels, but genuine leather only. Italian.

Shawl and sweater—pastel color, preferably blue.

Pearl earrings.

It's a list of the things Mrs. Natello would like next time.
Shoes and clothes aren't an issue. I'll easily find those at the
boutiques. But earrings will pose a problem. My husband
usually buys me gold, so I don't have a pearl pair in my jewelry collection. And I can't risk buying them because I already
got a gold pendant less than two weeks ago. If I start buying

jewelry too often, Rocco will notice and demand I wear some of the new pieces.

Below the list, four sentences are added.

I can't sleep at night because of the worry, passerotta.

Please consider telling Don Ajello somehow, or let me do it. Please.

I love you, Ravi.

I brush my thumb over my mother's neat handwriting. Since I was a kid, my mom loved hiding short notes for Vitto and me in our room and waiting for us to find them. It was never anything important, only a few words such as: "We're having your favorite pizza for dinner" or "I heard you did well on your test. Nice work!" written on folded sheets. The notes were never signed but we always knew they were from Mamma. My father was never the openly touchy-feely kind, and his handwriting looked as if a crow dipped its leg in ink and wrote the thing.

A sad smile pulls at my lips. Mamma has always tried her best to compensate for my father's lack of affection and to make me and Vitto feel loved. Knowing the truth about my marriage and keeping silent is killing her, but I made her promise that she won't say a word to anyone.

Before I married Rocco, I imagined myself finishing college and starting a family. I hoped I would have a husband who wouldn't just be a figurehead, but a man who would truly love me. Two, maybe three kids to spoil. And a home full of warmth.

It was a nice dream.

I don't dream anymore. The only thing I have now is the resolve to get myself out of this nightmare.

In the early days after my wedding, I deluded myself with the notion that I would find a way to tell someone what was going on and ask for help, but Rocco took away my phone and forbade me from speaking to anyone except the house-keeper and maids. My mom and brother were the only people I was allowed to see, but always under supervision. Having me locked in the house would raise questions, so Rocco insisted I go to get manicures and do some shopping. That way, people wouldn't suspect anything. Either Rocco or a bodyguard was always with me whenever I left the house. Without means to contact anyone and being under constant surveillance, my hands were tied. Secret notes between my mom and me were the best we could do, and only when we managed to trade them without my security detail noticing.

Rocco loves dragging me to dinners and parties with other Cosa Nostra members, and there are always many people. I hoped that someone would figure out what was going on, but it didn't happen. In public, Rocco has been extremely careful not to lash out at me when there are other people close by, and he has never hurt me in front of witnesses. But I'm sure some people have noticed. Like the guard at the gate, when I was sporting a huge bruise on the side of my face three weeks ago. He had come to Rocco's window, asking something about shift change, and I saw his eyes widen when he'd seen me. But he quickly looked away.

After a month, I kicked my hopes out of my head and decided I needed to save myself. There's no such thing as a knight in shining armor. Not for me, at least.

In one of the notes, I requested Mom to ask Melania, my childhood best friend, to get me the Viagra placebo pills. In the next one, I told her to see which of her clients would be interested in buying my unworn clothes. The half sister of Capo Cosimo, the cranky old lady for whom my mother has worked for decades, said yes. I had to resort to buying the clothes she wanted because Mrs. Natello is much taller than me.

The sound of leaves being crushed under the tires reaches me from beyond the open balcony door. I crumple my mom's note and put it in my pocket to dispose of later. With one last look in the mirror, I grab my coat off the back of the chair and rush out of the room.

There's work to be done.

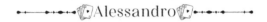

Alessandro

"Report on yesterday," Rocco barks the moment I step inside his office.

"As planned," I say. "Shopping. Lunch. Her mother's place. Back to the mansion."

Rocco furrows his eyebrows and leans over his desk, obviously less than thrilled with my account.

"I need you to be more specific than that, Zanetti. Did she meet or speak to anyone? What did she and her mother talk about while you were there? Did they mention me? I want to know everything, including the order she made at the restaurant."

"We visited five stores where she bought a bunch of clothes and shoes. She didn't meet anyone or speak with anyone other than store employees. We didn't go to a restaurant. She grabbed a pastry from a bakery at the mall."

"Filling?" he asks.

I tilt my head. "What?"

"What was the filling, Zanetti? Ravenna is not allowed to eat sweets unless I specifically allow it."

I fist my right hand at my side. The sick bastard controls what his wife eats. "It was a cheese pie."

"Good. Proceed with what happened at her mother's place."

"They talked," I say through my teeth.

"About?"

"About the clothes she bought. And then we left."

Rocco takes a pen off the desk and starts tapping it on the rim of the glass offset before him in a slow, uneven rhythm. The sound is extremely irritating, threatening my already thin restraint. Each time he is in my field of vision, I need to employ every damn self-control technique I know, so I don't just kill the motherfucker on the spot.

Does he ever think about the woman whose life he took? My wife lay in a puddle of her own blood, in the middle of the street for almost half an hour until the ambulance arrived. That day, a few blocks away, an upper floor of the city parking garage collapsed, killing and injuring several people. Traffic was tied up for miles. Fire and police departments assisted with rescue and evacuation. Medical personnel were busy triaging and getting the injured to the nearby facilities. Amid the chaos, it took too long for the emergency vehicle to get to Natalie. One life in a city of millions. One death that shook my world. Of course, he doesn't spare a thought for her. He probably forgot it ever happened.

But I will make him remember when the time comes. He will remember the woman he killed when I cut his wife open in front of him and make him watch as the life slowly seeps out of her.

The image of Ravenna Pisano sprawled on the floor, covered in blood, flashes before my eyes. I've always found it comforting to imagine the way I would kill the motherfucker's wife, like finally fulfilling a life-long promise and shedding the weight of the burden I carry, but now, instead of the peace of mind, something else rises within me.

It's denial.

The image of Mrs. Pisano's bloody face blurs in my thoughts and transforms into an unknown woman.

I dig my nails deeper into my palm as I clutch my fist and focus on the pen Rocco is still hitting on the glass, trying to shove Ravenna Pisano's likeness back where I envisioned it to be. It doesn't work.

"And nothing else happened, Zanetti?" Rocco asks. "Nothing unusual?"

I shift my eyes off the pen he's holding and meet his gaze. His wife secretly hiding clothes at her mother's place would probably count as unusual. As well as having her friend give her an unknown substance from the pharmacy.

"No," I say.

"Good." He throws the pen back on the desk and powers up his laptop. "Ravenna is probably waiting for you by the front door. She has her weekly spa appointment scheduled."

Of course she does. It seems like the only things that interest Mrs. Pisano are shopping and beauty treatments. My mind goes to the scene from yesterday when I watched her scrub her mother's kitchen so the older woman wouldn't further hurt her back. It doesn't add up.

Nodding, I leave the office.

Just like her husband said, Ravenna Pisano is standing by the front door, holding her coat over her arm. I reach out to take the coat from her, but she quickly takes a step back.

"Please, don't," she says.

"Why?" I ask.

"Just . . . don't." She puts on her coat, opens the door, and steps outside.

I follow her as she rushes down the stone steps and stops on the last one with her head tilted up toward the sky. There is nothing above that would attract her attention, only gray clouds. She stands like that for almost a minute, breathing deeply and staring at the vast nothingness before heading to the car.

Situated in a modern building, the Wellness Center takes up the entire second level and promises its patrons nothing less than heaven and luxury. That is if one is to believe the sign in the lobby directing us to this place. As Mrs. Pisano walks toward the reception desk, the click of her heels echo off the marble floor, somehow complementing the soothing sounds of nature playing from well-hidden speakers.

"Mrs. Pisano." The girl on the other side of the desk smiles. "I'm glad to see you again. Hazel is waiting for you."

"Thank you." Mrs. Pisano nods and turns to face me. "You need to wait out here. Men are not allowed inside."

I raise an eyebrow.

"This is a female-only spa, Alessandro. There are naked women in there. Please, wait here. I won't go anywhere."

The whole explanation spills out in one breath, and the tone of her voice is slightly higher than usual. She's nervous and trying to hide it. Why would she be nervous about her spa appointment? I focus on her face and nod.

"I should be done in four hours. It's a complete body wrap and face cleansing treatments and then a massage afterward.

It takes a long time." She motions to the door on the left. "See you later."

I watch Mrs. Pisano as she disappears, then take a seat on one of the white leather chairs set against the wall and wait. Elegantly dressed women come in and leave, passing under two huge crystal chandeliers that hang from the high ceiling and illuminate the white and gold posh interior. A strange, sweet scent of flowers and coconut tickles my nostrils. It permeates the air as if someone dumped a ton of bath salts somewhere nearby.

My eyes scan the elaborate space and I spot a brochure lying on the coffee table, getting a glimpse of the extravagant prices. Jesus, no wonder this place looks like it can rival an art gallery or a small museum. There are even paintings that decorate the opulent walls. I wouldn't be surprised if the price tag on those is in five figures.

Turning away from the white marble sculpture standing by the reception desk, I concentrate on the door that Mrs. Pisano went through earlier. It's identical-looking to the six other doors leading off this reception area. Nothing special about it except for the fact that, in the past hour, none of the other clients have walked through that one. I take a quick look at my watch, then leave my spot and head toward the exit.

The Wellness Center building is nestled between two smaller ones. The one on the left is office space—cubicles with desks and computer equipment are visible through the floor-to-ceiling windows. The building on the right, however, seems to be residential, its windows and balconies facing the spa. I'm certain there's one that will have a view of the room that Mrs. Pisano entered, so I head inside the apartment building.

There are five residences on each side of the second-floor hallway. I stop at the third on the left and ring the bell. A man in his early thirties opens the door and swiftly steps back when he sees the gun in my hand.

"I need to have a look from your balcony," I say.

The man's face drains of color, and he quickly moves to the side. He doesn't utter a word as I walk across the living room to open the sliding door and step outside.

Most of the windows belonging to the Wellness Center are frosted, obscuring everything that happens inside. There are two, though, in my direct line of sight, that aren't. These clearly don't belong to treatment rooms or other spa facilities because I can see office space with several desks inside. At one of them, Ravenna Pisano is perched in front of a computer, vigorously typing something on the keyboard.

Another woman is seated next to her, holding a thick blue folder and a pen. The desk is facing away from the window so I can see the lit monitor, but I'm too far away to be able to discern what they're working on. I watch them for a couple of moments, then leave the apartment and its freaked-out resident, returning to the spa to wait while my charge finishes her "beauty treatment."

Later that night, after I drop Ravenna Pisano off at home, I drive back to the Wellness Center. The entire time my thoughts are filled with what happened that afternoon. When Mrs. Pisano came out, all she did was thank me for waiting. Our trip back to the mansion passed without a word. I glanced at her a couple of times through the rearview mirror, and she seemed way too tense for a woman who supposedly spent half her day at the spa. The tension didn't leave her tiny frame when we arrived, and she exited my car. She passed by me as I held the door open for her and entered the house never once looking me in the eyes.

I reign in my thoughts and focus on the task at hand. There is a fire escape on the back side of the building, and I use it to get to the second floor. After a quick recon, I pick the lock of the emergency exit door and neutralize the security system. I didn't have time to get the floor plan for the building, but finding the office I'm after isn't hard. The blue folder I spotted earlier in the hands of the woman sitting with Ravenna Pisano is still lying on the desk. I open it and leaf through the printouts within.

Supply orders. An invoice for the lease on the location. A dry cleaning receipt. More statements for items the spa center requires.

I set the folder where I found it and power on the computer. The monitor lights up, displaying the login screen. Above the blank password field, the username reads *Hazel* with the word *Accounting* next to it.

Why in the world would a capo's wife secretly deal with a spa center's accounting?

CHAPTER
five

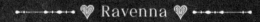

💜 Ravenna 💜

THERE'S SOMETHING SOOTHING ABOUT WATCHING the sunset when silence envelopes the surroundings and no one else is around. Well, no one except for my bodyguard who's been the ever-present dark shadow following me around for the last seven days. I take a quick glance back at Alessandro, who is standing by a tree about fifty feet away, his arms crossed over his chest.

With my previous bodyguards, I had no issues ignoring their presence, but that's not the case with Alessandro. It's hard to overlook a mountain of a man who pursues your every step. And even when he's out of sight, I can still feel his proximity. He, on the other hand, pretends I'm a faceless, loathed task he needs to fulfill.

It's been a week since he took on this role, and his behavior hasn't changed since the first day. He does his job and doesn't talk to me unless it's absolutely necessary. He won't even look at me directly, his eyes are typically focused somewhere over my head. But a few times our gazes connected, and I could still see the despise in his depths. He hates me just as he did the moment I met him. I don't know why. I just know that he does.

I reach out to carefully break off a frozen rose flower in front of me, and look at the fragile and wilted yellow petals in my hand. The roses were in full bloom when I first came to this house just over a year ago. It was also the day I met my future husband.

Both of Rocco's maids had caught a stomach bug, and since my mother often cleaned houses for Cosa Nostra members, including for one of Rocco's security guards, she was called to fill in. I came with my mother to help because she's been having back problems for years. The doctor told her she wasn't allowed to do heavy manual work, but what I earned at my accounting job and the diner wasn't enough to cover my father's medical bills, so she had no choice but to work, too.

We arrived at seven in the morning and left after nine in the evening. I saw Rocco only in passing then. I was mopping the foyer when he came home and went into his office, leaving wet footprints all over the floor I just washed. He was yelling at someone on the phone and hadn't even noticed me, but even that brief encounter rubbed me the wrong way.

We came again the following day because the house was too large for two people to scrub it clean in one go. I was dusting one of the sculptures in Rocco's office when he came in and started shouting at me to be more careful. I can still recall the degrading way he looked at me then. As we were leaving, I swore to myself I would never set foot in that house ever again. Fate had a different plan for me, unfortunately.

I crush the frozen petals in my hand and throw them

away. Turning around, I head toward the small gazebo off to the side. The living shadow follows me.

It's too cold for the mere wool sweater I'm wearing, but I can't make myself go back into the house to get a jacket. I'd rather risk getting a runny nose than go inside that dreadful place if I don't absolutely need to.

One of the chairs inside the gazebo has a cushion, a slight barrier against the cold. I turn it so it's facing away from the house and take a seat. A few moments later, the crunch of frozen leaves alerts me as Alessandro comes to stand somewhere at my back. Closing my eyes, I tilt my head toward the setting sun and inhale, letting the smell of chilly winter air fill my lungs.

"Do you have a nickname?" I ask.

A few more leaves get crushed under his feet, a little closer this time.

"Yes."

His voice has such a pleasant timbre to it. Like the purr of a big, wild cat. A panther on the prowl. Just before he eats you up. I wait for him to continue, but the only thing I can hear is a distant whir of a vacuum cleaner coming from the mansion.

"And, will you tell me what it is?"

"Yes."

I lift my hand and press my fingers over my mouth to stifle a laugh. He really likes his answers monosyllabic. Or maybe he doesn't like the idea of talking to me. I should probably leave the man alone but I like the sound of his voice too much. And since we're both facing away from the house, no one can tell that we're talking.

"What is it, then?" I prod. "I bet it's something short."

"Az."

72

A giggle escapes my lips. It doesn't get shorter than that. I like his full name better.

"Rocco mentioned you worked for the don before you were transferred here," I say. "Security detail, as well?"

"Yes."

"For the don?"

"His wife."

I try to remember what Salvatore Ajello's wife looks like, but can't. They both attended my wedding, and I recall people gossiping about her, however, I was too distracted that day to pay attention. "How is she?"

A few moments of silence ensue before he answers, and when he does, I almost fall off the chair at his response.

"Whacky."

"I'm not sure it's wise to call the don's wife whacky out loud." A snort escapes me as I chortle the words.

"Maybe."

I glance over my shoulder. Alessandro is leaning on the tree by the gazebo, his gaze fixed on me. Suddenly, as if everything else fades from existence, his hard, dark eyes capture mine, and I find myself unable to look away. Alessandro pushes off from the tree and, taking a few large steps, comes to stand right behind my chair.

"But you're good at keeping secrets." He lifts his hand and places his index finger under my chin, tilting my head up. "Aren't you, Mrs. Pisano?"

There's that hostility in his eyes again, but his touch is so gentle, barely there. I blink and quickly look away, his finger slipping from my face. Pulling my legs up, I wrap my arms around my folded knees and turn my gaze to the expanse of orange sky above the horizon. The sound of retreating steps echoes behind me as Alessandro walks away.

I don't try to see where he's going, too absorbed in the still lingering feel of his fleeting touch and the fluttering it inflicted in my chest.

A few minutes later, I hear him approach again. Or maybe I just feel him. I'm still focused on the sky when something soft and fluffy lands on my back. I look down, staring at the edges of the blanket Alessandro placed around my shoulders, while the last rays of the setting sun sink behind the bare branches of the trees.

CHAPTER
six

―――・――・――・❦Alessandro❦・――・――・―――

I STEP ON THE LAWN AND HEAD TOWARD THE GARAGE, making sure I walk a few more feet over to the left than I did yesterday. The camera mounted on the lamppost by the driveway covers a wider angle than I thought, and I need to determine how much wider.

Every morning when I arrive at the Pisano mansion, I take a seemingly casual stroll around the grounds, and to anyone who might wonder, it probably looks like I'm just walking around while waiting for my charge to get ready. However, there is nothing random in my intent.

The map of the Pisano property, which is pinned on my wall, has all camera positions marked with a circle around each, showing the approximate area it covers. I don't rely on approximation, so every morning, I take the path I believe will avoid the camera-monitored spaces. When I get home at night, I play that morning's recording, note the spots where the cameras picked me up, and adjust my route the next time. During the ten days of reconnaissance, I've established most of the locations on the driveway and the front lawn where cameras don't reach. A week or so more, and I'll have the whole property scouted.

The door on the second-floor balcony opens, and Ravenna Pisano steps out, wearing a long white satin robe. I take a step behind a thick beech tree so I can watch her without being seen. Her black hair is gathered in a bun, as always, and even from this distance, I can see she's wearing heavy makeup. It creates such a contrast with her delicate gown as it flutters in the wind. She resembles one of the marble statues scattered around the lawn. Cold. Untouchable.

Her husband called me this morning, giving me her schedule for the day and asking if I have anything to report. As I do every morning, I said nothing out of the ordinary transpired the previous day. But the thing is, what Rocco Pisano considers ordinary is anything but.

His wife doesn't seem to have any friends or even acquaintances. Other than her mother, she never meets anyone. Shopping, spa treatments, lunches . . . she always goes alone or with her husband. Yesterday, I took her to a park where she spent three hours just walking around before I drove her home.

I don't know why the fuck I can't stop thinking about her. From the moment I set eyes on her, she's been constantly popping into my head. I have no business having thoughts about Rocco Pisano's wife other than deciding how I'm going to kill her, but the notions that flood my mind have nothing to do with her body covered in blood. Just the opposite.

I imagine my fingers in her hair after I pull it out of that damn bun. My hands on her milky white skin, exploring her sinful body while she moans under me. Trailing soft kisses along the line of her delicate neck where I had planned to slice it open. Just thinking about her makes me hard.

The logical part of me feels sick about that. I haven't touched a woman for eight years because neither sex nor any other kind of physical indulgence have interested me in the least. Revenge was my only desire. I lived for it. Nothing else mattered. And now, I'm lusting after one of my targets. It's like fate has decided to royally fuck with me.

Ravenna Pisano turns around and goes back inside, closing the balcony door in her wake. I stay hidden behind the tree for almost half an hour, trying to push away the images of her naked body under mine. And failing.

"I'm just going to grab some breakfast and then we can leave," Mrs. Pisano says as she descends the grand staircase that bisects the house into the two wings, then crosses the foyer and heads toward the hallway leading to the east part of the main floor.

The enormous dining room is in the opposite part of the house, and it's where she always has her meals, even when she eats alone. It's rather idiotic, in my opinion, for her to sit by herself at a table long enough to seat twelve, but it seems that's the way things work around here.

I follow her down the hallway which leads to the kitchen, using the opportunity to commit this part of the house to memory. Only the maids and the housekeeper have gone into this passage, so I've avoided it while Rocco has been home because I don't want to raise suspicion. But he left early this morning, before my arrival.

"Could I get some ham and cheese, Abby?" Ravenna Pisano's voice reaches me from the room further down the hall.

"I'm sorry, Mrs. Pisano," the housekeeper's clipped voice replies, "but the boss said only bread and water."

I stop in my tracks a step away from the door leading to the kitchen.

"May I get milk instead of water?"

The satisfaction in the housekeeper's tone of voice isn't lost on me as she replies, "Mr. Pisano was very clear in his guidelines on the meals I'm to prepare for you. Should I call him and ask about your request?"

"No, of course, not. This is perfectly fine, Abby."

I grit my teeth and step inside the kitchen. Ravenna Pisano is standing by the counter, holding a glass of water in one hand and a plate in the other. A plate with a single piece of bread on it.

"Get out," I say.

Both women look at me with surprise and shock in their eyes. I meet the housekeeper's gaze. "Now, Abby."

She blinks at me in confusion and rushes across the kitchen toward the door. As she passes, I reach out and grab her upper arm.

"And keep your mouth shut, unless you want me to shut it for you." I bend to whisper in her ear. "Permanently."

Abby nods and dashes out of the kitchen. I close the door once she's through and turn to face Mrs. Pisano, who stares at me with wide eyes.

I walk past her and pull out a chair from a small table next to her. "Sit."

She regards the chair for a few moments, then places her glass and plate on the table and takes a seat.

I head to a big black fridge in the corner and open it, scanning the items within. I locate milk and cheese, but I don't see ham anywhere. After I move some of the contents around, I find two packs of sliced ham behind a row of condiments. I slam the fridge doors closed and carry the food to the table where Mrs. Pisano is sitting with her eyes glued to her plate.

Tempering my disgust with this fucked-up situation, I place the groceries in front of her in the same order she asked for them—ham, cheese, and, finally, a jug of milk—then I turn around and leave the kitchen.

The traffic light changes to red. I pull to a stop behind a white truck and look in the rearview mirror. Mrs. Pisano is sitting with her eyes focused on her lap.

She hasn't uttered a word since she exited the kitchen this morning. I took her on another shopping spree and then to her mother's place, where she again covertly left some of the things she bought. A sweater and a shawl this time.

The initial time I witnessed this, I thought the clothes may have been for her mother. But once I had a chance to consider what was happening, I realized that both women are roughly the same size. Since all those items seemed too large for her, the clothes Mrs. Pisano stashed behind the couch must be for someone else. Before we leave, I noticed her slip a piece of jewelry under the cushion of the sofa. We didn't visit any jewelry stores today, so I assume it's something of hers.

The light turns green, and I move my eyes back to the road, but the scene from this morning lingers in my mind.

"Why?" I ask.

It's been eating at me for hours. Why would that son of a bitch control what his wife fucking eats? And, more importantly, why in hell do I give a fuck?

"Excuse me?"

"The breakfast," I say.

When she doesn't reply, I glance in the rearview mirror, expecting to find her glaring at me for daring to ask. She's not glaring. The expression on her face is hard to interpret. Her lips are pressed tight, and her eyes are bulging. An instant later, she bursts out laughing.

It's like magic. Unrestrained, high-pitched laughter that reminds me of chirping birds. I should be watching the road, but I can't take my eyes off her. I'm so captivated by the sight that I ease my foot off the gas pedal so we don't crash and stare at her.

"I'm sorry, but *the breakfast*?" She snorts and erupts into another round of giggles. "Do you have something against compound sentences?"

I want her to keep laughing but I'm not sure how to manage that. In all the time I've spent in the Pisano household, I don't think I've seen Ravenna Pisano laugh once.

"Maybe," I say.

She shakes her head and wipes under her eyes with her fingers. "*The breakfast* is one of Rocco's things. He likes to emphasize that he's the sole provider in our household, so, sometimes, when he's not home during a meal, I only get bread and water as a reminder."

My grip tightens on the steering wheel. "How often is *sometimes*?"

"A couple of times a month."

A horn blares somewhere behind us. I step on the gas pedal and turn my focus back to dealing with traffic. When I look in the rearview mirror a moment later, Mrs. Pisano isn't smiling anymore.

We drive the rest of the way to the mansion in silence. I try really hard to keep my eyes on the road, but they keep wandering to that damn mirror every couple of minutes. After I park in front of the house, I pick up the shopping bags from the passenger seat and get out. Mrs. Pisano has already left the car and is walking toward the front door, clutching the sides of her white coat at her chest.

Ravenna

I've been so deep in thought that I realize Alessandro has followed me up the stairs only after I come to a stop in front of my bedroom door. Taking a deep breath, I turn around and reach out to take my bags, but when my fingers wrap around the ribbon handles, he doesn't release them.

"Has your husband been hurting you?" Alessandro's deep voice comes from above my head.

My body goes still. I swallow and, not looking up, shake my head.

His huge hand enters my field of vision as he takes my chin between his fingers and tilts my head up. I should be intimidated by his towering over me while his dark piercing eyes bore into mine, but his touch is featherlight, and he doesn't make me feel threatened. His gaze is steady, and I realize his eyes aren't black, but the deepest shade of blue.

"I could have sworn they are black," I mumble.

"What?"

"Your eyes."

The tip of his thumb starts moving to the side, tracing the line of my jaw. A tingling starts in my stomach. I close my eyes for a moment and enjoy his touch.

"I asked, is he hurting you?"

Can I trust him? Should I risk telling him the truth? If it was just my life on the line, I would. But I can't risk the lives of my mother and brother. If Rocco finds out I'm trying to escape, he would probably kill us all.

"No." I open my eyes. "Of course not."

Alessandro nods and releases his hold on the bags. The finger on my chin lingers for a moment longer before he turns around and heads back down the hall.

I take off my coat, then carry my purchases to the bed and start putting away the things I've bought. Silk blouses. Cashmere sweaters. Shoes that cost more than six months of my mom's rent. Rocco insists that I wear only particular brands, preferably something where the logo or labels are visible. Sometimes, I feel like a walking billboard, advertising just how rich my husband is.

People love to talk behind my back, especially at parties. They gossip about how well I did, snatching a prize like Rocco. A real-life fairytale about a poor girl who ends up married to a capo. One who showers her with expensive jewelry and clothes. They have no clue what happens behind closed doors, and how those shiny trinkets are used to cover up the bruises.

I would gladly trade it all to get my old life back.

My family, who I'm allowed to visit only under supervision. Friends, who these days turn their heads in the other direction when I happen to unexpectedly meet them while I'm out. I've stopped calling, so they think I believe I'm too good for them now. And my dreams of going to college and finding a good job so that I can help my mom. I want those back.

But most of all, I wish I still had my hopes of getting married for love. The realization that I'll probably never have a family, was the hardest blow. I'm not sure if Rocco is capable of having kids, but even if he is, I could never bring a child into this mess. The Viagra placebo tablets are not the only pills Melania has been supplying me with.

Once I have all the shoes and clothes put away in the closet, I reach for the last bag and take out the black velvet dress. Rocco sent me the link to this particular garment a few days ago, ordering me to buy it for the upcoming party. Like all other dresses he makes me wear, it's short, tight, and shows too much cleavage. I put the awful gown on a hanger and walk out onto the balcony that overlooks the front yard. It's chilly outside, but I don't mind.

Close to the iron gazebo that's located some distance beyond the garage, a figure of a man lurks. Alessandro doesn't seem to be bothered by the cold as he stands, unmoving, and observes the surroundings. I lean my shoulder on the balcony doorway and follow his gaze, trying to figure out what he's looking at. He's at the fringe of a nice enough garden, but there is nothing overly interesting there. Scattered trees, rose bushes that are all dry now, and a few life-size marble sculptures Rocco had ordered. My husband believes that these make the garden look more sophisticated.

Alessandro tilts his head up, looking over at the garden light a few feet in front of him, then looks to the right toward the driveway, where a lamppost illuminates the wide access route. A few seconds later, he heads toward the mansion. He looks deep in thought as he walks straight ahead, then changes course, slightly wavering to the left for a dozen or so feet before turning back to the house. When he reaches the edge of the driveway, he shifts his track once again. The corner of my lips spring upward. What is he doing, going around in a zigzag?

As he reaches the edge of the lawn, he comes to a stop

just below my balcony. I step forward and lean over the railing just as he looks up. Our gazes meet.

The wrought iron railing under my palms feels hot compared to the coldness in my bodyguard's eyes as he watches me.

"Get inside," he barks.

"Why?"

His gaze moves from my face to my silk blouse. "It's cold."

With that, he turns around and heads toward his car parked in the driveway. The fallen leaves and road salt crunch under the tires as he reverses and drives toward the gate, disappearing from view. It must be six already since that's when his shift ends. He never leaves a minute early, even when there is nothing for him to do.

Maybe I could ask him to take me to one of the malls in the neighboring borough tomorrow. I can pretend I'm searching for something particular, and that would allow me to spend more time with him. I like the feeling of having him near, even if he doesn't talk much. I could pretend to stumble again, like I did a few days ago and hoped he'd take my hand to steady me. He did. And for those few seconds, while his huge fingers held mine, I felt like no one could do me harm.

My father's face rises in front of my eyes, his preaching words fill the recesses of my mind. *Marriage is for life, Ravenna. The sanctity of marriage is the foundation of our society.*

Well, I seem to recall something about husbands loving their wives, and there being an equal amount of respect and understanding when it comes to marriage, too. None of those things reside in this house. I hate my husband with a passion so strong that, each day, it's becoming harder to hide. Does it make it okay, then, to be attracted to another man if my husband is a bastard?

Later that night, I wake up covered in sweat. It's not the first occurrence. The difference is, this time, it's not a nightmare about something my husband has done. It's a dream about *him*. My bodyguard. The sweat is not the product of fear but of the overwhelming pleasure that engulfed my dreams where he slammed into me—again and again—as his brooding dark eyes bore through mine.

Chapter
seven

Envy. Distrust. Scheming. All well hidden behind false smiles and chic outfits. Rocco Pisano truly enjoys every kind of circus and having a spotlight on him.

I take a few steps toward the corner where I have a better visual of the room, and clasp my hands behind my back, regarding the people milling around the massive conference hall.

This is supposed to be a business banquet of sorts. Pisano didn't share the specifics when he told me I was to escort him and his wife. It doesn't make a difference, all these events are the same no matter what their purpose is. Most of the people present are businessmen. I do spot a few armed security personnel hanging around the perimeter of the room, just as I am doing. Nothing unexpected, there are usually of few of those attached to some VIPs. The location is public and proficient at hosting these sorts of shindigs, so likely no unusual situations will arise. But I never leave anything to chance. I learned well before I ever got pulled into a secret government program that the extent of shit that could happen is greater when the expectations are low. So, I scan all four exit points once more, assessing the amount of time that will be needed to reach each one.

If I had a choice, I'd take the closest just so I can escape a guy in a tuxedo giving a speech on stock fluctuations and throwing a few lame jokes from a raised platform on the opposite side of the venue. He seems to be the only deadly hazard in this place, threatening to bore guests to death with his nonsense and forced humor.

When I'm done checking the egress points, my gaze wanders back to the Pisano couple. Rocco is laughing at a stupid joke the guy on the stage has just rambled off. His hand rests against his wife's upper back. She's laughing, too. A picture of a happy married couple enjoying the party.

If one disregards the small details, that is.

The way Ravenna Pisano is clutching the glass in her hand. Or how every few minutes she discretely pulls the hem of her dress. The tension in her body when Rocco's hand glides down her back.

My eyes zero in on Rocco's fingers as they grip his wife's hip, and I have to bite the inside of my lip to keep myself from growling. The interest I've developed in the woman I'm planning to kill is highly disturbing. As is as the unexplainable urge to walk up to them and remove her husband's hand.

Blaze sparks in the pit of my stomach as anger boils inside my chest. I shouldn't be pissed off that he's touching her. She's his wife. And yet, my nostrils flare and my eyes squint as an unwelcome thought barrels into my mind. He shouldn't be allowed to touch her.

Gritting my teeth, I make myself look away from Rocco's bony fingers to observe the people around me, but less than a minute later, my gaze is drawn to Ravenna Pisano again. A polite smile is still gracing her face as her eyes meet mine, but there is no trace of laughter in those green orbs watching me from the other side of the room. Just the opposite.

In one of the rare missions when I was sent to save lives instead of to end them, I was in charge of saving a kid held for ransom. The boy's father was Kruger's buddy, a big shot who was neck-deep in shady business, so the official rescue channels were out. I can still remember the look in the boy's eyes while the kidnapper was holding a gun to his head. It's the same look I see in Ravenna Pisano's eyes now.

Dread. And despair. Fuck! The relationship she has with her husband shouldn't matter because I will be killing them both in the end. The fear in her eyes shouldn't bother me. But it does.

The man on the stage finishes his speech, thanking everyone for being here. Rocco lowers his head, whispering into his wife's ear, and I catch relief ghosting across her face. She nods and steps away from him, heading in my direction. The dress she's wearing tonight is skintight and black like her hair that's again pulled up into a bun. The huge diamond earrings and a matching necklace around her neck reflect the light from the crystal chandeliers overhead. Most of the women present are wearing similarly expensive jewelry, but it doesn't escape my attention that Ravenna Pisano's diamonds are the largest in the room.

How would she look without all that makeup and extravagant trinkets, I wonder. A spit-second thought, and the image of Ravenna Pisano naked forms before my eyes. I push that image away in that same instant, but I can't make myself look away from the real woman walking my way.

She stops before me and tilts up her head, her glassy pools drawing me in. "Could you take me back to the house?"

A beat, a breath, and I break eye contact. I give a slight jerk of my head toward the nearest doors and usher her out of the room.

When we reach the coat check, a staff member approaches us, carrying our jackets. He passes me mine and turns toward Mrs. Pisano, holding her black coat out for her to put on.

I yank the coat from his hands. "Back off."

Mrs. Pisano glances at her coat in my hands, then meets my gaze with a question in her eyes.

"Security precaution," I bite out.

She arches one perfect black eyebrow, turns, and slips her arms through the sleeves. The moment her coat is on, I head toward the exit, absolutely refusing to analyze my behavior. The man was an unknown element. He presented a possible threat. Case closed.

The wind blows in my face as we step outside and trudge toward the parking lot. Mrs. Pisano is on my left, trying to keep up with my long strides while her unfastened coat flaps with each strong gust. My car is less than three hundred feet away. It's not that cold, but I stop and wrap my hand around her upper arm, turning her to face me.

"What's wrong?" she asks, looking around.

Ignoring her question, I start buttoning her coat. There are only three buttons and the fabric is too thin. Stupid fancy shit—good for nothing, especially not for keeping a person wearing it warm. When I'm done with the buttons, I raise the lapels so her neck is covered.

"Security precaution, as well?" There's a barely detectable trace of amusement in her voice.

"Yes," I mumble and resume my tracks toward the car.

I try to keep my eyes glued to the ribbon of road beyond the windshield as I drive, but they still drift to the rearview mirror every few seconds. Mrs. Pisano is sitting in silence, clutching her coat to her chest. I blasted the heat the moment I got into the car, but it seems she's still feeling cold. My grip on the steering wheel tightens, turning my knuckles white. I *don't care*, I tell myself and look back at the road. *I. Don't. Care.*

She sneezes.

Shit. I steer to the right and park at the curb. Vehicles zoom by as I exit and walk around to the back, yanking open the passenger door.

"Shoes. Off," I say.

Ravenna Pisano raises her eyebrows in surprise, probably thinking I've lost my fucking mind. I'm afraid she might be right. I bend and, holding her ankle, lift her leg a bit so I can remove her heels. First the right, then I do the same with the left.

"Legs under your ass."

I wait for her to rearrange herself, then take off my jacket and lean in to drape it over her lap. Her forehead is just a few inches from mine, and I can feel her breath on my face. The subtle powdery scent envelops me, urging me to inhale a lungful of it. I tuck the sides of the jacket around her and meet her gaze.

"Next time we go on one of your shopping sprees," I say, glaring at her, "you're buying a proper coat, or I'll buy one for you. Understand?"

The corners of her eyes twitch, and a small smile pulls at her lips. "Congratulations."

I furrow my brows. "For what?"

"That was a beautiful, complex sentence. You're doing great." Her smile widens.

Is she teasing me? I narrow my eyes at her, expecting her to stop smiling under my mean glare.

"Are you trying an intimidation technique on me, Alessandro?"

"Yes," I bark.

She tilts her head up a bit and the tip of her nose touches mine. Her lips are so close that only a minuscule move would be needed to taste them. Fuck! I lean away abruptly and slam the door shut, hurrying back behind the wheel.

When we reach the mansion, I escort Mrs. Pisano to the front door without a word, then turn around and head back toward my SUV. The light over the garage illuminates the metal bay door hiding Pisano's precious vehicles from view. I've been here for two weeks and still haven't put my plan in motion. I could lie to myself and say that I just want to be fully prepared before I take the next step, but I'm well aware this delay has nothing to do with readiness.

It's *her*. Ravenna Pisano and this damn fixation I seem to have developed for her. I'm disgusted by the fact that I've started to care for the woman who is married to Natalie's killer.

I get in the car and head down the driveway, promising myself that whatever spurred me to care about Rocco's wife, ends now. And I purposely ignore the fact that, for a fleeting moment, my eyes flicked to the rearview mirror and the reflection of the window on the left side of the house.

 Ravenna

The slam of a door wakes me from my sleep. I sit up and listen to the steps echo through the hallway, getting closer, and then stopping just on the other side of my door. My pulse jumps into a gallop. Everything remains eerily quiet for a couple of moments, then I hear the door to Rocco's room open and close, and a sigh of relief leaves my lips. He went to sleep. I lie back down, but five minutes later, the sound of Rocco's door opening causes every muscle in me to tense.

Uneven steps drawing nearer. A thump, followed by a curse. I grab the bedcover and pull it up to my chin. The knob turns, and the light from the hallway falls inside my room.

"I'm home, bellissima," Rocco's slurred words hang in the air.

He's drunk. I make myself stay still, hoping he'll go away if he thinks I'm asleep.

"You know, I was thinking. Those pills must have been out of date," he says approaching the bed. "So, I got myself a new batch."

No. No. No.

"Let's see if these work better." He grabs at the bedcover and rips it off me.

I will myself to turn and look. Rocco is standing at the foot of the bed, wearing only an unbuttoned white shirt, a wine stain on its front.

"Spread your legs for your husband."

I stare at him as panic rises and spreads through every nerve of my body. He climbs on the bed and crawls up, looming over me. His hand shoots out, tearing open my pajama top, then grabs at the band of my shorts and pulls them down along with my panties.

"I'm getting hard," he mumbles, then grips my hand and presses it on his still semi-limp dick. "See? Everything is working as it should."

He laughs like a maniac, then drops down onto my body. The smell of alcohol and sweat invade my nostrils.

"Wider!" he snaps.

I spread my legs slightly, and he starts grinding his penis at my opening. Clenching my teeth, I force myself to remain motionless and impassive. The sounds that leave Rocco's mouth remind me of an animal in pain. Wheezing. Short breaths. Moans, as he presses himself to me, brushing his dick on my pussy. Then he stops suddenly and groans. A moment later I feel his cum, warm and sticky, between my legs.

"That was good, bellissima," he says between labored breaths. "It'll be even better next time."

I lie unmoving as he climbs down and heads toward the door. Only when I hear the one across the hallway close, do I spring from the bed and run into the bathroom.

It takes me twenty minutes to scrub myself until I feel somewhat clean again. Rocco doesn't force himself on me often, and since I started switching his Viagra with the placebo Melania has been providing, it happens even less frequently. At least he left the new bottle of pills on my nightstand. It means I can make the switch again. Rocco gets mad when he can't get an erection. He's never got hard enough to actually penetrate me, but I feel disgusted by the mere grinding of him against me. I'd rather face his wrath and blows than have him do that.

I sit on the wooden bench under the window with my forehead pressed to the glass. There's no way I'm going back to bed before I change the sheets, and that needs to wait till tomorrow. I can't risk going downstairs and running into Rocco again tonight. Thinking about what just happened still makes me want to puke.

It's nearly four in the morning, but I can't sleep. Wrapping a blanket tighter around me, I close my eyes, only to open them again a minute later.

I need to find a way to get more money. The amount I collect from the clothes my mom sells to Mrs. Natello is a lot, but not enough. And I have to be careful so Rocco won't suspect anything. I make sure to buy an array of clothes in every shop, but only one item out of the bunch for my mom to resell. That way, if Rocco asks to see what I've purchased, I have something to show him. But it's too slow-going.

The stuff I bought this month was worth eighteen grand, but Mrs. Natello only paid nine, saying she won't spend more than 50 percent for secondhand garments, even though they all still had price tags attached. So, I've decided to give Mom some of my jewelry to sell. Hopefully, Rocco won't notice. Maybe I could implore Hazel to let me help her with accounting twice a week. The money she pays me isn't much, but every penny counts.

As I vacantly stare at the lawn, still lost deep in my thoughts, a shadow moving behind a tree attracts my attention. The security guards are not allowed this close to the house. Could it be an animal? I lean forward, pressing my nose to the cold glass pane, but nothing seems out of the ordinary. My tired brain is probably playing tricks on me.

I must have started to doze off when a loud bang startles me. I scan the grounds and the garden beyond my window, and something orange at the top of the garage catches my eye. Another bang ensues, then a few more. I scream as the roof of the garage caves in. Stunned and unable to move, I watch as the flames consume the building, and its ruined frame gets swallowed up by the raging inferno and the billow of smoke.

CHAPTER eight

"I DON'T FUCKING CARE THAT THE CARS WERE insured!" Rocco roars into the phone. "It's been three days. I want the person who worked on the electrics in my garage found and dealt with!"

He cuts the line and slams his phone on the desk's surface.

"It took me six months to acquire one of those cars," he barks. "Now, they are all gone. Because of some idiot who didn't do his job properly. How the fuck does a fucking electric panel catch fire all of a sudden?"

Yeah. Such a shame.

"I need you to take Ravenna to the hairdresser," he continues. "She'll visit her mother afterward, and you'll get a few hours free. Then, I need you back here at eleven. Armed."

"All right. Situation?" I ask.

"There's a shipment of drugs being handed over to-night, and we're a few men short to deal with it. Some of the guys who are supposed to work this job got pulled away by Arturo. He's essentially gone off the deep end, been driving around town for weeks now, searching for his missing sister. I need you to fill in."

I nod and turn to head out.

"Zanetti."

His voice takes on that smugness and condescension he can never hide. I halt in my tracks and turn back to face him. It takes everything in me not to put my fist through his ugly mug, wiping that self-absorbed expression off it.

"Do you have anything to report? Any strange behavior as far as my wife is concerned?"

"No," I say, just like I do every morning when he calls me to debrief. "Nothing out of the ordinary."

As is usual when I accompany Mrs. Pisano to her mother's place, I'm standing by the wall, my gaze fixed beyond the window. Her mother had fallen asleep on the sofa, and my charge headed out of the main room, saying she'll wash the dishes before we leave. I'm mulling over her actions when the sound of breaking glass carries from the small kitchen area. My head snaps to the side, zeroing in on Mrs. Pisano, who's standing in front of the sink, holding her hand under the stream of water.

"Ravi?"

"I'm okay, Mamma. Go back to sleep." She looks down at her hand. "Shit."

I cover the short distance between us and stand behind her. The blood is oozing from a nasty cut in the middle of her palm. "Let me see."

"I'm fine," she mumbles as she tries to grab a kitchen towel with her other hand. "It was just a chipped cup."

"Let. Me. See."

Her hand hovers over the cloth. Slowly, she looks up, and those guarded greens meet my stare. I turn the water off and take her hand in mine, inspecting the cut. It's not deep, but it is rather long, crossing diagonally across the whole surface of her palm.

"First aid kit?" I take a napkin from the holder and press it on her palm. Her hand is so damn small compared to mine.

"I don't know," she says in a barely audible voice and points to my left. "Maybe in the drawer where my mom keeps her medicine."

There's no first aid kit in the drawer, but I find a disinfectant spray and a small roll of bandage. I remove the napkin and spray her cut. Mrs. Pisano sucks in a breath, but doesn't complain, and watches me in silence as I wrap the length of the bandage around her hand.

"Please don't tell Rocco."

I look up and pin her with my gaze. "Why?"

"Just don't. Please."

I place my palms on the counter on either side of her, caging her in, and lean forward. "What happens to the clothes and the other stuff you buy when you leave them with your mother?"

Ravenna's eyes go as wide as saucers. "Did you tell my husband?"

"No."

She blinks in confusion. "Will you?"

"Nope." I tilt my head to the side and study her. "Are you selling that stuff? Do you need money?"

A mix of uncertainty and trepidation flares in her eyes. Her pulse picks up, hastening her breaths, as well. It lasts but a moment before she pulls herself together, straightening her spine.

"Rocco never puts a spending limit on my card." She juts her chin slightly.

"That's not what I asked."

"Well, that's the only answer you'll get."

The corner of my lips curve upward. I've never seen her talking back to Rocco like this. She is usually skittish around him. My size tends to alarm most people, especially women. They get spooked whenever I'm near, whether there's a real cause or not. Taking this assignment, I kind of expected that Ravenna would be, too. She's not. Seems like there is much more to Ravenna Pisano than meets the eye.

"What are you doing at the spa? The invoices, receipts . . . Accounting with Hazel?"

Ravenna's breath hitches, but her lips remain tightly pressed. It's obvious she won't give me an explanation. I lean forward until my lips brush the shell of her ear.

"Will you ask me not to tell your husband about that, too?" I ask.

When she tilts her head to the side, our cheeks touch. Her powdery scent teases my nostrils, urging me to fill my lungs. I grip the counter harder, suppressing the urge to crush my lips to hers. Closing my eyes, I count to ten.

This woman is too tempting. She's a distraction I do not need, but here she is anyway, jeopardizing my self-control without even realizing it.

"Do I need to ask?" Ravenna whispers.

"No. You don't need to ask." I allow myself another

fleeting second of her touch, then take a step back. "We should go."

Ravenna

"What happened to your hand, Ravenna?"

I jump in my chair, almost knocking over the plate in front of me, and quickly hide my bandaged hand beneath the table. Rocco is standing on the other side, glaring at me.

"I asked you a question, bellissima."

"I . . . cut myself when I helped Mamma with the dishes this morning," I blurt out and regret it the moment the words leave my mouth. Rocco is obsessed with what other people think of him. And by extension, me.

"Do you know that we're going to dinner at my father's this weekend?" he snarls as he walks around the table. "Some of our business partners will be there! Do you want them to think I allow my wife to do menial work?"

"I'm sorry. It won't happen again."

He grabs my upper arm and pulls me up from the chair. I whimper and try moving away, but his grip only tightens.

"Please. You're hurting me."

"You've earned it." He squeezes my arm harder, and I cry out. "I never punish you unless you deserve it. Do I?"

"No, Rocco."

"I'm glad we agree on that." He leans into my face. "Zanetti will take you to buy a dress to wear to dinner. Make sure you pick well so my business partners forget you're a cleaning lady's daughter."

I nod. "I'll go first thing in the morning."

"Afternoon. Zanetti is coming with me tonight as backup, and we won't be back before morning."

"Backup?" I say, breathless. "Is it something dangerous?"

"Are you worried about me, bellissima?"

Worried about *him*? Is he really that delusional?

"You know I am." A lie.

"It's just a drug deal. Now, get out of my sight."

As soon as he releases his hold, I turn and run out of the dining room. Rocco has always been easy to enrage, but ever since he's taken on the responsibility for some of Arturo's duties, he's become worse. The garage fire has only ignited his militant tendencies.

Once inside my bedroom, I climb into bed and snuggle under the blanket. I wish I could kill him. Or have the money to pay someone to do it for me. Often, when I'm lying awake at night, I imagine sneaking into Rocco's bedroom while he sleeps and raising the gun he keeps in his drawer. I've never fired a weapon, so the bullet would likely end up in the wall or the floor. Still, it makes me feel better, imagining the shots that would hit his chest. Other times, I imagine wrapping my hands around his neck and squeezing with all my might. Oh, how I would enjoy watching his bulging eyes stare at me as he struggles for breath. Yeah, I have very intense feelings for my dear husband.

A loud ping breaches the silence in the room, making me freeze. It takes me a few moments to realize what it is. Reaching out, I take the phone off the nightstand and stare at the notification on the screen.

New text message.

I rarely receive any. Rocco installed a device management software on my phone that only lets me communicate with people on my contacts list. And he is the only one with a passcode that allows him to add contacts or change permissions. For months, there've been exactly five numbers on my list. Rocco's. The housekeeper's. And the numbers for the three security chiefs—one for each shift. His most trusted people. But another number had been added three weeks ago.

I click on the notification and the new chat frame fills the screen. Well, *fills* isn't exactly accurate since it contains only one word.

19:47 Alessandro Zanetti: Hand?

I can't help but smile. It's so like him. I touch the tip of my finger to his message. It's just one tiny word, but warmth spreads inside my chest from simply looking at it. Judging by the glares I usually get from him, he hates me for some reason. Still. Except when he thinks I'm cold, or hungry, and now when I'm hurt. He cares enough to ask.

I type a quick response, then hit send.

19:52 Ravenna: Fine.

I stare at the screen for ten minutes, wondering if he'll send something else, but the phone stays silent. I should probably delete the conversation. As benign as it is, if Rocco sees it, he will be furious. He may even hurt Alessandro because of it. I bite my bottom lip, type another message, then quickly delete the whole exchange.

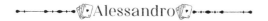

Alessandro

The structure of the abandoned factory that was picked as the meeting point still has its walls and roof pretty much intact, but it's freezing inside because most of the windows are broken.

Rocco has his arms crossed over his chest as he stands and watches two SUVs rolling through the facility's back entrance. Until Arturo returns, Don Ajello has split the responsibilities of handling the drug business between two capos—Cosimo and Rocco. Both are in charge of construction and real estate deals for the don, but now also bear the brunt of extra work. Based on the irritated look on Rocco's face, he is not happy having to get his hands dirty. There's a huge difference between negotiating property contracts in an upscale restaurant over a bottle of expensive cognac, and standing in the dead of night at a cold, rundown factory in the middle of nowhere.

I take the phone out of my pocket and quickly glance again at the message Ravenna sent me earlier. It's the fourth time I've done that so far.

20:02 Ravenna: Be careful tonight.

The thuds of the shutting car doors come from the direction I'm facing, so I put my phone away and assess the newcomers.

There are several criminal organizations and gangs in New York. Those who mind their own business or cooperate with Cosa Nostra are allowed to flourish. Others cease to exist in very short order. The group of men who have just exited the vehicles belong to the set that has been allowed to conduct their operations in this territory. That allowance, so far, has been lucrative for both sides.

Cosa Nostra began doing business with the Serbian syndicate several years ago, after Ajello took over as Don. I'm not certain about the extent of Cosa Nostra's business dealings with the Serbs, but from what I've heard, they move close to

50 percent of Ajello's drugs. They also run a club that presents as an entertainment place for high-end clientele, but in truth, it's a neutral ground where most of the underground transactions are negotiated.

This club happens to be a place where the Serbian boss conducts his main business—dealing in black market precious stones, diamonds mostly. A true jack-of-all-trades, as Ajello alluded, he probably has his fingers and toes dipped in other realms, as well. The don has been trying to plant someone within the Serbs' organization for a couple of years now, without success.

Drago Popov—the head of the Serbian outfit—approaches, and the expression on his face tells me he's not happy to see Rocco.

I met Drago recently when I had some personal business to conduct. In a leather jacket and black jeans, he doesn't look like a typical high-profile criminal. In fact, he seems rather ordinary. The key word here is *seems*. But I know a killer when I see one, and Drago Popov belongs to that label. Knowing Rocco, he's going to underestimate the man, believing he wields the upper hand.

"Where is Arturo?" Drago asks in heavily accented English.

"Arturo is not available. I'm here in his place." Rocco gives him a chin lift. "I want to see the money first."

The Serbian leader raises an eyebrow, then turns to the blond man standing on his right. *"Ko je ovaj idiot?"*

"Capo," the blond guy says.

Drago *hmms* and heads back toward his car. "We'll talk when Arturo is back."

"Hey!" Rocco yells. "Come back here or you can forget about any further deals."

I take the opportunity, while Rocco and his men are focused on the retreating group of Serbs, to head over to Rocco's new sports car. He bought the convertible the day after I burned down his garage, along with all his expensive toys inside. This one, I plan to blow up at some point, too, but not yet. Maybe in a week or so.

Two other vehicles are parked in front of it, blocking me from everyone's view. I crouch beside it and slide my arm underneath, checking the device I planted last night. It's a very sophisticated gadget, and it cost me a small fortune, but it will be worth it.

Making bombs was never my strong suit. Sergei Belov ran point on missions that required our unit to blow shit up. He could make a bomb, using only the stuff one might have in the kitchen, in under five minutes. I may not have the skill set to make them, but I damn well know how to use them.

Rocco is still shouting, threatening Drago that he's going to tank his business. The cocking of guns echoes through the space. Shit is about to hit the fan. Just as I finish arming the bomb, the first gunshot pierces the air. The overhead light fixture explodes, sending shards of glass down around me. I fucking hate it when I'm right.

I switch on the receiver, making sure the signal is live, and take out my gun. A bullet hits one of the windows of the car just ahead. A few of our men have taken cover behind it and are shooting at the Serbian gang members. Gunfire rages all around.

Rocco is squatted on the other side of a low concrete wall, two of his security men flanking him. A bit to the right, another security guy is sprawled on the floor. He caught a bullet to the thigh, but he's alive.

"Back in the cars!" Rocco yells.

I straighten and aim toward the group of our opponents, covering for Rocco's men as they get inside their vehicles. After changing the magazine, I glance over the raised roof of the sports car. Two of the Serbian gang members are unharmed and are trying to help the wounded get inside the SUVs. I made sure none of my shots were lethal. From time to time, small brawls between our crews are not uncommon, it's how illicit business works. As long as no one ends up dead, dealings among us continue.

Rocco rises and sends a bullet to the back of one of Papov's men. Drago pushes the wounded guy into the rear of the vehicle and turns toward Rocco, aiming at his head. I lift my weapon and fire, hitting the Serbian's shoulder. The gun falls from his hand, clattering onto the floor.

As he's getting into his car, Rocco gives me a chin lift, a thank you for saving his life. The idiot has no idea that an expiration date was stamped over his pitiful existence the moment I found out he killed the last family member I had left. And I'll be the only one who gets to end it.

CHAPTER
nine

 Ravenna

I LOATHE VISITS TO ROCCO'S FATHER. NOT ONLY BECAUSE he's a misogynistic pig, but because my husband has an extremely sick need to show off in front of his dad. We've been to Elio Pisano's three times, and on each occasion, the experience was worse than the last. Considering that the business partners will be present tonight as well, it's bound to top all previous occurrences.

I finish fixing my hair and look at myself in the tall mirror. The tight red dress with its ridiculously low neckline that I purchased for this event makes me feel like a slut. Before marrying Rocco, my tastes skewed to casual clothes—jeans and tops, sometimes simple dresses. I favored comfort and pastel colors. I also wore my hair down and never put on makeup, except for special occasions. Rocco insists on a prim and proper hairstyle of a tight, sleek bun and heavy makeup because, in his eyes, it makes me look older and classier. He caught me clean-faced once when he came home from work early. I had to apply a double layer of concealer and foundation for the following week to hide the bruise on my chin.

With one final look in the mirror to make sure everything is as it should be, I leave my room and head downstairs.

Rocco is standing at the bottom of the stairwell, talking with someone on the phone. When he hears me coming, he looks up and nods. I guess my outfit is approved because he turns away and continues with his conversation in a hushed tone. As I'm descending the stairs, my eyes wander to Alessandro who is standing by the front door, and I almost stumble from the intensity of his gaze. Does he like what he sees?

Since my life fell apart like a house of cards, I've been feeling like crap. I'm a punching bag for a perverted man who makes me dress like a call girl so his friends can salivate upon seeing me, only to have him "punish" me for it afterward. But there is a palpable difference in my bodyguard's reaction compared to Rocco's. My husband's face showed satisfaction upon seeing me literally half-naked. An amply revealing outfit means that more men will be ogling me. The expression on Alessandro's face, however, is completely blank, but the look in those steely depths shows disapproval.

I want to laugh and cry at the same time. For months I've detested the heated looks other men have been giving me because it meant I'm going to pay for each one. And now, when I secretly yearn to have *his* lust-filled eyes on me, I'm gifted with disdain instead. Well, these days, I'm used to that, too. Even though it feels more pointed somehow. Breaking our locked stares, I walk toward the front door, looking straight ahead.

Rocco walks up to his shiny new convertible that's parked on the driveway and holds the passenger door open for me. He was in an exceptionally good mood when he drove it home from the dealership and never even commented when I mentioned having spa days on Saturdays, as well. With the end of the year approaching, there is more work to be done, and Hazel jumped at my offer to come twice a week.

Swallowing the bile that rises each time I have to touch my husband, I take his outstretched hand and slide inside the car. Rocco walks around the hood and gets behind the wheel, jabbering about the horsepower and the speed the new car can reach.

"That son of a bitch Cosimo will die of envy when he sees this baby." He laughs as he brushes the white leather upholstery. "I heard him telling Pietro that he was eyeing this exact model but didn't want to spend a hundred grand. Do you know that he still drives that tin can he bought four years ago?" He makes a disgusted face. "Some people have no self-respect."

Sometimes he reminds me of a spoiled child who has a tantrum if anyone has a shinier toy than him. Cosimo happens to be an especially touchy subject for Rocco. Whether the other capo realizes it or not, Rocco's in an all-out duel with the elder man. He tries to best him at every turn. Whatever Cosimo gets, Rocco needs to surpass. Whatever Cosimo wants, Rocco needs to possess first. I think it's all because the don seems to defer to Cosimo's advice more, and Rocco can't handle it.

Rocco continues rambling as he starts the engine and drives toward the gate. I pretend that I'm listening to his nonsense while my eyes wander to the side mirror. Alessandro's SUV is following closely behind us. I can't see his gloomy face in the mirror's reflection, but I can almost feel his eyes on the back of my head. He didn't say anything when he drove me to the Wellness Center this morning, even though we both knew I wasn't going there to have a facial. And when we went by my mom's place afterward, I'm pretty sure he noticed me slipping a purse I got for Mrs. Natello behind the sofa. He didn't comment on it. Why hasn't he said anything to Rocco?

I recall Alessandro's hardened glance when he asked if Rocco had hurt me. The tick in his jaw when he questioned me about the things I buy. The edge in his voice when he assured me of his silence about my time at the spa. Maybe he hates my husband more than he dislikes me.

I dreamed about him again last night. We were in an elevator, facing each other, while a dozen Zippo lighters hovered overhead, throwing yellowish light on Alessandro's face. I wasn't scared of the tight space as I would be in reality. It was as if Alessandro's presence alone chased away the fear and anxiety. He took a step toward me, grabbing the two sides of my dress. The sound of ripping fabric filled the small space as he tore the dress off my body in a single motion. I was naked underneath.

His eyes held mine while he undid his zipper and released his cock, then grabbed under my ass and lifted me, pressing my back to the cold elevator wall. The chill dissolved when his rough palms caressed my smooth skin. His touch seemed so real. As did the absolute bliss once he buried his cock in me with one swift plunge. The flames suspended above us flickered to the rhythm of Alessandro's thrusts, making the scene even more surreal.

Like in the previous dream, he fucked me without mercy for what felt like hours, not a single word uttered aloud the entire time. It was raw. Wild. Unapologetic. And I enjoyed every second of it. I was free. When I awoke, I was so drenched that I had to change my underwear.

"Make sure you behave, bellissima," Rocco says, pulling me back to earth.

I look up at the windshield and regard the shape of a

big white house visible over the fence that stretches down the street. We're almost there. I take a deep breath, trying to mentally prepare myself for what's to come.

"You know the rules," Rocco continues. "No talking unless someone asks you a direct question. No one is interested in what you have to say."

"Yes, Rocco." I nod.

When we park in front of Elio Pisano's house and head toward the front door, I steal one fleeting glance over my shoulder. Alessandro is walking a few paces behind us, a towering shadow on a snow-covered landscape. Our eyes meet for a fraction of a second, and my heart leaps in my chest as his gaze burns through mine.

"When can I expect a grandson, Rocco?"

My body goes stone-still upon hearing my father-in-law's question. I don't dare move my eyes from the plate in front of me.

"Ravenna is still young," My husband says next to me. "We're planning to wait for a couple of years."

"You are thirty-five," Elio roars. "You don't have time for waiting. What if the first one is a girl?"

"Maybe Rocco wants to enjoy having his wife only for himself a little longer." A man sitting further down the table snickers. "I know I would."

Everyone around the table bursts out laughing. I take the edge of the tablecloth between my fingers and squeeze.

"Makes sense. There's nothing grosser than a woman's tits after she's done breastfeeding. Make sure you book a plastic surgeon for her right after," Elio jeers then nods toward my right hand, noticing my stilled movement as I was about to set down the fork. "What happened to her hand? Are you being too rough in bed, Rocco?"

"I would never," Rocco says with a grin, and another burst of laughter ensues.

"Let's go play cards and relax. Rocco, send your woman home." My father-in-law stands up, motioning for the rest of the men to follow. And just when I thought I couldn't feel worse, his next words prove me wrong. "Did you know that my son got his wife in a game of poker?"

I can't take it anymore. Grabbing my purse, I rush toward the other side of the dining room. I don't stop when I reach the foyer, just continue at the same pace to the front door where Alessandro is standing by the wall in his usual stance, spine ramrod straight and his hands clasped behind his back. I grab the knob and, without waiting for him, dash outside. Only when the cold fresh air hits me, do I find the ability to draw a breath. When Alessandro comes outside, I'm already standing by his car, shaking from the cold. I completely forgot to grab my coat on the way out.

I expect him to ask what the fuck is wrong with me, running out like that. He doesn't. Instead, he takes off his coat and holds it out for me. My eyes start to twitch, tears are threatening to spill as I glance at the coat he's holding. I'm shivering from cold but I don't dare take it. If Rocco sees me accepting my bodyguard's offering, Alessandro will be as good as dead.

"Ravenna."

My heart skips a beat. It's the first time Alessandro has used my name. I tilt my head up and find him watching me, his eyes focused on my cheek. He raises his hand, cupping my face, and brushes away the stray tear with his thumb. Tiny hairs at the back of my neck lift at the sensation of his skin touching mine. I can feel every callus on his palm as he strokes under my eye one more time before removing his hand.

"Now, Ravenna." His voice is deeper than usual, and there is a strange incensed tone to it, almost as if he's mad about something but trying to hide it. Snowflakes are caught in his black hair and on his suit jacket. I hadn't even noticed it was snowing until this moment. He raises the coat in front of me again.

I look toward the house and only once I'm sure there's no one in sight, I turn around and slip my arms into the sleeves. On Alessandro, the coat reaches his knees. It swallows me up to my ankles.

I shift my gaze to Alessandro's hand, holding open the door to the back of the car, then walk around him. Tugging on the handle, I hoist myself up onto the passenger seat, shutting the door behind me. Then, I wait.

A few seconds later, the driver's side opens, and Alessandro slides behind the wheel. He doesn't say anything. Not then, and not during the hour-long drive back to the mansion.

Alessandro

The only light in my bedroom is from the laptop in front of me, throwing the pale glow onto the notes and picture-covered walls. I stare at the photo of Natalie, absorbed in her warm brown eyes that seem to return my gaze. Looking at this image has always calmed me. Hurts as well, but it helps me stay focused on my purpose. Every time I fall asleep, her face is on my mind.

The day before I set foot in the Pisano mansion, I visited her grave and reaffirmed my vow that I'll avenge her death. An eye for an eye. Rocco Pisano's wife for mine. I swore to it.

However, looking at Natalie's picture now stirs different feelings in me, the same ones that have been brewing in my soul. Remorse. Shame. Guilt. They've been eating at me for a while because it's not the brown eyes I see when I fall asleep anymore. It's the green ones. Instead of dreaming about killing Ravenna Pisano in cold blood, I'm imagining how it would feel to have her under me, moaning as I take her, declaring her mine.

Earlier tonight, when I watched Ravenna walk next to her husband, his arm around her waist, I nearly exploded in anger. The urge to remove the motherfucker's hand off her was barely containable. I wanted to grab her and shout, "She's mine!" for everyone to hear.

It's madness. And this madness needs to stop.

I click the icon in the upper left corner, and the camera feed from outside Rocco's house fills the screen.

When I came into Rocco Pisano's household, the plan for his demise was already set in stone, thought out to the smallest detail. I imagined my vengeance plan as a big rock fortress rising toward the sky. Solid. Unshakable. Unless an unintended variable arises, making it necessary to act sooner than intended, the plan stays in place. No exceptions.

The printed-out timeline of every fucking stage, all steps strategically spread over the course of two months, hangs above my bed. The garage was phase one. The second is destroying his construction business and making him look like an incapable fool in front of the don. Roco's finances would be the next. Only after I have finished with the material stuff, had I planned to move forward with phase four—playing with his head.

Constant fear for one's life, knowing that there is a threat lurking in the shadows, is the most intense torture. The uncertainty. Looking over your shoulder all the time. The plan was to make Rocco believe someone is trying to kill him and to drag that stage out for weeks until the mere pop of a wine cork makes him shit his pants. Offing his father would come after that. And at the end—his wife. Just before killing the fucking Rocco Pisano and burning down his pretty house to ashes.

On the screen, Rocco's white convertible enters the camera's frame and parks on he driveway. I glance at the detonator at my side. The signal from the bomb I placed under his sports car is still active, ready to be activated remotely. If executed well, being blown into oblivion is a very quick and rather painless death, unfortunately. And the demise I have in mind for Rocco Pisano is neither quick nor painless. I've planned to blow up this car in two weeks, as a scare tactic. And when I put a plan in motion, I never deviate from it.

My thoughts drift to Ravenna, seeing her stand on the snow-covered driveway while the wind blew a few strands of hair that escaped from her bun. I shake my head trying to get rid of the image. Instead of disappearing, the scene continues replaying in my mind, looped on her sad face and the tear sliding down her cheek.

My rock-solid fortress starts shaking. Long thin fissures appear on its sides, and one big chunk of its fortifications breaks off.

Its distant thud thunders through my mind as Rocco exits the car and heads toward the mansion. I feel the aftershocks as I pick up the detonator and place my thumb over the red button.

Eight years of searching and planning . . . compromised. All because of a tear from the woman I swore to kill.

A drop of water upon a stone. Tenacious.

Rocco climbs the stairs, reaching the front doors.

Drip.

I press the button.

The car blows up, its sleek sporty body propelled a few feet into the air in a torrent of fire, smoke, and debris.

A smile pulls at my lips as I watch the orange glow on Rocco Pisano's terrified face while he lies sprawled on the ground. It might be from the blast, but I'd bet it was from the shock. I wonder if he pissed himself.

Well, I leaped from phase one to phase four. Time to realign and get back on track. The son of a bitch will lose everything he holds dear before I'm through with him. His gilded life is about to fall apart.

I keep my eyes on the screen as I pick up my phone and dial Felix. The call rings twice, then disconnects. I hit it again.

"What?" he roars.

"Did you get me in?"

"It's one in the morning!"

I switch the feed to another camera which has a better view of Rocco. "So what?"

"I go to bed at eight!" Felix hollers.

"Stop whining and answer me."

"Do you know what's in the pot? Diamonds! You'll need at least half a million worth of rocks to play with them."

"I know. Did you get me in, Felix?"

"Yeah, yeah, I got your crazy ass in. Players are not allowed to arrive directly, so they will be sending a vehicle for you. Secrecy and all that. You'll get the pickup time and location the morning before the game."

"Good." I switch the feeds again. Rocco and some of the guards are in the process of trying to put out the fire. "And where are we with the body I asked for?"

"*We* aren't anywhere. *I'm* being the goddamned undertaker and digging around for you. I need the date when you want it delivered."

"Just take it when a suitable candidate turns up and store it for me until I call."

"Store it?" he shouts. "It's a fucking dead body!"

"You have a freezer, don't you?"

"And what should I say to Guadalupe if she decides to make carne asada and finds a fucking dead body in the freezer?"

"Who's Guadalupe?"

"My girlfriend," he snaps.

My eyebrows hit my hairline. "You're ninety."

"I'm seventy-five! And for your information, Lupe says I don't look a year over fifty."

"Tell her, 'Sorry, baby, it's just work.' She'll understand. And maybe take her to get her eyes checked."

"Oh, go to hell, Az."

The line goes dead.

I grab the black velvet pouch lying on the desk next to the laptop and take out a small green rock, lifting it toward the light. Drago Popov certainly has a nice product.

CHAPTER
Ten

CRACKING THE WINDOW JUST A TAD AND MAKING sure I remain hidden behind the curtain, I eavesdrop on the conversation happening on the driveway below.

"I could have died, Nino!" Rocco howls. "If the bomb went off ten seconds earlier, I would have been toast! I have a fucking crater in my driveway."

"I'll have the car checked out. Maybe the techs will be able to find something." Nino—the head of the don's security—approaches Rocco's car, or what's left of it, and places his hands on his hips. "Shit."

"I think it's that Slovenian motherfucker. Drago," Rocco says.

"You mean Serbian."

"Whatever. We had a skirmish a few days ago, and some shots were fired. This is payback."

"Who fired first?" Nino asks.

"I did. That arrogant asswipe refused to deal with me! I had to make a point."

Nino pinches the bridge of his nose. "Boss won't be happy with how you handled that, Rocco. I would keep myself out of sight if I were you."

"They started it!"

"I'll call Drago and try to reason with him."

"When is Arturo coming back? I have my own shit to run. Our construction projects are falling behind schedule, and property acquisition deadlines are breathing down my neck. I don't have time to deal with the lunatics he collaborates with."

"No idea. There's still no news on his sister. He's losing it." Nino sighs and heads toward his car. "Someone will come to collect the wreckage later today."

I move away from the window and head into the en suite to take a shower. Like always, I leave the bathroom door wide open so I don't feel as if the walls are closing in on me. It's hard enough to deal with the shower stall, but at least the glass sides help in keeping my anxiety at bay. When they don't fog up too much.

The smell of smoke and burned plastic permeated every part of the house, making me feel dirty and sick. The windows of the ground level had to be barricaded and are being replaced. They were shattered by the blast. When it happened, the explosion was terrifying. The loud bang jarred me awake. I ran to the window to see what had happened and saw the flames consuming the wreck. For a brief moment, I thought Rocco was inside the car when it exploded. And I was relieved.

As I turn off the water and exit the shower stall, I find Rocco standing in the doorway. He's got a spiteful expression on his face like he's ready to wring my neck just for the sheer pleasure of it. I take a step back and plaster my naked body to the cold tiled wall.

"My father's friends wanted to know why my wife left so

quickly last night," he says and takes a step inside the bathroom. "One of them asked if you perhaps didn't like their presence. Or mine, for that matter. Is that true?"

"No," I choke out.

"It certainly seemed that way." His hand shoots out, wrapping around my upper arm. "I'm in a really bad mood, bellissima. Pay attention to your behavior, or you won't like the outcome."

"I will." I nod.

"Of course, you will." With his other hand, he pulls the gun out of the waistband of his pants and aims at the overhead light. The shot reverberates through the small space, and the fixture shatters—raining debris from above and shrouding the bathroom in semidarkness.

"No," I whisper.

"Yes." A sinister smile spreads across Rocco's face as he exits the room, closing the door in his wake. The darkness envelops me.

I spring to my feet, running blindly toward the door. Just as I find the knob, the sound of a turning lock echoes in my ears.

"Rocco!" I scream, as panic builds inside my chest. "Please! Please, don't!"

There is no answer. Only a receding snicker.

I close my eyes and lower myself to the floor, trying to get my breathing under control. I wasn't such a doormat at the beginning of our marriage. The first time Rocco locked me in the closet and turned off the light, I told him to go fuck himself. I sat on the floor, expecting him to come back. Minutes passed. Then hours. I started hearing things. It was probably just noise from downstairs, but to me, it felt like it was right there. Beside me. Although I've never been afraid of the dark—not even when I was a kid—being shut into that small dark space and hearing strange noises all around me, spooked me. When Rocco finally let me out the following morning, I was close to losing my mind. He has done it twice more since then, each time when he was particularly unhappy with my behavior. It left me terrified, and my claustrophobia was born.

My body starts to shake, whether it's from the rising panic or the rapidly cooling floor tiles beneath me, I'm not sure. Probably both. I'm still dripping after the shower, and the air around me grows chilly. My muscles cease up, and I can't make myself stand to search for a towel. Enduring the strikes of his fists is easier than this. I wrap my arms around my naked form and rest my head on my knees.

I wish I had kept Alessandro's coat. The idea of wrapping myself into it makes me feel a little less cold. I don't know why I keep thinking about him. Living with Rocco has made me despise men in general.

When I daydream about the possibility of meeting someone new should I manage to escape my husband, a sick feeling forms in my throat. Before my life with Rocco, wondering about a partner usually consisted of questions such as, *would we like the same things? What if our tastes in music differ too much? I'm an early riser, so what if he prefers sleeping in?* That kind of nonsense. It didn't feel like nonsense then. Now? Now the first thing I think about is, *will he hit me, too?*

Since the days of Rocco's first blows, I started paying attention to the couples around me. From time to time, I'd notice the subtle tells where the seemingly perfect marriage on the outside, was anything but. Just like mine.

Closing my eyes, I imagine Alessandro sitting beside me, his hand holding mine.

"Seventy-three," I whisper.

It feels strange talking aloud when there's no one around, and my voice sounds weak through my chattering teeth.

"Seventy-one," I continue. "Sixty-nine. Sixty-seven. Sixty . . ."

The click of the lock alerts me to the opening door. I look up and squint at Rocco. The light spilling from the bedroom outlines his shape, making him look even more menacing. For a frightening moment, I feel as if I'm at the gates of hell, with Cerberus barring the exit.

"Get dressed," he snaps. "I'm having dinner with an associate and I'm taking you with me."

I watch him as he leaves, and when I hear the bedroom door shut, I rise from my spot in the bathroom corner. Thousands of needles pierce my legs as I drag myself toward the dresser by the bed where I keep my delicates. A white ornate clock is atop it, showing it's two o'clock in the afternoon. He kept me in the bathroom for what felt like days, but it was only six hours.

I put on my bra and underwear and look at my reflection in the mirror. I should sneak a screwdriver or another tool into the bathroom and closet, and hide them somewhere so that next time Rocco locks me inside I can try to dismantle the lock. That idea never popped into my thoughts before today. All this time, it's as if Rocco managed to not only beat down my body and mind but my sense of worth, as well. I stopped fighting him and let him shape me into his obedient dog. With one last look in the mirror, I turn around and head into the walk-in closet.

When I get downstairs, Rocco throws a disgusted look at my black blouse which has a modest neckline, but his lips widen into a smile when he notices the short red skirt that barely covers my ass.

"We're going to be late." He grabs my hand and drags me toward the front door.

We exit the house, and I blink in confusion. Four vehicles are parked on the driveway, with the chief of the first security shift standing next to the one in front. A rental car is next in line—it must have arrived while I was locked away—and two other vehicles are bringing up the rear. Rocco rarely takes bodyguards with him when he attends his meetings. Most of them are with people who are not involved in illegal activities. The only constant security detail has been assigned to me, and it had nothing to do with his concern for my well-being.

My eyes wander to the SUV at the back and the man sitting behind the wheel. My heart beats faster, as it does each time, when I spot Alessandro. He has aviator sunglasses on and seems to be looking straight ahead, but I can feel his gaze on me.

"Get in," Rocco snaps and ushers me into the passenger seat of his rental car.

The vehicle in front of us purrs to life, and it heads toward the gate. Rocco starts the car and follows. I look in the side mirror and notice the last two cars driving behind us. The whole situation is like a scene from a movie—a presidential convoy when he departs the residence.

"What's going on?" I ask.

"Someone is trying to kill me, that's what's going on," Rocco barks.

I take my sunglasses from my purse and slip them on my face, secretly observing Rocco as I do. At first glance, he seems angry. His jaw is clenched and a scowl mars his face. But I look harder, and there are tells that don't escape my notice. The way his eyes dart to the rearview mirror and to the sides every so often. Beads of sweat gathered along his hairline. And finally, his breaths, coming faster than normal.

A smile threatens to pull at my lips, and I'm narrowly able to hide it. Rocco Pisano, the man who proclaims to have the biggest balls in the world, is scared shitless.

The hum of several dozen people talking at once. Laughter. The clang of the cutlery on the plates.

Each sound drills a small hole into my temples. I lift the fork to my mouth, but I don't feel like eating. My throat feels sore and, even though the room is well-heated, I'm cold.

"Are you all right, Ravenna?"

I look up and offer a faux smile to the woman sitting on my left. Rocco introduced me to her and her husband when we arrived at the restaurant, but I can't remember her name.

"I think I'm coming down with something," I say.

"Oh, I'm so sorry, sweetie." She looks toward Rocco who is engaged in a deep discussion with her husband about real estate. "Rocco, Ravenna is not feeling well. Maybe you should take her home."

"Oh?" Rocco tilts his head and pins me with his gaze. "Are you sick, bellissima?"

"No." I quickly shake my head. "I'm okay."

"Sure? Maybe you should head home and get some rest." He leans to the side until his lips are just next to my ear and whispers, "I have a big game tonight. Make sure you're ready when I get home in the morning."

A shudder runs down my spine.

Rocco is a frequent poker player. He usually plays at Luigi's with the other Cosa Nostra men, but he doesn't find those games challenging enough. They simply sustain his addiction. Every three months, however, there is a poker tournament held at an undisclosed location outside of the city, and Rocco has been obsessed with it.

The game is an invitation-only event, and the attending players are concealed. Their identities and presence are kept secret, even from their competitors, but Rocco still loves to brag about it, especially in front of the other capos. The previous tournament was just after our wedding. Rocco won and, when he came home—high on adrenaline and full of himself—he woke me up in the dead of night and demanded I beg him to fuck me. I spat in his face when he told me to remove my clothes and kneel on the floor. He hit me with such force that I ended up there anyway. The following morning, I woke up to a message on my phone. It was a close-up photo of my sleeping mother, a gun pointed at her head. It was a threat of what will happen if I dare to disobey him again.

"Okay." I rise, ready to leave the table.

Ever the doting husband in public, Rocco stands up as well and waves his hand at Alessandro, who's been waiting by the exit with the other two security guys. As Rocco's kiss lands on my cheek, my eyes wander to Alessandro while he's approaching us with a murderous glare in his eyes. It looks like he's back to hating me.

"Take my dear wife home," Rocco says and strokes my hand before he sits back down.

Alessandro follows me out of the restaurant and to his SUV in silence. He doesn't say a word as he starts the vehicle and pulls out onto the street. I manage to keep it together for almost an hour, but as we turn onto the road leading to the mansion, anxiety skyrockets in my chest.

"Please stop," I choke out.

Alessandro immediately pulls to the side of the road. The moment we park, I get out and lean my back on the side of the car. Closing my eyes, I focus on taking deep breaths, trying not to think about what will happen when Rocco comes home.

I don't hear Alessandro's approach around the car. But it doesn't matter. Even with my eyes tightly shut, I can feel him standing before me.

"You know," I say, as the wind tingles my face, "when I was a kid, I thought I was going to be a math teacher."

"Why?"

"I like numbers. And kids. I guess that's how I saw myself." I sigh. "You? Where did you see yourself?"

Silence stretches before he answers. "In jail."

The last thing I feel like doing is smiling at the moment, but his response makes my lips curve up anyway. "Wanna elaborate?"

"No."

Of course not. I wrap my arms around my middle, but I doubt it's because of the cold. A heartbeat passes, and then, a slight caress feathers my face. My eyes snap open to find Alessandro leaning over me. His left palm is braced on the car, just next to my head, while he traces the line of my jaw with the back of his other hand.

"What's wrong?" he asks.

"Nothing. And everything."

"It's either nothing or everything. Can't be both." His eyes peer into mine. Steady. Enigmatic.

"Why do you care? You don't even like me."

"I'd say that neither *like* nor *dislike* are suitable terms in this situation, Ravenna."

I arch an eyebrow at his cryptic words. "No? And what is?"

"Something raw." His face is shrouded in shadows which heighten the sharp lines of his face.

"What?" I whisper.

Alessandro's touch vanishes from my face. He lowers his head until his lips hover close to mine, just a few inches apart.

"I'm still trying to figure it out myself," he says and leans into my body.

I should be timid, having such a hulk of a man pinning me down. With the mess my psyche has become as a result of abuse by my husband, I should feel threatened by Alessandro's size and strength. But instead of fearing his closeness, I want him nearer still.

My most recent dream invades my mind. Thoughts fill with images of him rocking into me against the elevator wall and me screaming in pleasure. How would it feel? Would it be like I envisioned?

"Ask," he says.

"Ask what?"

"The question I see in your eyes."

I shiver at the timbre of his voice. "I was wondering if it would feel like in my dream?"

"What?"

"You," I whisper.

Something flickers across Alessandro's face upon hearing my words—a fleeting emotion, there one second and gone the next. He clenches his jaw and takes a deep breath, steeling his self-control so it seems. Our faces are so close that I can feel his warm exhale caress my mouth.

I tilt my head up ever so slightly. The tip of my upper lip touches his bottom one. It's not a kiss. Just the tiniest brush, but it hits me right in the core of my being. I don't dare move. I don't even breathe.

A vehicle zooms past, its rumbling sound breaking the spell. Alessandro takes a step back.

"We should get going," he says. "I have somewhere to be, and I'm already late."

I nod and quickly get inside the car.

Alessandro

The organizers of the poker tournament certainly made sure they keep the identity of the players a secret.

I get out of the car and look toward the scantly lit one-story house. There are no other vehicles around, so I assume that each player was scheduled to arrive at a different time. A man waiting at the front door escorts me inside, across the unfurnished hall, and into a small room on the left side of the building where another man, wearing a three-piece suit and black gloves, is seated behind a desk covered in a black tablecloth. I guess that makes him an inspector.

"Quality check," he says and taps the surface of the desk with his palm.

I reach into my pocket for the velvet pouch, undo the string, and let the contents spill over the ebony surface.

The inspector grabs a small magnifying glass and, taking one of the rocks, lifts it toward the light. The gemstone shines in the brightness the same way Ravenna's eyes do when she smiles.

"Green diamonds. Nice," he murmurs while looking at the stone from all sides. "Very nice. Popov's?"

"Yes."

"Exceptional quality." He places the diamond on a small scale. After he checks the weight, he makes a note in a leather-bound notebook and moves to the next one.

There is no specific requirement on the size or color of the precious gems that will be used as stakes for the game, as long as each is worth at least twenty-five grand. One stone equates to a chip. It doesn't matter if the actual worth is over the minimum value. For people who attend this particular game, a few grand here and there don't matter.

I move my eyes to the page where the inspector is jotting down the estimate, scanning over the numbers. If Drago fucked me over on even one rock, they won't let me participate.

After the jeweler checks all twenty of my diamonds, he places them back into the pouch and nods at the man who escorted me here.

"He's good," he says and returns the pouch to me. "Steven will be your host for the evening. I wish you a great game, sir."

My host ushers me to a curtained-off space somewhere in the depths of the house. The alcove is encased in heavy black floor-to-ceiling curtains that hang on either side of the door, creating a funnel-like tunnel to a curved bench and chair placed at the far side. At the end, a window—set just above the bench—allows me to see beyond. Once I walk up and take a look, I realize that the curved bench is actually a round table, partitioned by the curtain dividers and the window screen, which appears to be a one-way glass. I can see out, no one can see in.

I take a seat at the table, contemplating my surroundings.

The game is set for four players, judging by the three other screens marking the spots. A dealer's seat is the only one left not concealed, occupied by a stocky man in a bow tie. The black curtains, though sturdy, drape in soft waves. Their color reminds me of Ravenna's hair. It's like she is haunting me everywhere I go.

The hunger that has burned in me by having her body pressed to mine hasn't dissipated, even though it has been hours since I left her at the mansion. I brush my thumb over my bottom lip, recalling the touch of hers in that fleeting moment. It took all of my self-control not to grab her that instant and bite at her tempting mouth.

I expected that problems may arise, that something may jeopardize my plan of vengeance or make things harder along the way. But I didn't expect these to come in a shape of a woman with jewel-like eyes, who's been constantly invading my mind. I want her out of my head. I wish I could take a fucking pair of pliers and dig out every single thought about her. It probably wouldn't help. Even now, two hours after I dropped her off, I still have her scent in my nose.

My host comes to stand on my right, so I refocus on where I am. The small gap between the window and the table is barely ten inches high, just enough to allow my hands to slide through. Everything else is hidden behind the one-way glass screen.

The other three players are already in their seats, their faces hidden, but I can see their presence through the gaps. I'm assuming they each have a host at their side, just like mine is hovering close by. The man across from me has his right hand on the table, holding a lit cigar between his fingers. A thick gold ring with a red jewel is on his forefinger. Rocco Pisano.

I smile and place the pouch with the diamonds in front of me. Let the game begin.

"We're done," says the host to my opponent on the left.

Through the gap under the screen, I spot the man in a white suit slowly rise and leave his enclosure. His host follows him. The player to my right departed half an hour ago. That means only Rocco and I remain.

I lean back and observe Rocco's hands visible beneath the one-way glass. He's gripping the edge of the table so hard, that his knuckles turned white. There's only one diamond left in front of him. Just enough for the ante, but he won't be able to continue the game. All other stones used in the game so far are now mine.

Rocco's hand shoots to the side, grabbing the wrist of his host standing to his right, pulling him closer. There is murmuring, and then the man steps back.

"We would like to continue with checks, if you'd allow it," Rocco's host says.

I raise an eyebrow. Only precious stones are allowed as chips, and when you're out of them, you're done. Switching to checks is allowed only if all other players agree, and the "house" accepts the responsibility for handling the transaction. It is almost never done, due to one very specific reason: The player who uses anything other than stones to place a bet loses the option to fold, and he's forced to call, match, or raise the bet. He must continue playing until the round ends.

Keeping my eyes on Rocco's hands which are yet again gripping the table, I nod and throw a single emerald toward the center of the table.

"Approval granted," my host declares, and the dealer proceeds with the next hand.

Obtaining the details on how much money Rocco Pisano has in his bank accounts, both legitimate and overseas wasn't easy. It took Felix a few weeks to get that information for me. The total is a little over two million. I was rather surprised by that sum. Based on how much he spends on cars, I would've expected ten times that amount.

When the time comes to place a bet, I take twenty gems from the pile in front of me and slide them forward. I can't see Rocco, but I can imagine the look on his face. He sits unmoving for a couple of moments, then takes out a checkbook, scribbling something with curt, angry moves. His host accepts the check Rocco hands him.

"One million," the man declares and places a house chip in lieu of Rocco's check in the middle of the table.

I can barely stifle a laugh. Not only did the stupid motherfucker call my bet, but he also doubled it. He must be desperate to get his diamonds back. I take the rest of my stones and push them forward, raising the total bet to two million.

Rocco Pisano has two options. To match my raise by adding another million. Or to raise again. However, according to the rules of this tournament, the new raise must be double the sum of what I just put forward. And I know he doesn't have enough money left in his accounts to do that. He reaches for his pen and writes another check.

"One million, amounting to a total of two million dollars," Rocco's host says and adds another house chip to the table.

"The bet has been called. Please show your hands," announces the dealer.

Since I was the one who made the last raise, I should be

the one to show my cards first. It seems like my opponent is too eager because he throws his cards down, and his hysterical laugh fills the room. I look down at his hand. Full house.

Rocco is still laughing when I place my cards on the table, then his laughter dies. Silence descends over the room, and only the sound of labored breathing can be heard from behind Rocco's screen.

"We have royal flush here," my host announces and turns to face me. "Congratulations, sir."

I wait while the inspector approaches the dealer and replaces the chips with the equivalent number of stones. He then slides the diamonds toward me, and my host collects them and places them into my pouch. I take out four rocks and hand them over as a fee to the tournament organizers. With the transaction complete, my host motions for me to follow him out. Glancing at the screen to where Pisano is still sitting, I smile and leave the room.

The car that brought me to this location awaits when I exit the building. The driver is hovering by the back door and springs to open it as I approach. I stop before him and lift one gem in front of his face.

"Sir?" he asks as his eyes go wide at the sight of the shiny rock.

"I need to borrow this car." I throw the diamond at him. "I'll leave it at the same spot where you picked me up."

"Yes, yes. Certainly." He nods eagerly as he shuts the rear door, rushing to the driver's side to get that one open instead. "Just leave the key in the glove box. I have a spare."

The moment I get behind the wheel, I floor it, peeling out of the driveway.

When I get close to the Pisano mansion, I find a spot where I can get the car off the road and park behind some bushes which will conceal it from view should anyone happen to drive by. The remaining distance, I cover on foot. My analysis of camera placements on the perimeter wall and at the gate, as well as the field of view they cover, leads me to a location with direct sight of the entrance but falls into a blind spot. Then, I wait.

Half an hour later, headlights appear down the road, nearing the gate.

I know men like Rocco Pisano—arrogant, self-important bastards who can't deal with the reality when someone bests them. They often need a way to shake off their ire when faced with their own failure, and usually with violence while blaming someone else. In the weeks I've been with Pisanos, I haven't seen Rocco hurt his wife, but something still doesn't add up. I can't get that haunted look in Ravenna's eyes out of my head.

An angry man may resort to violence, but a scared one will likely seek a hole to hide in. I want to make sure Rocco is the latter. So, as his car stops at the gate, waiting for the metal door to slide to the side, I take out my gun and aim at the back of the car. Then I empty my magazine into the rear window, fender, tail lights—anything I can, but avoid actually hitting Pisano.

The security guys rush out of the guardhouse, guns raised, and head toward the car to check on their boss. By the time they start combing the terrain around the gate, I'm already partway to the other side of the property where last week I hid a rope with a climbing hook in one of the bushes.

Getting over the wall poses no problem, but going across the yard takes me more than ten minutes because I need to zigzag my way along a specific path that keeps me out of the view of the cameras. When I reach another blind spot by the west wing of the mansion, I throw the hook up where it catches on the balcony handrail. The skin on my hands feels raw from climbing the rope with no gloves on by the time I get to the top. I pull the rope up and crouch behind the parapet so I'm hidden from view.

The glass door is closed, and the curtain is pulled over it, but the white sheer material still allows me to see through it. Ravenna is sleeping curled under a blanket. I'm not even sure when I started thinking of her as "Ravenna" instead of "Mrs. Pisano," but that's what she is now. I can't handle labeling her as a Pisano anymore. That asshole's name is too filthy for her to bear.

I shift my attention to the bedroom door on the other side of the room and take the gun out of my holster.

The yells and hustle of the security guards as they search the grounds draw near. They must be moving this way.

What the fuck am I doing—keeping watch over the woman I'm planning to slay? Risking exposure because I need to be sure that the son of a bitch won't be hurting her? I shake my head as if it'll help clear my fucked-up mind.

Maybe Felix was right. Maybe I've gone insane, but not because of the gore and violence I've seen and done. The trigger for my madness is sound asleep only a few feet away.

CHAPTER
eleven

 ❤ Ravenna ❤

I PULL THE BLANKET TIGHTER AROUND ME. WHY IS IT so cold? Did I leave the balcony doors open? I'm not sure. The last thing I remember is lying in bed, glaring at my bedroom door, and expecting Rocco to arrive. Maybe I dozed off.

Sitting up, I glance at the clock on the dresser. Half past five in the morning. Rocco didn't come to my room last night. A sigh of relief leaves my lips. It's possible he got drunk after the game and went straight to bed upon returning home, but that seems unlikely. He gets even more riled up when he drinks. Whatever the reason, I was spared last night, but it doesn't mean I'll be lucky again next time. Dread floods my veins and a shudder of disgust runs through me.

A slight movement catches the corner of my eye, and I look at the balcony doors, finding them closed. It's still dark outside, but even with the curtains disrupting the view, I recognize Alessandro's imposing form. He's there in one breath, and then just disappears in another.

I rush toward the balcony doors, wrapping the blanket

around me as I do, and slide it open. Cold morning wind blows into my face, making the long sheer curtains flutter on either side of me while I take in the empty terrace. I've nearly convinced myself that I only imagined seeing Alessandro out here when my eyes get caught on a metal hook grappled over the railing. I move two steps forward and look down over the edge.

"What the . . .?" I mumble as I watch my bodyguard swiftly climb down the rope attached to the hook.

Alessandro is still several feet above the ground when he leaps and gracefully lands on his feet. My jaw hits the floor. How can someone his size be so agile? I'm still in a state of shock when he looks up and our gazes collide.

"The hook," he says calmly as if scaling onto people's balconies is the most natural thing in the world.

I glance at the hook, then back at him.

"Now, Ravenna."

Without breaking our eye contact, I unhook the metal thing and let it fall to the ground. Alessandro bends to collect his equipment and then casually walks away, heading toward the garage. When he's halfway there, he makes a sharp turn to the right and continues in that direction for a dozen or so feet. He reaches the oak tree next to the garden fountain and changes direction once again. What the hell is he doing? If someone sees him, he's dead.

But there's no one around this close to the house, except Rocco who's probably asleep, is there? Just the cameras. I survey the lawn, taking in the lampposts and the cameras mounted on them. I'm sure those are still recording. The security in the guardhouse monitors the stream twenty-four seven, but I don't see any of the men rushing out here to apprehend the intruder.

Alessandro heads right, toward the back lawn, out of my sight. I rush out of my bedroom to the hallway. There is a big window at the end, and I reach it in time to see my bodyguard swinging his grappling hook over the outer wall. The dimness of predawn makes it hard to make him out clearly, but I'm pretty sure that just before he starts climbing, he glances back at the window where I'm standing. Moments later, he disappears over the wall.

Right as I get back to my bedroom, my phone vibrates on the nightstand.

05:47 Alessandro: Go back to sleep.

I stare at the message, then type a reply.

05:47 Ravenna: What were you doing on my balcony?

Several minutes pass before he responds.

05:54 Alessandro: My version of a spa treatment. Kinda like yours every Wednesday and Saturday, Ravenna.

Laughter surges in my chest, threatening to burst. I bury my face in the pillow and let it out.

I dozed off again, finally feeling more calm after spending a restless night dreading Rocco's return. When I wake just after eight, I've got the worst headache on earth and my nose won't stop running. I rarely get sick, so I don't keep any medicines in my room. Maybe one of the maids has something? Rocco has forbidden me from leaving my room without makeup, but he should have gone to a meeting he mentioned last night. It's probably safe for me to quickly go downstairs and get something for the pain. I exit my room and head down the hallway when I hear the door to Rocco's bedroom open.

"Ravenna!"

I take a deep breath and slowly turn around to face him. His eyes travel over my nightgown and then drift up, stopping on my makeup-free face.

"Where the fuck do you think you're going looking like that?" He takes a step forward.

"I just need to get some medicine from the kitchen, and I'll come back upstairs to get ready."

"And what have I told you about walking around and looking like something the cat dragged in?"

His hand wraps around my neck, making it hard for me to draw air. I grab at his fingers, trying to pry them off, but his hold only tightens.

"Don't defy me, bellissima." He brings his face close to mine. "I'm not in the mood to deal with your disobedience. If I must, you won't enjoy your punishment."

With one more squeeze, he lets go of my throat, and I double over, coughing and struggling to fill my lungs.

CHAPTER
Twelve

•───•───•◦♦♦◦Alessandro◦♦♦◦•───•───•

T HE FRONT DOOR OF THE PISANO MANSION OPENS
as I'm exiting my SUV. Rocco rushes out, carrying a
big folder under his arm, and heads down the stone
steps toward one of the other four cars parked on the driveway.
His suit jacket is unbuttoned, and I can see that he's wearing
a bulletproof vest under his dress shirt. I size up the car he's
getting into. It's not one of those fancy convertibles he likes,
but a sturdy SUV with heavily tinted windows. Seems that last
night's events scared him enough to start using an armored
vehicle. Good. I wait until the entourage leaves the driveway,
then head inside the mansion.

One of the maids is standing at the foot of the stairwell,
polishing the wooden banister with a sour-smelling chemi-
cal. Ravenna doesn't seem to be around, so I turn toward the
east wing. I tried catching a nap when I got home this morning, but I couldn't stop thinking about her.

Unease settles in my guts. From the moment I climbed
off that balcony, I had a feeling that I should have stayed until
Pisano left the house. And my instincts have never been wrong.

Ravenna is not in the kitchen. The housekeeper is the only one there, putting groceries into the fridge.

"Where is Mrs. Pisano?" I bark.

The housekeeper jumps, startled. "Still sleeping."

It's nine o'clock. Ravenna is always up before I arrive. I turn around, intending to calmly walk down the hallway to check out the dining room and the library, but end up running. She's not there either. Fuck! I'm halfway up the stairwell, heading to check her bedroom when my phone rings. I fish it out of my pocket and see her name on the screen.

"Can you drop me by the pharmacy?" she asks when I take the call. Her voice sounds raw.

I grip the banister to the point my knuckles turn white. "Why?"

"I think I caught a cold."

My hold eases, blood returning to the extremities.

"I'm downstairs," I say and put the phone away.

That's when I notice the maid still at the bottom of the stairs. She's busying herself by pretending to polish wood but, I spot her watching me from the corner of her eye. I can almost see her inquisitive glower. Shit. I completely forgot about her. It seems I forget things quite often whenever Ravenna Pisano is in the picture. Ignoring the maid's stare, I pass her by and stand by the front door.

Ten minutes later, Ravenna appears on the top landing. As she descends the stairs, I scan down her body, from the top of her head to her black heels. She seems okay, but I eye her up and down again to make sure. Her powdery scent invades my nostrils as she rushes past me through the door.

Once we're inside my car, I take a closer look at her through the rearview mirror and notice dark circles around her eyes that are visible even under her makeup.

"The pharmacy is right here." Ravenna takes a tissue from her purse and wipes her nose.

I park the car and follow her inside. When the man at the cash register rings up her purchases and starts putting them in a small paper bag, I take note of the contents. Nose drops. Pain and fever meds. Vitamin C.

As we're approaching the car, Ravenna stumbles, and I reach out to steady her. Her eyes zero in on my fingers wrapped around her forearm, then move up until our gazes connect.

"You need to be in bed," I say and release her arm.

"I have to check on my mom."

My eyebrows furrow. She's barely able to stand on her own, and I'm fairly certain she's running a fever. Without taking my eyes off her, I lift my other hand and press my palm on her forehead, finding it hot. Her emerald irises return my stare, but she doesn't move away.

"I'm taking you home," I say, but I don't remove my palm. She's wearing a long dark-green coat and a matching scarf that's wrapped around her neck. Both make the color of her eyes pop on this dreary day.

"Okay," she whispers.

I nod and let my hand drop to open the car door for her. She looks at the back seat, then heads around and opens the passenger door, taking the seat at the front. I should tell her to sit in the back.

I don't.

I do tell her to move before we're in sight of the gates. I don't trust anyone not to open their yaps and let Rocco know they saw her sitting beside me. I'm still not sure what happens in that house, but I'm not doing anything to jeopardize her safety and well-being on *my* account.

When we reach the mansion, I follow Ravenna inside. I don't think she even notices me walking behind her, too focused on finding a tissue in her purse and blowing her nose. Why in hell do I have a ridiculous urge to make sure she goes straight to bed? I should hate anything and everything that's connected to Rocco Pisano. His wife included. Especially his wife. At the same time, I *need* to know that she's okay. And that's all kinds of fucked-up.

Ravenna starts ascending the stairs, but then stops at the third step and falls into a fit of sneezing. The sound reminds me of a little kitten. It's hard to believe, but she looks regal even when she sneezes. Shaking my head, I lean forward and scoop her into my arms.

"What?" Ravenna gulps in surprise, then sneezes again.

I carry her up the stairs, keeping my eyes fixed directly ahead, trying to ignore the overwhelming enjoyment of having her so close. Denying myself the need to pull her even closer against my chest. Her face is just a fraction away—I can feel her breath fanning my neck. When I reach the landing, I carry her down the hallway and lower her to the ground in front of her door.

"Um . . . thank you. It wasn't really necessary, but"—she sneezes, then looks up at me—"thank you."

I watch her, noticing how red her nose is from wiping it with a tissue at least a hundred times, and how tired she looks. I want to take her back in my arms, as if it would somehow make her feel better.

Instead, I just nod once more.

Ravenna blinks at me and then smiles. My breath catches the same way it did the very first time I saw her.

"People really need to dig to get a word out of you, Alessandro." She cocks her head to the side.

The scarf around her neck has come loose, and my eyes fall to her throat. Or more precisely, to the vibrant red marks on it. Murderous rage ignites in my chest. I plant my palms against the door on either side of her and lower my head until our faces are only inches apart.

"Was it Rocco?" I say through gritted teeth.

A gasp leaves Ravenna's mouth.

"When, Ravenna?"

She turns around, twists the knob, and disappears into her room, closing the door behind her. I squeeze my hands into fists and take a deep breath. And another one. He dared to touch her. Hurt her. It must have happened this morning, after I left.

Taking out my phone, I open the tracking app. I didn't have a chance to put a tracer on Rocco's new car, but I do have his security vehicles tagged. And where Rocco goes, they follow.

The highest level of this unfinished garage gives me an unobstructed view of the surrounding area. I lower my bag to the ground and look down at the construction site on the other side of the street.

Rocco is standing by a makeshift table placed off to the side. The man, who looks to be a site manager, is across from him and is currently staring at the blueprints spread out between them. Rocco's security men—five of them, with hands never leaving their holsters—are spread in a ten-foot radius around him.

I crouch next to my bag and start reassembling my rifle. There are not many sniper rifles designed to be assembled on the spot. Most are intended to be transported and used as complete units because each time the precision weapon is disassembled and reassembled its accuracy is impacted. This beauty has the barrel and optic assembly in one piece, so it remains zeroed in and ready to fire. It cost more than my car, but the alternative would be carrying a meter-long weapon around. Only a lunatic would do that. Well, a lunatic or Kai Mazur.

None of the guys in my old unit were exactly sane, but Kai Mazur was a unique type of crazy. He reminded me of a trained bloodthirsty animal who never forgot his feral nature. I wonder if they found him in a fucking jungle, taught him to feign civility, and pushed him into the program. Kai was the only member of the team who was sent on missions before he reached the age of eighteen. I think our commander, Kruger, eventually regretted recruiting Kai and kept sending him on the most dangerous missions with the hope he wouldn't return. But that maniac always came back. Except for that one time he got picked up because he was strolling through the city with a damn sniper rifle on his back in the middle of the day. Attracting the attention of local law enforcement was a big "no" in our line of business, but I'm pretty sure Kai did that on purpose, just to rile up Kruger.

I finish assembling my weapon and take cover at the unfinished parapet wall. Rocco, still in a heated discussion with the site manager, leans forward over the table, his palms planted on the wooden surface. I look through the scope and aim at the bastard's head. So easy. It would be so fucking easy to end his life here and now. I imagine the bullet passing through his temple and dwell on the idea of his brain matter exploding through the other side, but then, I shift my aim lower until I'm zeroed in on the middle of his right hand. The hand that's responsible for the bruises on Ravenna's neck.

And I squeeze the trigger.

 Ravenna

He saw.

I can't believe I forgot myself and let Alessandro see my neck. I always make sure I cover the bruises with foundation, but I was so exhausted this morning that I decided to use the scarf to hide them. Applying a full face of makeup drained what little energy I had.

I reach for the pain and fever meds on the nightstand and take two pills. My head feels like it's going to explode. Bundling myself under two blankets, I close my eyes and let myself drift to sleep.

Bang.

I squeeze my eyes shut and throw the blanket over my head.

Bang. Bang.

"Mrs. Pisano!" the maid's voice carries through the door.

"I'm sleeping," I choke out and turn toward the wall.

"Nino needs to talk with you, Mrs. Pisano. He said it's urgent."

I sit up. What would the don's head of security need with me?

"I'll be downstairs in fifteen minutes," I say and drag my-self out of bed.

After a quick shower and putting on a new layer of makeup, I leave my room and head downstairs. The fever had broken while I slept, so I feel slightly better. It doesn't show on my face, however, so I made sure I put enough war paint on to hide that fact. When I enter Rocco's office, Nino is standing by the desk. Alessandro is a few steps behind him, his back leaning on the wall.

"There has been a shooting, Ravenna," Nino says.

"A shooting?" I don't understand why he is telling me this. Nobody ever tells me anything about the "business."

"Someone tried to kill Rocco. It was a sniper, but he got away before we managed to locate him," Nino continues. "Rocco is at a private hospital. Doctors are trying to save his hand."

"His hand?"

"Yes." Nino nods. "The shooter missed. The bullet hit Rocco in his right hand."

My heart rate skyrockets, a wave of emotions surges through me but I'm too overwhelmed to make sense of any specific one. I move my eyes from Nino to the shadow loom-ing at his back. There are no words that could describe the look in Alessandro's eyes as they pierce mine. Bottomless, dark-blue depths regard me with unblinking determination. So full of rage and spite, but also satisfaction. He tilts his head to the side and moves his gaze to my neck where the bruises are hidden under several layers of concealer. Then, back up until our eyes meet again.

And I know.

The sniper didn't miss.

"Ravenna," Nino asks. "Are you okay? Do you need to sit down?"

I make myself look away from Alessandro and shake my head. "I'm fine, Nino."

"There won't be any visits allowed today, but Zanetti can take you to see Rocco in the morning," he says and looks over his shoulder at Alessandro. "Go pack. I want you back here in three hours."

"Pack?" I ask.

"Zanetti will stay in the mansion with you until Rocco gets released."

I definitely should have sat down. Fairly certain my heart is about to punch its way out of my chest. "All right," I manage to say. "Anything else?"

"That's all. I'll let you know when Rocco is out of surgery. Don't worry, these doctors know what they're doing, and it's not the first time they've treated Cosa Nostra men."

I follow Nino with my eyes as he leaves the office. When he's out of sight, I take a deep breath and face Alessandro who is still silently leaning against the wall on the other side of the room. He straightens and heads toward me. Each step he takes feels like a zap within my chest. He stops in front of me, his huge body towering over my frame, and I tilt my head up to meet his gaze.

"It was you, wasn't it?" I whisper, staring into his eyes.

Alessandro doesn't reply. He just regards me for a couple of moments, then lifts his hand and lightly brushes my cheek with the back of it. It's a very light touch, but it still feels like I've been hit by lightning. Without moving his fingers from my face, he bends until his mouth is just next to my ear.

"If your husband still has his hand when he comes home,"

he says in a deep, controlled voice, and a shudder ripples down my spine, "I'll correct it immediately."

His touch disappears, and I close my eyes for a second, mourning the loss of his warmth. When I open them again, he's gone.

CHAPTER Thirteen

•————•—•————•🂠Alessandro🂠•————•—•————•

I PUSH THE BLUEPRINT OF THE PISANO MANSION WHICH Felix provided inside my dresser, and reach for my jacket and the shoulder holster on the chair. I had set my alarm for five in the morning so I could have enough time to check out the east wing before the housekeeper and the maids start their shifts at eight.

When I arrived with my bags last night, the housekeeper proposed I take one of the guest rooms in the west wing. I've already explored that part of the house in detail over the last couple of weeks, so I declined. Instead, I moved into a small room in the east wing, one that was probably meant to be a storage space but got outfitted for household staff at some point. It has only one narrow, horizontal window, high up on the wall. From the outside, no one can actually see inside, especially because the AC unit and other utility meters are in the way. It's also close to the kitchen and laundry room which I haven't had the opportunity to recon so far.

I step out and head down the hallway toward the laundry room, passing the kitchen and a few more empty staff bedrooms along the way. The blueprint showed that there is an unfinished sublevel space below the main floor of the house, but the schematic didn't have the entrance to it marked. I find the basement door on the far end of the laundry room, behind one of the shelves holding cleaning supplies. It's locked.

I take out my phone and check the camera feed from the entrance gate. The security guards are in the middle of their shift—acting rather lax, actually—and no cars are in view. Putting the phone away, I take out my set of lock picks. The basement door has only a standard lock, and it takes less than twenty seconds to unlock it. When I descend the steps, I look around the vast space. It's only one room with a furnace and the water tank off in the corner, duct piping and electrical wires running along the exposed beams. There is nothing else except thick support pillars.

I take my time inspecting the heating unit and the pipes, then check the walls until I find an electrical panel. With that done, I move to the support pillars, making calculations in my head. The house might be smaller than I originally expected but overloading the circuits won't be enough. The pillars will have to go, too. I do another round to make sure I haven't missed anything, then return to the laundry room.

Striding down the hallway, I intend to head upstairs and check out the upper floor, when I hear sounds in the kitchen behind me. Isn't it too early for the maids to be here? A look at my watch confirms it's not eight, yet. I turn around and retrace my steps, only to stop short when I get to the kitchen doorway.

There is a woman standing by the open fridge, searching for something inside. Her face is hidden behind the appliance door, but I'm certain I've never seen her here before. She's wearing black leggings and an oversized gray sweater with the sleeves rolled up. Her feet are bare. Long black hair is falling down her back in soft waves.

"Who are you and what are you doing here?" I bark.

She jumps with a yelp, closes the fridge, and turns to face me. My eyes flare in shock.

"Good morning," Ravenna mumbles.

I can't stop staring. If I saw her walking down the street, I probably wouldn't have recognized her. Ravenna is a hundred times more beautiful without makeup. She looks like a fucking angel who descended from heaven, and I find it impossible to take my eyes off her. She is also much younger than I thought.

"Um . . ." She tilts her head to the side and picks up one black strand between her fingers, twirling it. "Are you okay?"

No, I am not okay.

Although I've never been attracted to women who wear a lot of makeup, I've been mesmerized by Ravenna, even when she wears lavish clothes and has a ton of crap smeared over her face. But seeing her with her hair hanging freely, framing her angelic face, I feel like I've been sucker punched, unable to draw in air.

"I need to go to the hospital and then check on my mom after," she says.

My gaze moves down, stopping at her throat. The bruises on her neck are a deep purple color today, and looking at them rekindles the rage in my stomach. It's my fault. I should have stayed on that damn balcony and killed that motherfucker the moment he went inside her room, no matter the consequences.

"Alessandro?" Ravenna steps forward and inclines her head.

I carefully reach out and move her hair back so I can have a better look. The black strands feel like silk on my palm.

"I like your hair," I mumble.

Ravenna's lips curve upward. "I like your hair, too." She lifts her hand and hesitates for a few moments, then glides her fingers over the side of my head.

"It's really short." She smiles.

I should fucking leave, not discuss damn haircuts, but I can't make myself move.

"Habit."

With my hand on her neck, I trace the shape of each bruise with the tip of my finger. Her skin is so soft, and to see it marred in such a way makes me want to go to that hospital, cut off the bastard's hand, and make him eat the damn thing.

"Was that the first time?" I ask through clenched teeth.

"Yes." She shrugs. Her hand is on my upper arm now, and I can feel the warmth of her touch even through the fabric of my shirt and suit jacket.

She's lying. I should have realized way sooner that her husband was hurting her. There were so many signs pointing out that something is wrong between them, but I was too blinded by my hate and focused on vengeance that I chose not to dwell on them.

I still don't want to. I don't want to care. It would mean kissing my revenge goodbye and breaking the promise I made to myself and to Natalie. That can't happen. I might have deviated from my plan so far, but I am going to execute it in full at the end. These stupid feelings that started growing in me, wrapping around my ice-cold heart like fiery claws, need to be extinguished. I hate Ravenna Pisano, and my stupid heart better remember that.

The sound of female chatter and hurried steps reach us from the direction of the hallway. The maids have arrived.

Ravenna quickly pulls her hand from my arm and steps away. "I'll be ready in twenty if that works for you?"

I nod and leave the kitchen.

Ravenna

Not one word.

The man sitting next to me shot off my husband's hand because it was used to hurt me, but he hasn't said a single word to me since we got inside his car. But I did catch him looking at me when he thought I wouldn't notice—a sideways glance as I was sliding onto a passenger seat instead of the back one. A squinty glimpse while I rummaged through my purse looking for a new pack of tissues. A peek through the reflection in the side window as I was trying to find the switch on the dashboard to turn up the heat. I can't stand it anymore.

"So . . ." I ask. "Cat got your tongue?"

Nothing. Alessandro keeps staring at the road straight ahead.

"Looks like it." I blow my nose in the tissue. "Shame. I quite enjoy your one-word monologues."

He grunts. The man fucking grunts at me.

"Sorry, I don't speak that specific dialect. Can you try again?"

This time, I get a sideways stare, then he looks back toward the road.

"Does my presence suddenly bother you, Alessandro?"

I hear the squeak of the leather as he tightens his hold

on the steering wheel. The moment is brief before the tendons on the backs of his rugged hands relax. I swear to God, I don't understand this man. I shake my head and focus on the buildings we're passing by. We're almost at the hospital.

"You shouldn't have shot Rocco," I say. Maybe Alessandro is worried that the don will learn of what he's done? Punish him for it? Blame me? "Don't get me wrong, I'm glad you did. But it's obvious you're regretting it now. Why else would you act like—"

The car suddenly swerves to the right, and I scream and grab the door handle like my life depends on it. I squeeze my eyes shut as we barrel toward the streetlight. I assume we missed it because the SUV comes to a screeching halt a split second later. The car door slams, and I'm left in silence.

Tentatively, I open my eyes and watch Alessandro as he walks past the car, stopping several feet ahead on the sidewalk. The biting wind seems to have little effect on him even though he's not wearing a coat. It still lies on the vehicle's backseat, just where he threw it when I chose to sit at the front.

He turns partway, not quite toward me but enough that I catch his fleeting glance, and throws his head back, facing the sky. What's he doing? Seeking help from above? With his hands on his hips, the restlessness wafting off him is nearly palpable. I watch as he finally drops his head forward, chin nearly hitting his chest. He slowly shakes it side to side, and I have a distinct impression that an internal struggle just went on within him.

Finally, he looks at me through the windshield, our eyes catch and hold. His seem to burn as he strides toward me, his gaze unbreaking. The closer he gets, the faster he moves. A predator with prey in sight.

Approaching my side, he grips the handle and opens the

door with a forceful yank. The air cracks as he leans inside, his muscled bulk invading my space. The look in his eyes is positively feral, like he wants to annihilate me on the spot.

"This is why," he grits out through his teeth and, grabbing the back of my neck, slams his mouth to mine.

I don't breathe. I can't! It seems like even my heart has stopped beating through these fractured seconds while his lips stay pressed to my own. Before I have time to process or react, Alessandro releases his hold and abruptly pulls away.

"Fuck!" he barks, hits the roof of the car with his fist, and slams the door shut.

No longer still, my heart is thumping through my ribcage as I watch him walk around the front of the SUV and get back behind the wheel. He puts the car in drive and pulls onto the street. Lips pressed tight, and eyes glued to the gray concrete ribbon beyond the windshield, he won't even look at me now. I, on the other hand, can't make myself look away from his gruff profile.

I don't think a kiss has ever shaken me so much, especially one so swift. Or so angry. I'd only had two boyfriends before I married Rocco, but neither made me feel like Alessandro's all-too-brief kiss had done. God, I want him to kiss me again.

I dreamed about him again last night. I've come to crave these nightly visions. This time, I was on top, riding his cock as his hands moved over my stomach and breasts, and up to my throat. That should have frightened me—his hands wrapped around my neck. Rocco often holds me down when he forces himself on me. He likes to remind me of his power. But even in the dream, Alessandro's fingers at my throat didn't faze me. My subconsciousness knew I could trust him. I came so hard, that when I woke up, my pussy still trembled at the thought.

What happens now? I press my thighs together, helpless to stop the clench inside my core.

Alessandro parks in the hospital lot and walks around the front of the SUV to open the door for me. His stance is rigid, gaze focused somewhere across the sea of cars. I exit the vehicle and head toward the visitor's entrance, while he follows a few paces behind.

I stare at the white door at the end of the hospital hallway. I don't need to be directed to my husband's room. There's only one door with a guard on either side of it. I've been fixated on that door for what seems like hours while standing in the waiting room, but I know it couldn't have been more than just a few minutes.

"Please, stay here," I say to Alessandro without turning around, then head down the hall.

When I enter the room, I find Rocco lying in bed, head raised to allow him more comfort. The wall-mounted TV on the opposite side is showing the news. The monitor beside the bed tracks his vitals—heartbeat, blood pressure—giving off a steady beep once in a while. His right hand is hidden from view, wrapped in a thick layer of bandages.

"It's still there. For now."

I tense upon hearing Rocco's voice and make myself look at him.

"It was those Serbian bastards. Can't be anyone else," he continues. "But they will be dealt with soon enough. I've made arrangements for some of my guys to hit that club of theirs and kill everyone there."

"The don won't like you acting without his approval," I

say. The head of our Family is very strict on how things are handled.

"One of them almost shot off my damn hand!" he snarls. "The doctor said they're going to keep me here for three weeks at least. Three weeks!"

I can feel the pressure in my chest ease off ever so slightly. Almost a month without him.

"And then, that sleazy motherfucker, Cosimo, called me, saying how sorry he is for what happened, and that he'll be taking over my obligations. And, how it's such a shame I won't be able to attend Giancarlo's fucking party tomorrow," he rambles on. "He always acts like he's better than everyone else, when we all know he's getting special treatment only because he's banging the don's mother. I won't be going, but you are. And after, you're going to tell me everything that happens there. I want to know who was present, and what was said about me."

I take a deep breath and squeeze the purse in my hand. Rocco might have bought me tons of expensive jewelry and extravagant clothes, but I'm never going to feel like I belong in that circle. Money was always scarce in my family, and I feel awful being surrounded by so much wealth because I know that my mom and brother can barely get through a month on what my mother makes. I detest going to the Cosa Nostra gatherings.

"Are you listening to me, Ravenna?"

I bite the inside of my cheek as a memory of me curled on the bathroom floor pops into my mind. The realization that I never tried to pick or break the lock to get out eats away at me like acid.

"I don't want to go to that party," I blurt out.

Rocco glares at me and leans forward. I take an involuntarily step back and bump my back into the door.

"Who the fuck cares what you want!" he yells and launches the TV remote at me. I barely have time to duck and avoid being hit in the head.

"You'll do as I say, and you'll watch yourself. I'll have Zanetti report to me on your behavior. Is that clear?"

"Yes," I choke out.

"Good. Now, get out! I can't bear to look at you!"

I fling the door open and dash out of the room. Running down the hall, I ignore the curious stares of people as I pass them. Only once I've reached the sidewalk in front of the hospital do I stop. My heart is beating out of my chest and I'm struggling for every breath.

A hand lands on my upper arm, long strong fingers squeezing lightly.

"Did he do anything?" Alessandro's voice rasps over my back.

I close my eyes and shake my head. Pathetic. Rocco was in bed, almost ten feet away from me. He wouldn't have been able to hit me, but I still panicked and ran away like the coward I am. It's hilarious, how I always believed myself to be confident. I never shrank from confrontation. Once, I caught an older boy from school bullying my brother. I kneed him in the junk. And look at me now. Fucking terrified because that bastard raised his voice.

"Ravenna."

A shudder runs down my spine. I love how Alessandro says my name.

Slowly, I turn and look up at his hardened face. Even in my four-inch heels, I still need to tilt my head way back to be able to meet his gaze.

"What did he do?" he asks through clenched teeth.

"He didn't do anything." I blink to keep the tears from spilling. I don't know why I feel like crying. Maybe I'm mourning my pitiful attempt at standing up to Rocco. "He just yelled. I got spooked. It's stupid."

Alessandro's nostrils flare, and he lowers his head, leveling with my face. There's a dangerous glint in his eyes, and if it was any other man in his place, I would have probably recoiled. Once bitten, twice shy, people say. But I don't back away.

Since I've met him, Alessandro has gifted me with a plethora of different looks. There was despise. Anger. Irritation. Even hate, especially in the beginning. I haven't felt threatened by him even once.

"He will. Never. Touch you again," he says in a hushed voice.

It's been a very long time since anyone stood up for me. Especially a stranger, or at least not a family member. I'm not sure I can trust myself to believe.

"You can't promise that," I whisper. If Alessandro confronts Rocco in any way, my husband will have him killed. Or he'll do it himself.

"Yes, I can," Alessandro says and smiles.

I can't look away from his mouth, captivated by how sinfully attractive such a wicked grin could be.

As we head toward his car, the back of his hand accidentally brushes mine. Biting the inside of my cheek, I move a bit closer and hook my pinkie with his.

Alessandro stops.

I halt, too, but I don't dare glance at him. A moment passes. Alessandro resumes walking, and I follow. He doesn't pull his hand from mine.

When we reach my mom's apartment, Alessandro takes his spot by the door as usual, and I head to the kitchen where Mamma is preparing lunch.

"You're later than usual," she whispers while reaching for an onion. "Did something happen?"

"Rocco got shot."

"Is he dead?"

"No. He's in the hospital." I pull some carrots out of a bag and start peeling one. "How much did you get for the bracelet?"

"Eight grand."

Shit. I'd hoped for at least ten. "I'll see if I have a necklace that's not too distinctive and bring it next time."

"What if Rocco notices?"

"I'll just say I lost it."

My mom throws a quick look at Alessandro, who seems extremely interested in the window on the opposite wall, then focuses back on the onion she's chopping. "And where will we go when we've got enough money?"

"As far as possible."

"He'll come after us, Ravi. You know that."

I close my eyes for a second. Lying to my mom is the last thing I want to do, but she would never agree if she learns the truth.

I knew from the start that escaping my husband would be nearly impossible. He has the funds and connections to find me no matter where I go, so I've decided that I won't be staying with Mamma and Vitto. I'll get them settled somewhere far from New York, with enough money to last them for a few months, and leave. I'm the one Rocco will be searching for, and I won't let my family become the collateral damage. He'll probably kill me when he catches up with me. No one crosses Rocco Pisano and lives to talk about it.

"We'll figure something out when the time comes," I say. "Where's Vitto?"

"Still sleeping. He went out with his friends last night and came back this morning."

"What friends?"

She just shrugs, avoiding eye contact.

"Mamma?"

"I made him promise me this was the last time. He won't do it again."

"He went with Ugo?" I screech. "Darn, Mamma. Did they go to that bar to play cards again?"

"He said they just went to watch. He doesn't play cards anymore."

"And you believed him?" I throw the half-peeled carrot on the counter and march through the living room to my brother's bedroom.

Vitto is sprawled across the bed, still in his jeans and hoodie. The curtains are pulled over the window, barring the outside light. I flip a switch, turning on the lamp on the right, and step over a pair of sweatpants on the floor, reaching for the black backpack on his desk.

"Yo, Ma?" Vitto grumbles sleepily. "Turn off that lamp."

I open the backpack and empty the contents onto his desk. A half-full bottle of soda. Empty snack bag. Earbuds. Some change. More trash. And a bundle of money.

"What the fuck is this, Vitto?" I yell.

"Ravi?" He sits up and squints at me. "What are you—"

"Explain!"

He looks at the cash in my hand and leaps off the bed, grabbing my arm. "That's mine. Give that back!"

"Gambling again? After everything? How could you?!"

"It's my life! You don't have the right to tell me what I can't do!" He wraps his fingers around mine, trying to pry them open.

"But you can ruin mine?"

"Fuck you, Ravenna!" he yells in my face.

A thick arm wraps around Vitto's midsection from behind. I stare in shock as Alessandro carries my brother out of the room, then I run after them. Vitto tries his best to free himself, thrashing around with his legs dangling a foot off the ground and shouting obscenities along the way. Alessandro puts him down in the middle of the living room and points to the sofa.

"Sit down."

"What the fuck, man?" Vitto hollers. "Who do you think . . ."

Alessandro takes a step forward. "Sit. Down."

My brother drops down onto the sofa and crosses his arms over his chest.

"Now, apologize to your sister."

Vitto looks at Alessandro sideways, then turns to me and tucks his chin. "I'm sorry, Ravi."

I shake my head and come to sit on the sofa next to him. Alessandro walks back to his place next to the front door, but he keeps his gaze fixed on my brother. My mom is still in the kitchen, her hands gripping the counter and her head hanging low. I can't see her face, but I know she's crying by how her body shudders.

"You need to stop, Vitto. It's not a game." I take his hand

in mine and cast a look at Alessandro. He's still watching us. "You know what happened the last time."

"But it turned out good, Ravi. You live in a nice place now. Rocco has a ton of money, and he always buys you fancy clothes. You have a great life and—"

"Shut the fuck up, Vitto," my mom snarls from the kitchen.

"But it's the truth, Ma. If it wasn't for me, she wouldn't be rich. I have to wait at least a couple more years before I'm allowed to join Cosa Nostra and start making money like Rocco."

My mom storms into the living room and grabs my brother by the front of his hoodie, jerking him around. "Did you ever wonder why your sister wears sunglasses almost every time she comes here?" she yells into his face.

"Mamma, don't." I grab at her forearm. "Please."

"Did you, Vitto?" she keeps yelling while tears roll down her cheeks. "Because she doesn't want us to see the bruises! Rocco has been beating her from the start. You fucked up and she had to pay the price! And you are still doing it."

Vitto stares at Mamma, then turns to me. "Ravi? That's not true, is it? You like Rocco. You told me so yourself."

I press the heels of my palms to my eyes and shake my head. Mamma promised she'd never tell my brother the truth.

"Jesus fuck," Vitto chokes out. "I'm going to kill him. I'm going to fucking kill him."

He springs off the sofa and runs to the front door.

"Vitto!" I jump to stop him, but there's no need.

As my brother reaches the door, Alessandro wraps him in a bear hug. Vitto thrashes, shaking his head left and right, trying to headbutt Alessandro. But my protector just stands there, his furious eyes scorching right through me.

"Stay there," he says and opens the door, carrying my brother outside.

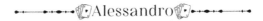

Alessandro

"Let me go, you motherfucker!" The kid twists, his spit flying everywhere.

I put him down and pin him against the hallway wall. "Calm down."

"I can't fucking calm down! That son of a bitch has been hitting my sister! I'm going to kill him."

"You're not going to kill anyone."

"Just watch me!" he yells and tries to free himself. I put a bit more pressure into my hold.

"And do you want your sister to watch you being dragged to jail? Or even worse, attend your funeral? Because, believe me, there is nothing more excruciating than seeing the casket with your family member lowered into the ground."

The kid stops thrashing and tilts his head up to look at me.

"Now, you're going to calm the fuck down, go back inside, and hug your sister. You'll tell her you love her, and that you won't be making any more problems in the future."

The kid stares at me, then nods. "And what about Rocco? If he's going to . . ."

"Rocco Pisano had his death sentence signed years ago," I say. "He won't touch your sister again."

"How do you know?"

"Because you can't hit anyone if you don't have any hands. And because I'm going to kill him before he ever has the chance to go near her again." I release the kid. "Go inside. Tell Ravenna I'll wait for her out here."

He turns around and narrows his eyes at me. "You're really going to kill him."

"Yes."

"I hope he'll suffer."

An easy smile breaks across my face. "Very much."

No longer the hot-headed teenager of just a few minutes ago, Vitto gives me a look that of a man who understands the gravity of this situation and goes back inside. I lean my back on the wall across from the apartment door, listening to the hushed words coming from within, but I don't move any closer to hear them more clearly. I'm barely hanging on by a thread, and if I hear any more about how that son of a bitch hurt her, I'm going to storm that hospital and separate the asshole's head from his body.

Ravenna walks out a few minutes later, her gaze cemented on the decrepit floor.

"I'm sorry you had to witness that," she mumbles.

I reach out and lift her chin. Her eyes meet mine. Sad. Haunted.

"Why did you marry Rocco?" I ask. "Were you in love with him?"

An anguished laugh escapes her lips. "My brother thought it would be fun to challenge Rocco to a game of poker. Vitto lost. And I was a part of debt settlement."

I stare at her. Stories have been circling that Rocco won his wife in a card game, but I thought it was nothing but some bullshit gossip.

"Who knows?" I ask through gritted teeth.

"That Rocco's been beating me? Other than my mom, no one. Maybe one of the guards who saw the bruises."

165

"His name?"

Ravenna's eyes widen. "Why?"

Why? Because I need to find the cocksucker who saw her hurt and did nothing. I squeeze my eyes shut, trying to erase that idea from my mind. *She* is my target. The fact she was being abused should have no impact on me. I will not jeopardize my plan any further because of her. She means nothing to me.

I move my hand to her cheek, cupping it into my palm. The skin under my fingers feels so soft, like down feathers.

"His name, Ravenna."

"Federico."

The bald guy on the second shift who works the gate. I nod. "Anyone else?"

"No. Rocco was very clear about what would happen to my mom and brother if I told anyone." She slumps her shoulders. "My mom has been selling the clothes and jewelry I give her. In a few more months, I should have enough money for the three of us to escape. But until that happens, I have to endure."

I tilt her chin back up. "Endure?"

"You think I'm weak? Just letting it happen and doing nothing?" Ravenna shakes her head. "I tried fighting back. The first time Rocco slapped me, I tried smashing a table lamp over his head. He hit me so hard that after I couldn't eat solid food for the rest of the week."

Like a blast from a fucking grenade exploding in my brain, I feel the quake of my stone-cold fortress. The tremors shake the foundations of my revenge plan. Yes, in the beginning, I did think she was a weak, shallow, trophy wife whose only interests were buying clothes and parading around like a holier-than-thou queen. She fooled me, too.

Or, better said, I let myself be fooled because it was easier to hate her that way. She's been trying to fight that son of a bitch from the start, and when she couldn't do it with brawn, she resorted to outsmarting him. Alone.

"You're far from weak, Ravenna." I brush her cheek with the back of my hand while another enormous chunk of my fortress breaks away and crumbles into a cloud of dust.

When we arrive back at the mansion, I escort Ravenna to the front door, then turn around and feign a casual stroll through the grounds, heading toward the guardhouse. There's a blind spot close to the old oak tree. Knowing that cameras won't be an issue here, I stop and take out my phone.

Overriding multiple feeds without my laptop isn't possible, but I can scramble one with the software on my cell. I select the camera overlooking the guardhouse and pull up a dummy recording I prepared a few days ago, making the switch. Now, no one will see me slipping through the door when the moment is right.

I take cover in the shadows and wait, pressed against the outside wall of the guardhouse, not far from the pedestrian gate that's just next to the main one. The window lets me see what's going on inside.

Federico and another security guy are sitting in front of the monitors at a desk covered in containers of fast food. Fifteen minutes later, the other man exits the guardhouse and heads toward the trees, probably to take a piss. Federico remains, his attention focused on the wall of monitors before him. I slip inside and approach from behind. Slapping my left palm over his mouth, I simultaneously grip his neck with my other hand by pressing on both his carotid arteries.

It's not a Vulcan nerve pinch and not like in the fucking movies when the opponent falls unconscious instantly. In reality, you need to keep the pressure on both points for at least seven seconds to cut off the flow of blood to the brain. When Federico's body sags, I clasp his nose and grab a hamburger from one of the takeout boxes, stuffing it deep into his throat. He comes to fairly quickly and starts jerking, gasping for breath, but I keep his mouth and nose shut. The fight leaves him several moments later, and his body sags again. For good this time. I let Federico's bulk slack in the chair, with vomit trickling out of his mouth and down his chin, then slip out of the guardhouse.

As I'm striding back toward the mansion, I look up to the second floor and the last window on the left. Ravenna's light is off, but I can see her silhouette behind the sheer curtain. I pause and take out my phone, dialing her number. She disappears from the window, then comes back a few moments later. The curtain moves to the side, revealing Ravenna with her cell in her hand.

The ringing stops and the call connects, but she doesn't say anything. The only thing I can hear is her soft breathing.

"Tomorrow morning at six," I say into the phone. "The library. Wear something comfortable."

A few beats of silence before she whispers, "Why?"

"Because it will work better." And because I'll make sure she never feels defenseless ever again.

I end the call and watch her. A distant light from the driveway lamppost casts its glow on Ravenna's face. She keeps looking at where I stand, then nods. The curtain falls over the window. A moment later, she disappears from view.

I should have killed her the minute I set foot in this house. I haven't. And now, I'm no longer capable of doing it.

CHAPTER
fourteen

I WALK INTO THE LIBRARY AND LOOK AT THE TALL, wooden bookshelves covering every wall. The first time I entered this room, I was amazed by the number of leather-bound tomes filling the beautiful, vintage shelves. Each bookcase is arranged to hold books of a similar color.

It didn't take me long to realize that the books weren't there because my husband liked to read, but because they made the room look good. Rocco loves having cocktails served here for his friends so they could *ooh* and *ahh* upon seeing the lavish space. The only thing that matters to my husband is what people think. Without houseguests, the only visitors to this room are me and one of the maids who clean the library twice a week.

Alessandro told me he'll wait for me here at six, but it's ten after according to the clock on the left side of the room, and he's nowhere in sight. I have no idea why he asked me to come here. Deciding to return to my room, I turn around and collide with a wide male chest. I tilt my head up and up until I meet Alessandro's gaze.

"Sorry I'm late," he says. "There was an incident."

"An incident?"

"One of the guards choked on his food last night. Nino came to bring his replacement."

"The guard is dead?"

"Very much." Alessandro nods, then walks past me, heading toward the big window overlooking the garden.

I blink, staring at his retreating form. Alessandro's appearance is always very formidable, regardless of what he wears. It's not just his size, which does have a big impact on the overall impression. It's the combination of his silence and cold aloofness that cling to him like a second skin. Even in navy-blue sweatpants that hang low on his hips, and a white T-shirt that stretches tight over those wide shoulders and enormous back, Alessandro looks like he's capable of wrestling a dozen men without breaking a sweat. As I admire his muscular body, he approaches the window and pulls the curtain over it.

"Less than two hours before the staff arrive," he says looking at his wristwatch. "We better start."

"Start what?"

Alessandro stops right in front of me. "Your first self-defense class," he says, and before I have time to process that statement, he wraps both of his hands around my neck.

I freeze. He's not hurting me, and his hold is mostly loose, but I still can't move.

"Free yourself."

I stare at him.

"Now, Ravenna."

"You're more than double my weight," I mumble.

"Closer to triple, probably, but that's not important. I'm not asking you to knock me out. Just to get out of my hold."

"Why?"

He bends, closing in on my face. "Because knowing you can escape will help you keep your cool. And getting free will allow you to take control of the situation."

I close my eyes and take a deep breath. Alessandro's hands remain around my neck, and I like them there. "Even if I free myself from Rocco's hold, he'll catch me, eventually. And it'll only be worse then."

"Look at me."

When I open my eyes, Alessandro moved even closer, his forehead almost touching mine.

"I already told you. Your husband will never put his hands on you again." He's so near I feel his breath on my skin. "This is not about Rocco. It's about you, Ravenna. So, you don't ever feel helpless and can always protect yourself. Now, try to get out."

I regard him—his scowling face and those dark-blue eyes, then wrap my hands around his wrists, pushing them to the side. Nothing happens. Not even an inch of movement.

"You are competing strength for strength with me," he says. "Most men will be larger and stronger than you."

"So, what then?"

"Fight against my weakest points. My thumbs." He lifts his right hand off my throat and places it at the top of my head. "Step back with your right leg. Then bend." He pushes my head down and guides it under his left arm. His grip on my neck disappears. "You're free."

"Your hold was loose."

"It won't be next time. Again."

His fingers come around my throat again, but his clench remains lax. "Leg. Bend. The whole body, Ravenna, not just your head. Again."

I keep practicing, but only a small part of my brain is

concentrating on the actual move. The rest is too focused on Alessandro's hands on my neck. His fingers in my hair as he guides me when I don't dip low enough. The closeness of his body.

"Do you need a break?" he asks after the twentieth or so time.

Yes. No. I'm not sure. My brain is foggy, and I'm not certain if it's from repeating the same move over and over, or because of him being so close. I think it's the latter. And I want more of his touch.

"Let's do it a few more times," I breathe out.

Alessandro nods and places his hands around my neck. I don't make a move to bend. Instead, I lift my hands and wrap my fingers around his wrists. Or try to, at least. His wrists are thicker than my ankles.

"We've already established that approach won't work, Ravenna."

"I remember," I say and hold his gaze. Alessandro's eyes move down to my lips. God, I want to feel his lips on mine again—so much.

His hold of my neck relaxes, and his hands move up to cup my face in his palms. His expression is completely unreadable, utterly contrary to the dangerous look in his eyes. By all appearances, he seems unperturbed at having us so close to each other, but I see the truth in his burning gaze. My heart rate doubles under that stare. Those dark-blue orbs look like they want to eat me alive—a big, hungry, wild cat ready to pounce. And I wouldn't object.

I slide my hands up his forearms, feeling the taut muscles under my palm. He shifts his stance, and my heart skips a beat.

"Let's try something else," he says abruptly. The next instant, I find my back plastered to his front, his arms locked around me. "This is called a rear bear hug. What would you do?"

I shake my body left and right, but it doesn't budge his purchase. His arms stay tightly wrapped around me.

"I'm bigger and stronger, and in a position of advantage with no weak points you can exploit. I'm controlling your whole body. You need to make it harder for me. What should you do?"

"I don't know," I say.

"Open your stance and drop your weight. Yes, like that. Now, you can stomp on my foot. Or hammer me in the balls."

I look at him over my shoulder. "Why not try that first?"

Alessandro bends his head until his mouth touches my ear. "Because by widening your stance, you're making it harder for me to throw you on the floor and pin you down."

I know he won't hurt me, but being defenseless should frighten me at least a little. It doesn't. Instead of being scared, I bite my lip and lean back onto his chest, imagining what it would be like to be pinned under that body. Would it feel like in my dream?

Alessandro buries his nose into my hair and inhales. His hold grows tighter, but it's only his left arm that's encircling me now. His right hand is slowly drifting over my yoga shorts down my stomach, and lower still.

"I don't understand how a woman could fuck me up so badly, Ravenna." His palm slides over my mound and presses onto my pussy, making me gasp. I want to turn around so much, but his embrace is too vigorous. "Years of planning. Ruined."

Fingers caress my pussy. Hard. The thin fabric of my shorts is barely a barrier. Wetness pools in my panties. I widen my legs and grab at his forearm, grinding myself against his hand. Alessandro's mouth moves to the side of my neck, biting the sensitive skin.

"From the moment I set my eyes on you, you invaded my fucking mind like a plague, Ravenna," he says next to my ear and places a kiss underneath it. He's angry. Frustrated. I can hear it in the tone of his voice, and it's completely at odds with the gentle way his lips nibble at my skin. "Scrambling my brains so I can't even think straight anymore."

I moan when his hand grabs at the waistband of my shorts, pushing them down together with my panties. His palm glides back over my mound, and I feel his finger at my exposed core, sliding between my folds. Slowly. So slowly it feels like a punishment.

"I dream about you," I mewl, bending my knees and trying to get more of his finger inside me. He presses his hard cock to the small of my back, and I shiver at the contact. "I know it's wrong, but I can't make the dreams go away."

His finger slides deeper into me, and then he adds another, stretching me. "Tell me about your dreams, Ravenna."

"It's always you. Taking me. Possessing me."

A deep rumble leaves his throat, and in the next breath, I feel his tongue on my skin. "How?"

"In every way possible," I choke out.

Alessandro's body goes still and, for a few moments, the only movement I can feel is the rise and fall of his chest at my back. He curses. His teeth skim my throat as his hot breath ghosts over my skin, making me tremble. Withdrawing his hand, he spins me around, and I find myself pressed with my back to the wall.

"This wasn't supposed to happen," he says as his hands grip my ass, lifting me. His voice is raw. Strained.

I wrap my legs around his waist, taking his face between my palms. "I know," I say and press my mouth to his.

He bites at my lower lip, pulling it between his teeth, sucking at it while his cock nudges against me. My fingers shake as I slide them over his short hair, as does the rest of my body. I've imagined how this would feel for so long, and it's beyond my wildest dreams. We're only kissing, and I'm already close to combusting.

"Do you know why I'm here? Doing this job?" he asks as he trails kisses down my neck. His voice is gruff. There's an accusation in his tone.

I slide my hand between our bodies, undoing the string on his sweatpants, and release his cock.

"Why?" I blurt as I feel the tip of his hard length at my entrance.

Alessandro trails his lips along my chin to my mouth and stops once he reaches his aim.

"I came here to exact revenge on your husband," he says into my lips as his cock slowly slides into my dripping center. "And you were my payback, Ravenna."

There is so much resentment in his words. I should feel threatened. He just confessed his plan to end my life, but both my body and my mind ignore that uttered fact, too enthralled on claiming his lips.

Alessandro pulls out, then thrusts back in—to the hilt, pressing his body to mine. The air leaves my lungs as my walls spasm around his length. He doesn't move a muscle, just stands there with his body pinning mine, his cock nestled inside me.

"I hate you, Ravenna Pisano," he barks in my face, slamming into me one more.

The air escapes my lungs in short breaths, my vision blurs

as tremors rock my body. I grab onto his shoulders and scream while he drills me as if he wants to etch that statement on my bones. But I let go and ride the waves of pleasure.

"Tell me, Ravenna," Alessandro's hoarse voice says next to my ear midthrust. "Does your husband fuck you like this?"

I tilt my head and sink my teeth into his neck. "Why do you care?"

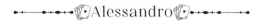

Alessandro

"Why do you care?" she whispers, and I feel those words wreak havoc in my head.

Why do I care? A thunderous sound rolls through the back of my mind as another massive chunk falls off the fortress I've created. I try to catch it, return it, but the piece only crumbles into nothingness.

"Answer me!" I roar into that angelic face, flustered and bathed in sweat.

I need to know. Just the idea of that asswipe having her like this is driving me insane. The verdict on my sanity is still undecided.

Ravenna's hand grabs the back of my neck, her long nails digging into my skin.

"Rocco is impotent," she bites out. "He never could . . ."

My body goes stone-still for a moment while my brain processes what I've heard. Fucking Rocco Pisano has never had her. I tangle my fingers in the long black strands at the back of Ravenna's head and bottom out in her pussy. Ravenna gasps, and I crush my mouth to hers, swallowing that sweet, sweet sound of her pleasure to save it for myself.

Keeping her head safe by cushioning it with my hand, I pound into her, finally collecting on weeks of frustration and sleepless nights she's subjected me to. I tell myself that my relentless pace is a punishment. Hers? Mine? I want to ruin her for making me betray my vow. Destroying everything I've lived for, for the past eight years. I will myself to believe it, all while a raging storm rages inside my mind. My fortress shakes and numerous fragments fall from its structure, casting aside the shards of my revenge. So fucking many, that I will never be able to collect and put them back in place.

I keep pumping into my raven-haired angel—a woman I vowed to kill—repeating the same mantra in my mind.

I hate her. Hate her.

Yet still, I can't make my hand move from behind her head, can't risk her getting hurt in the slightest, as we burn in madness.

Ravenna squeezes my arms, her nails digging into my skin as she trembles in pleasure. I quicken my pace, staring into her face. Sweat slides into my eyes, making them sting, but I don't consider wiping it away, I don't even dare to blink. I have to see her when she comes. The need to witness her undoing is primal and unrelenting. Ravenna arches her back, an ecstatic scream leaving her lips, as her pussy clenches around my cock. And with one last thrust, I bury myself into her and roar as my seed fills her. The sound is guttural and broken, a cry of triumph and defeat at the same time.

Closing my eyes, I press my forehead to hers. What have I done?

Soft, sinful lips touch mine. Warm breath fans my face. I return the kiss, even though it's the last thing I should do. I can't help it. Every stroke of our tongues, every small bite— heaven and hell at the same time. Pleasure and pain.

A part of me wants to stay like this forever, with her in my arms. But another part, it screams in anger, calling me a traitor. The battle for supremacy rages inside my soul, shredding it apart. The pain is almost physical, holding me in its grasp until one of the sides finally takes the win.

I release Ravenna's hair and move away from her lips.

"This won't happen again," I say, lowering her to the floor.

CHAPTER
fifteen

♥ Ravenna ♥

"I CAN'T BELIEVE SOMEONE TRIED TO KILL ROCCO!" Eleonora, Capo Giancarlo Medici's wife exclaims. "You must be devastated, my dear."

I pluck a glass of wine off the tray a waiter is holding and take a big gulp. "Yes. It's terrible."

"Do we know who did it?" She leans forward to whisper in my ear as if we're longtime confidantes. "I heard it was probably the Serbian clan. A payback for some quarrel they had."

"Maybe." I take another sip and move my gaze to the massive figure in a black suit standing in the corner of the room. As soon as my eyes fall on him, my heart starts to bleed once again.

Alessandro has been pretending that nothing happened between us this morning. He fucked me like there was no tomorrow, giving me the best sex of my life, then left the library without a word, slamming the door shut in his wake. I stood there—sweaty and flustered, his cum dripping down my legs—staring at that door for who knows how long. And I cried. Confusion. Hurt. Remorse. All those emotions raged inside my chest as I tried to understand what the hell happened and why he stormed out as he did.

You were my payback, he said.

Is that all I've been to him? Payback for something my husband has done? Were those kisses and caresses all just a lie? Yes, they probably were.

I look down at the wineglass in my hand and swallow. I've fallen in love with a man for whom I've been nothing but a revenge fuck. A sad laugh escapes me. I must be the biggest idiot who's ever lived because I thought he had feelings for me, too. I guess it's true what they say, there's nothing more blind or stupid than a woman in love.

"Well, I wouldn't be surprised if it was the Serbs," Eleonora continues. "All of them are absolutely crazy. Serafina told me she saw that Popov guy cut off a man's finger on the bar of his club. He did it in front of the patrons. An animal."

I tune out Eleonora's rambling and observe Alessandro. He's standing with his hands clasped behind his back, watching the crowd with a grim expression on his face. The entire evening, I've been trying to avoid looking directly at him because it hurts so much, but my eyes keep being pulled to him like magnets. Just as they are now.

After what happened in the library, I didn't see him until this afternoon when he took me to the hospital so I could do my wifely duty and visit my husband. The drive there took longer than the actual visit. Both Rocco and I knew we were doing it for show because, God forbid, someone may notice and comment that something is wrong between us. I stepped inside his room, delivered the things he asked me to bring, and left. It lasted less than a couple of minutes, but it still wasn't fast enough, and I couldn't wait to get out of there.

When I was done with that chore, Alessandro drove me

to the mall where I'd bought more clothes, and then he took me to my mother's place, where I left her with the stuff I purchased for Mrs. Natello. When we returned to the house, he disappeared into his room until it was time to head to this fucking party.

Alessandro looks up and, for a fleeting second, our gazes connect, but he quickly looks away. It stings. Especially since I've never felt as I did this morning, surrounded by his body, his hot breath on my face, and his cock inside me. I felt . . . free. Like nothing and no one could ever reach me, or hurt me again. His presence was an impenetrable wall, sheltering me, and protecting me from harm.

I should be ashamed of cheating on my husband, but I'm not. If I could turn back time, I would do it all over again. I want to feel Alessandro's body next to mine again, and it's not only about sex. It's him. Since the day we met, I've felt a pull toward him. I thought he felt something toward me, too. In my pitiful need to be loved, I let myself see the things that weren't ever there. He just wanted to bang his boss's wife as *payback*.

"Ravenna, my dear?"

"Sorry," I quickly look away from my bodyguard. "I was lost in thought."

"It's understandable. You must be worried about Rocco. Did they say when he can come home?"

Bile rises up my throat at that notion. "In a few weeks."

"Oh, so long? You must miss him. The two of you are such a beautiful couple." She smiles and starts to say something else but shouting erupts somewhere in the room.

I turn toward a group gathered at one of the tables, just in time to see an older man swinging his fist at another guy.

"I knew that man was trouble waiting to happen," Eleonora says next to me, nodding toward the younger fellow who avoided the punch and is now responding with a kick to his opponent's stomach.

"Who's that?" I ask.

"Damian Rossi. His brother is the don in Chicago." She smirks. "Ortensia says he's a beast in bed."

"He was allowed to come here?" I ask. Members of the other Cosa Nostra families are strictly forbidden from entering the New York area without our don's permission.

"Ajello has some sort of big business happening with his brother. Damian must have got the approval, which I'm sure will be revoked soon. That man, the one trying to strangle him, is Ortensia's husband."

Security guys approach Damian Rossi, trying to subdue him. In all the commotion, the betrayed husband yells something and reaches into his jacket. I don't see what happens next because a solid mountain of muscles masquerading as a black suit materializes before my eyes. A gunshot rings out.

Two large arms enfold around me, and I find myself with feet dangling off the ground as Alessandro carries me across the room. I can't see where he's going or what's going on because my face and body are plastered to his front. I can only hear shouts and another gunshot somewhere behind Alessandro. Meanwhile, he casually continues to saunter toward his destination. I understand that this kind of shit must happen often in his line of work, but shouldn't we run or something when there is gunfire raging all around?

"Are we going on a stroll?" I mumble into his chest.

"No."

"Maybe you could walk faster then?"

"No bullet will hit you, Ravenna."

Of course, it won't hit me when my whole body is covered by his! "It may hit you!" I snap.

"Chances of that happening are slim."

Behind us, the chaos in the room seems to have died down because now only quiet murmuring can be heard. I wouldn't doubt if the party guests have already switched from hysterics to gossip. Alessandro's measured steps come to a halt, and he lowers me to the floor but keeps his arms firm around me.

"Don't move," he says before finally letting me go and turning to survey the room.

I can't see anything except his ridiculously wide back, so I lean a bit to the side to peer around him. Damian Rossi is being dragged away by a couple of guys. He looks pissed off but unharmed. The other man, Ortensia's husband, is slumped in a nearby chair, holding a bag of ice to his chin. The rest of the guests are gathered in small groups of three or four, snickering among themselves and waving to waiters to bring more drinks. Typical.

"It's safe," Alessandro says.

I don't even look at him as I step around and head toward the bar where Eleonora is standing with Pietro. The feeling of being held tightly in Alessandro's arms won't fade. I want more. It's like an instant addiction that only he can feed. I despise it.

"Gin and tonic," I say to the barman and take a spot to Eleonora's right.

If my husband was here, he would have had a fit. Rocco Pisano's wife would never be seen with anything other than wine. Well, fuck Rocco. And fuck *Rocco's wife*. I'm my own person I have my own likes and dislikes. And I detest wine. He tried his best to suppress the person I am, and I let him. With every degrading remark, with every hit, I let myself sink deeper and deeper until almost nothing was left. It took being fucked and then discarded by my bodyguard for me to come to my senses.

"My God, that was awful," Eleonora exclaims. "One of the bullets damaged the ceiling. I don't think we'll be allowed to rent this place again."

"Probably not." I shrug, pick up the tumbler the bartender had set on a coaster before me, and take a big gulp.

"I need to find Giancarlo. Maybe he can reason with the manager. Pietro, can you keep Ravenna company?"

"Of course." Pietro nods. "How are you holding up, Ravenna?"

"Compared to my wedding, this is just a minor quarrel."

"Yes, I remember that night."

"Me, too. Very well," I say.

During my wedding banquet, the Irish mercenaries attacked while everyone was outside watching the fireworks. Several people died, and Rocco had to deal with the authorities until morning. He came home furious and tried to fuck me. Then, he beat me instead.

"Nino tells me Rocco lost one of his security people the other night. Federico, right? Poor bastard, to choke on his food like that."

The tumbler slips out of my hand, crashing to the floor. My gaze darts toward Alessandro where he is once again lurking next to a wall. His stance is rigid—spine ramrod straight, and his eyes fixed on Pietro.

"Ravenna? Are you all right?" Pietro asks.

"I'm fine," I whisper.

Is it just a coincidence? It can't be. He asked me the name of the security guard who knew Rocco hit me that very same night. My heart leaps in my chest. Maybe he feels something for me after all? *Stop*. I need to stop thinking about him. He made his feelings about me very clear this morning.

"You don't seem fine to me, Ravenna." Pietro places his hand on my upper arm.

I freeze, unable to move a muscle. Even without Rocco here to witness the touch, a wave of panic still engulfs me at the idea that someone will notice and tell my husband. That man has turned me into one of Pavlov's dogs.

"Do you want me to take you home?"

I don't want Pietro to drive me home. I want Alessandro to do it.

"Yes, that would be nice. Thank you." I smile.

Alessandro

I park next to Pietro's car at the Pisano mansion and grip the steering wheel until my hands hurt as I watch him escort Ravenna to the front door. Only once Pietro is back in his vehicle and pulls out of the driveway do I allow myself to leave my car. I would have snapped his neck otherwise. I hoped fucking Ravenna would get her out of my system, cure me of the damn obsession I've developed for her, but it has only made it worse.

I can't get my bearings where this woman is concerned. I might hate her, but my dick says I don't. The things she makes me feel are something I've never experienced before. Not even with Natalie. I loved my wife. But with Ravenna, my need for her is no longer a craving I can deny. She lodged herself under my skin, a tattoo on my psyche. When did protecting her become more important than killing her to carry out my plan?

Saving one woman means I'm betraying another, betraying the promise I've made at her grave. But taking Ravenna's life? I may as well put my own gun to my head.

I climb the stone steps and head inside the mansion. It's almost midnight, so there's no one around as I walk down the hallway to my bedroom. Once inside, I remove my jacket and holster, and pull out the house blueprints, spreading the schematic on the small desk tucked into the corner. I need to do something to make me stop thinking about Ravenna.

Two hours later, after I make the ninth mistake in marking the weak spots of the ground floor, I throw the pen across the room and push the papers away.

Leaving my room, I tread along the empty foyer and up the staircase to the second floor. It's well into the night and, other than the ticking of the grandfather clock on the landing, the house is silent. I turn to the left and head down the hall, stopping at the door to Ravenna's bedroom. The knob is cold under my palm as I carefully turn it, nudging the door open just a bit. Ravenna is asleep, her long hair spilled across the pillow. A fluffy white blanket is lying tangled at her feet.

I approach the bed and reach out to move a strand that has fallen over her face and neck. Not so long ago, I imagined slicing that delicate throat and watching her blood spill. But now? Now, just the idea of anyone hurting her in any way makes me go completely feral.

When I got this job and came here, it seemed like everything would be so easy. I had a goal and one way of reaching it. But I didn't count on Ravenna Pisano and her sad green eyes disrupting all to hell.

I need another distraction. Anything that would take my mind off Ravenna. And I need to move forward with my plan.

Reevaluate and adapt, I've been trained to do that. No plan survives contact with the enemy. So, time to shift.

Messing up Rocco's construction business will take focus and days of preparation, but, currently, I'm too wrought up to handle anything requiring either. I must have blood. Now! Seems like the moment has come for Rocco's father to die. Unfortunately, Pisano won't be there to watch.

I haven't had a chance to study Elio Pisano's house, and I don't know the movement of the security guys. From what I saw while escorting Rocco and Ravenna there, the alarm systems are very basic, but the whole property is heavily guarded. It would be too risky to try and infiltrate it without sufficient recon of patrols. But it doesn't matter.

Throwing one last look at Ravenna's sleeping face, I pull the blanket over her and silently exit the room.

Elio Pisano's home is nestled between two other houses. At the one on the left, the garden lanterns are lit, but the lawn around the house on the right is shrouded in darkness. It'll do.

I use the unlocked garden gate to enter the neighbor's property and creep along the fence wall that connects it to Elio Pisano's, approaching the maple tree that's growing over the divide. Its branches creak and bend under my weight as I ascend to scan the surroundings.

There are two guards at the main gate, but none along the outer perimeter. Inside the fence walls, however, there're at least five men patrolling the grounds, and more are stationed at the front door. I don't see any monitoring cameras except for the one at the gate, which seems to be the only entrance to the property.

I climb back down off the tree and walk along the fence wall until I reach the spot I've chosen as my entry point, extracting the grappling hook and rope from my backpack. During my missions with the Z.E.R.O. unit, we always used state-of-the-art pressure-powered grapnel launchers, but those are designed to secure access to very high-up locations and they tend to be too loud. Regular house walls require old-school equipment.

It takes me three tries until the hook finds its purchase. Using the rope, I climb the smooth wall, throw the hook to the ground on the other side, then jump down.

Most of the courtyard is well-lit, but there are trees and decorative shrubs scattered around. I use them for cover as I move toward an unguarded door at the back of the house. I'm almost there when a security guard rounds the corner and stops in front of the entrance. When he doesn't leave after five minutes, I use the shadows and foliage to reach a corner of the building. The guard's back is to me, and he is looking down at his phone. I approach him from the rear, press my palm over his mouth, and wrap my other arm around his neck. The man thrashes and tries to free himself, but I squeeze my arm tighter, snapping his neck.

I haul the body behind a bush and reach into my backpack to get the alarm jammer that's compatible with the security system I spotted installed in Elio Pisano's house. A minute later, I'm inside.

The layout of the house is similar to Rocco's—huge foyer and equally decorative wooden stairwell, frescos on the ceiling. A quick look around confirms there's no one in the vicinity. The stairs creak under my boots as I climb to the second floor and then turn left. All four bedrooms on this side are empty, so I head back the other way when I hear footsteps and the squeak of the floorboards. I press my back to the wall and take out my knife.

A man in a butler's outfit steps onto the landing. I have no idea what business he has roaming the house at three in the morning, but today is not his lucky day. I grab the front of his jacket and simultaneously swipe my knife across his neck. Blood pours over my hand as his body twitches a few times. I carry the dead butler to one of the empty bedrooms, then continue with my search.

I find Elio Pisano in the far bedroom. He's sprawled in the middle of the four-poster bed, wearing nothing but his boxer briefs—snoring. Reaching into the pocket of my tactical vest, I pull out a small box that holds a syringe and approach the bed.

For a few moments I just watch Rocco's father, enjoying the thrill of what will come, then I cover his mouth with my palm and bury the needle into his neck. Elio's eyes snap open, and I revel in the panic I see in them. His hand shoots out, grabbing my forearm, only to fall back down onto his chest. Limp, like the rest of his body.

I remove my hand from his mouth and watch his bulging eyes as they stare at the empty hypodermic needle in my other hand.

"It's a convenient little cocktail," I say as I put the hypodermic back into its box. "Military uses it sometimes. It paralyzes the body so the person can't move or speak."

I unstrap the knife from my thigh and place the edge of the blade on the tip of his thumb.

"You want to know the fun part? It doesn't numb the pain." I smile and slice off a part of the flesh from his finger.

Only once before have I witnessed a man scream with his eyes. It was more than a decade ago, a time when Kai went

AWOL following a mission, and Kruger decided to teach him a lesson afterward. He pumped Kai full of the same cocktail I'd just used on Elio and stabbed him randomly. But there's one very big difference between then and now. The look in Kai's eyes showed a scream of fury. Elio's eyes show only terror.

"Let me tell you a story." I move the knife up Elio's hand and forearm, making a shallow incision as I drag the tip. Enough to inflict significant pain without the possibility of making him bleed out. "It's a story of a woman who was taking a morning stroll through the neighborhood because she liked the smell of blooming trees in springtime."

I stop when I reach his elbow. There are certain parts of the body where the nerves close to the surface are more sensitive to pain. Fingertips. Knees. The arch of a foot. The tibia. Elbows. I bury the tip of the knife in the center of his, right through the ulnar nerve.

"A man in a souped-up car ran a red light and hit the woman as she was crossing the street," I continue as I twist the knife in his flesh. "He was drunk and driving twice the speed limit. And he fled the scene without ever looking back."

My nostrils fill with the smell of urine. When I look up, Elio's eyes are bloodshot, and a fine layer of sweat covers his forehead. I lean over him and drag the knife up to his neck, leaving a thin red trail behind.

"And the driver's daddy—a newly made capo trying to impress the new don of New York—made sure to cover everything up so well, it took me years to find the culprit."

I slide the edge of the knife across his neck, keeping the cut shallow, then trail a line down and stop right above his heart. When I have the knife in place, I bend my head until my mouth is just next to his ear.

"That woman was my wife," I whisper. "As you are dying

in a puddle of your own blood and piss, think about what I'll do to your son."

I grip the knife harder and plunge it into his heart, all the way to the hilt.

 Ravenna

The sound of a turning doorknob and the creak of wood floors under slow steps wakes me. My eyes snap open but I don't dare to move. For a moment, I think it's Rocco, coming to force himself on me. Then, I remember—he's not here. I sit up in the bed, clutching the bed covers to my chest, and notice Alessandro on the recliner by the balcony door. Based on the pale light peeping through the window, it must be early morning. He doesn't look like he's slept at all, and the strange outfit he's got on leaves me without a doubt.

"What are you doing in my room?" I ask, scanning his getup of black cargo pants and a long-sleeved shirt. A black military vest is dangling over the arm of the recliner. Other than in the library, during my self-defense lessons, I've never seen him wear anything but suits.

Alessandro doesn't reply, only keeps glaring at me.

"Leave," I snap. "You got what you wanted yesterday. It won't happen again. Out."

His nostrils flare and a guttural groan leaves his lips. I lower my eyes to his hands. He's gripping the arms of the recliner, his body taut. The sleeves of his shirt are rolled up to his elbows, revealing the strained muscles on his forearms. Dark red stains mar the back of his right hand and fingers.

"Is that blood?"

"Yes," he says through gritted teeth. "I was trying to distract myself."

"What kind of a distraction leaves a person with blood up to their elbows?"

"The killing kind."

I blink at him, waiting for the terror to race down my spine. It doesn't. The thought of my husband being home makes me want to run and hide, but the fact that Alessandro sits just a few feet from me after he apparently ended someone's life, doesn't scare me at all. The only things that terrify me are the need to curl onto his lap, and the belief that it will make everything better.

"And why did you need such an extreme distraction?" I ask.

"To stop thinking about you, Ravenna." He rises from the recliner and takes a few steps until he's standing at the foot of my bed. "I'm afraid it didn't work."

He grabs the edge of the bedcover. The fabric slips from my hands as he tugs and throws it to the side. In my sleep, my nightgown has ridden up to my waist, leaving my lacy blue panties on full display. My breaths quicken as Alessandro's eyes slowly travel up my body and stop at my mouth.

"Do you like Pietro?" he asks without removing his gaze from my lips.

"He was a friend of my father, and he was always nice to me."

Alessandro's eyes move up, meeting mine. "Let me rephrase the question. Do you want him to keep breathing?"

"Yes."

"In that case, please don't ask him to drive you home again."

His eyes glide down again and rest between my legs.

I bite my lower lip and lean back in bed, sliding my hand into my panties. "Why do you care who drives me home?"

"I don't," he barks as he grabs my ankles and pulls me toward the end of the bed.

The feel of his skin on mine as his palms slowly drift up my legs makes goose bumps break out all over my body. They follow the path of his caress as he hooks his fingers into the sides of my panties and meets my gaze. His eyes are two dark pools, and a storm is brewing in their depths.

"Tell me to stop," he says in a strained voice.

I press my lips together and lift my hips in invitation.

Something flashes in his eyes. The tempest clears for only a fraction of a second, letting me glimpse the hidden secrets beyond. There one moment and gone the next, obscured once more by passion and desire. I didn't have time to grasp what they were, his secrets remaining locked.

Once he slides the lacy material off, Alessandro kneels on the floor and buries his face between my legs.

A moan escapes me at the first stroke of his tongue over my slit. I've never experienced oral sex before, never even considered it. It's too carnal. Raw. I didn't think I'd feel comfortable letting a man get so personal.

Another slow stroke and then I feel Alessandro's tongue slipping into my core. I glide my fingers over his short hair and open myself wider to give him greater access.

"Faster," I whimper.

He ignores my plea and continues at the same pace, slowly sliding his tongue in and out. Torturing me. His palms caress my thighs, my skin burns everywhere he touches. When he reaches my ankles, he moves my legs apart, opening me even more.

"I've imagined doing this for days," he says between licks. "Eating your pretty pussy. Seeing if it's as sweet as I suspected."

"And is it?" I ask, absolutely shocked by my words.

"Yes. Even sweeter than in my fantasies. A forbidden fruit, sure to send me straight to Hades now that I've dared to taste it." I can feel his breath fan my skin as he inhales my scent. "I'm doomed."

A tremor starts at the base of my spine and then washes over me like a wave as he feasts on my pussy, each stroke of his tongue slightly quicker than the last. He moves his left hand along my inner thigh and slips his finger inside me while continuing to torment me with his mouth. My back arches as I suck in a breath. Wetness pools between my legs, dripping over his face while I tremble. Alessandro keeps lapping up my juices, sliding his finger in even deeper.

"Come for me, my emerald-eyed angel," he whispers between the licks and presses his lips to my clit, sucking on it.

White light explodes behind my closed eyelids. Alessandro keeps ravaging my clit, and just as I start to drift completely out of my mind, he slips another finger inside.

I scream.

It's loud and wild. A shrill of passion, but also freedom. The ecstatic cry of a liberated soul, finally freed of its shackles.

Alessandro places a kiss on my pussy and takes his fingers out, rising to his feet. I'm still shaking from the aftershocks as he picks up the blanket off the floor and covers me with it. Then, he turns and heads toward the door.

"Where are you going?" I ask.

He stops with his hand on the knob but doesn't turn around.

"Back to my personal hell, Ravenna."

CHAPTER
sixteen

 ❤ Ravenna ❤

As I EXIT MY ROOM TO HEAD DOWN TO BREAKFAST, the maid rounds the corner and rushes toward me. "The guard at the gate just called, Mrs. Pisano. Mr. Nino is coming to see you."

"Did he say why?"

"No. He just said it's urgent."

I rush along the hallway and down the stairs, wondering what could have happened. The maid dashes in front of me and opens the front door.

"Ravenna." Nino nods as he steps inside. "We need to talk."

"What happened?"

"Not here," he says in a grave voice.

"Okay." I lead him across the foyer to Rocco's office and close the sliding door once we're inside. Nino takes a seat on the leather sofa by the window and leans forward with his elbows on his knees.

"Elio is dead," he says.

I blink in confusion and lower myself onto the recliner

across from him. "I didn't know he was sick. We saw him about a week ago, and he seemed okay."

"He didn't die of natural causes. Someone broke into his house last night and killed him in his bed. It seems like they tortured him first."

I squeeze the padded arms of the chair as the image of Alessandro's blood-stained hand flashes before my eyes. The same hand that stroked my skin while he feasted on my pussy two hours earlier. I feel myself grow damp and quickly press my knees together, slightly appalled by my body's reaction.

"How did he die?" I ask.

"A knife through the heart."

"You know who did it?"

"No idea." He shakes his head, and I manage to hide a sigh of relief. "Could have been the Serbs. Rocco believes they are responsible for the hitman who shot him, so he sent mercenaries to attack Popov's club last night. Serbs could have been retaliating for the attack on the club, but the timing's too tight. There's no way they could have done it."

"Does Rocco know his father is dead?"

"No. I think it would be better if you told him."

I barely suppress a shudder. "Yes, I'll head to the hospital as soon as I get ready."

"Good. And make sure you don't leave the house without Alessandro until we find out what's going on," he says. "I'll see myself out."

When Nino leaves, I go back to my room to change and put on a new pair of panties. But as I'm standing in front of my underwear drawer, an unusual urge to rebel rises within me. I look down at the fresh pair of panties I've pulled out, then throw them back and close the drawer. As I will be seeing my husband, I'll do it while bearing the evidence of my attraction to another man.

I pick out a pair of pale peach pants and a jacket that comprise one of the few outfits I actually like wearing. Rocco prefers me in bold colors, such as blacks and reds. The only reason he let me keep this set is because of the jacket's big gold buttons that show the logo of the brand name.

My purse is on the dresser, and when I reach for it, I'm overwhelmed with loathing at the sight of it. Other women use purses to carry with them their most important items. Documents. Wallet. Their phone. The only things in my purse are a small makeup pouch, which I've come to hate, and two packs of tissues. My IDs are locked away in Rocco's safe, and I'm not allowed any money. I usually just leave my phone on the nightstand. What's the point of carrying it when I can't call anyone except my husband? My purse is just another reminder of the things he has taken from me. The things I let him take from me. My gaze moves from the purse up to the mirror above the dresser. I focus on my reflection, eyeing the big diamond earrings, reflecting the light off the stones and the sparkling gold. My long hair is gathered into a high bun, perfectly tight, and heavy makeup covers my face.

"Who are you?" I whisper. The woman in the mirror looks like me, but we have nothing in common.

There's no answer, of course. I stare at the stranger for a long time, trying to find more resemblance than the mere lines of my face, but I can't. That bastard made me lose myself along with everything else.

With one last look at my reflection, I grab my coat off the chair while pulling the pins out of my bun at the same time with my free hand.

As I head toward the staircase, the steady cadence of my heels is echoed by the delicate pings of the pins hitting the floor as I keep pulling them out one by one. By the time I reach the top landing, a trail of small black hairpins leads back to my room.

Alessandro stands at the foot of the stairs, a dark look on his face. This morning, he ate me out like a starved man having his first meal in weeks, and then disappeared. I can't stop thinking about his parting sentence. He said he was going back to his personal hell. What did he mean by that? I am his enemy's wife, yet there was no gloating, satisfaction, or triumph in his tone. He sounded defeated. There is something else going on.

My gaze moves from Alessandro's eyes to his lips. Can he still taste me? Will he come into my room again tonight? The sensation of his mouth on my pussy still lingers. It's more than the sexual act itself that shook me to my core. It's the way he touched me—as if I'm a precious, valuable thing. He said he hates me. His caresses tell me otherwise.

I'm aware of how a violent, angry man acts more than I've ever wanted to be. I can sense one, even through his smiles and pretense. Despite Alessandro's hostile words, my instinct for self-preservation wasn't triggered. Not even when he wrapped his fingers around my neck during that self-defense demonstration. Having his huge hand around my throat actually thrilled me. There is something so alluring about giving a man like Alessandro that kind of power over me. How easily he could have snapped my neck if he wanted to, but, instead, his touch made me feel safe. Protected. And it turned me on.

Because I know he wouldn't hurt a hair on my head.

"Why the fuck did you leave the house looking like that?" Rocco snarls from the bed. "You're not a goddamn peasant who walks around with her hair sticking out in all directions!"

I slip my hands into the pockets of my coat so he won't see them shaking, and take a deep breath. "I need to tell you something."

"I don't give a fuck!" His face flushes red as he roars and leans over the side of the bed, pointing to the bathroom door with his good hand. "Get in the bathroom and put your hair in order!"

"There's nothing wrong with my hair," I say. "Nino asked me to pass you some info."

"What info?"

"Your father is dead."

Rocco's body goes still, and several emotions race across his face. Shock. Denial. And then, a barely detectable excitement he's trying hard to hide.

The relationship my husband had with his father was always ambiguous. On one hand, he revered Elio and sought his approval relentlessly, while on the other, he despised his father for never showing Rocco respect. In public, Elio always boasted about how Rocco is one of the don's most trusted men, but behind closed doors, he enjoyed speaking down to his son, saying he's not good enough to become an underboss.

"How did he die?" he asks.

"He was killed at his home last night."

Rocco's eyes go impossibly wide. "You're lying!"

"I'm not."

Rocco's face turns an even deeper shade of red, his

nostrils flare, and the vein in his neck pulses. He reaches for his phone, which lies on the bed, and hurls it at me like a surly kid. I notice his intention in time and step to the side, letting his phone hit the door and crash to the floor. My eyes don't move off Rocco's indignant form as I crouch and pick up the cell.

"This is the last time you do that," I say. "I'm done being your punching bag. Next time you raise your hand to me, I'm going straight to the don."

"You slimy little bitch! I'll show you."

I throw the phone at him with all my strength, and excitement fills me when it hits him in the chest. Rocco grabs the side of the bed, yelling and shaking the railing. I simply turn and leave the room.

Alessandro is sitting in the waiting room on the other side of a long hallway, but he stands up when he sees me coming.

I approach him and search his expressionless face. "Can I get another self-defense lesson tomorrow morning?"

Alessandro's eyes narrow. He watches me for a few beats and then slowly nods.

We exit the hospital and head toward my car when a biker driving way too fast through the parking lot stops just a few yards in front of us. His bike is completely black, except for the prominent design on its body panel—a white skull with a thick cross over the forehead. Fuck. I grab Ravenna's wrist and pull her behind me.

"Do not move," I say, keeping the biker in my sight. "Confirm that you understand, Ravenna."

Silence stretches for a few moments before she replies, "Yes."

The rider dismounts the bike and removes his helmet. My eyes are locked on him as he approaches us with slow, measured steps until he stands before me.

"Zanetti. Was your buyer satisfied with the product?" His accented voice is steady and calm.

"They served their purpose," I say. "What are you doing here, Drago?"

Drago Popov looks up at the hospital building, zeroing in on Rocco Pisano's window. "I have some accounts to settle."

So, he knows Rocco is behind the attack on his club. Fucking perfect. "I'm afraid it's not possible."

"How so?"

"That account is held in reserve. By me." I glare at the Serbian leader, and I know he understands what will happen if he makes a move on a man who's mine to kill. People pass by us as they enter and exit the hospital, but no one pays much attention to our conversation.

"Personal debt?" he asks.

"Yes."

"You have a timeline for settling the account?"

"Within a week."

Popov casts another look toward Rocco's window, then nods and walks back to his bike.

"You have seven days, Zanetti. And that applies only to him. Not to others involved in the attack on my property and my people." He thrusts the helmet onto his head, climbs on his bike, and rides off.

"Who was that?" Ravenna asks behind me.

"Bad news."

A slight touch feathers the back of my hand as she drifts the tip of her finger along it and then hooks her pinkie with mine. I close my eyes and take a deep breath, hoping it'll stifle the need to take her into my arms. It can't happen.

This morning, after returning to my room, I stared at the ceiling for hours as I mentally made changes to my plan. The idea of fucking with Rocco's mind for several weeks disintegrated into dust. The notion of tying him to a chair while I torture him at my leisure—gone. I need to find a way to get into his hospital room and end him there. His death will be too fast, and that pisses me off, makes me want to hit something, but there's no other way. I can't wait until he is released. To preserve my sanity, Rocco Pisano needs to die as soon as possible. And then, I'll leave. I can try rationalizing that decision, find an excuse for myself, but it won't change the truth—I'm running away.

I spent a decade completing the most dangerous secret missions. Been shot at so many times, I've lost count. Held captive and tortured, twice. The last time I managed to escape on my own and, basically, dragged my blood-covered body back to base. And on top of that, I've nearly been blown to smithereens on more than one occasion. Then, came my years with Cosa Nostra. I wouldn't call this a safe work environment, either. The number of people I've killed thus far is in the triple digits. More than fifteen years of violence and death, and I've never fucking ran from a battlefield.

Until now.

And I will be running away, not from a more formidable enemy, but from a woman with emerald eyes. Her crystal depths are pulling me in, and I don't have the strength to re-sist the capture.

"Let's go," I say and head toward my SUV on the other end of the parking lot, tightly holding Ravenna's pinkie with mine.

She falls into step beside me as the wind whips her silky black strands into the air.

CHAPTER
seventeen

————•◦•◦•❦Alessandro❦•◦•◦•————

"**Y**OU ARE NOT ROTATING YOURSELF ENOUGH,"
I say and release my grip on Ravenna's hair.
A quick glance at my wristwatch tells me we
still have some time before the household staff get here in an
hour. "Again."

We've been practicing defense moves against an attack
from the rear for twenty minutes. Every time I pull on her
locks, even though I do it lightly and know that I'm not actually hurting her, it kills me. This is one of the most common
onslaughts a woman may experience, and it's important that
she learns to defend herself against it. Rocco won't ever hurt
her again, but it's good for her to have this training anyway.
The world is filled with plenty of assholes.

A murderous rage ignites in my stomach the moment
that thought forms. She shouldn't need to defend herself from
anyone, ever.

"Alessandro?"

I raise my hand and tangle my fingers in her strands, but

instead of twisting them in my grip, I let my palm slide down the silky lengths. Ravenna. The name suits her.

She turns around, the tendrils slipping from my grasp, causing almost physical pain in my chest at the loss of that small contact. What should I expect when Rocco is dead and it's time for me to go? I reach out and trace the line of her chin. What if someone dares to hurt her again and I'm not there?

"I'm leaving soon," I say.

Ravenna sucks in a breath, but she doesn't say anything as she locks her eyes with mine.

"You don't have to worry," I continue. "Even with me gone, you'll be safe. Always. I'll make sure of it."

"Interesting. Do you keep everyone you hate safe?"

"No." I grind my teeth. "Just you."

Ravenna

I watch the maelstrom in Alessandro's eyes. I've been too focused on his cruel words and his behavior, believing that he doesn't give a fuck about me. I should have paid more attention to his eyes. It's easy to lie with words and actions, but eyes always reveal the truth. And there is no hate in his now. It hasn't been there for quite some time. A different emotion lurks amid the anger and frustration. It's despair. I don't know what's going on in that thick head of his or the reasons for his lies.

"Are they for my sake, or yours?" I ask.

"What?" His thumb glides to the corner of my mouth, tracing over the shape of my lips.

"The lies, Alessandro. Are they for me or for you?"

His hand stills and his body stiffens at my words.

"They're for me," he says. His voice comes out sullen.

I want to leave him to his falsehoods, but I can't make myself turn away. He'll be gone in less than a week, as soon as he kills my husband. I may have missed out on college, but I'm far from stupid. The conversation he had with the biker revealed enough for me to put two and two together.

The thought of Rocco dead should excite me because I'll finally be free. But instead of reveling in that hopeful future, the only thing I feel is dread. With Rocco gone, Alessandro will be also.

"You know what?" I take a step closer, plastering myself to him. The proof of his lack of indifference presses into my stomach. "Both you and your lies can go to hell."

I turn on my heel, intending to walk out on him just as he did with me, when his arm wraps around my waist, pulling me to his body.

"I'm already in hell, Ravi," His free hand slips inside the waistband of my shorts and cups my pussy. "I've been there for a while."

A moan escapes me, and I grab his forearm as his finger slides inside my folds, teasing, driving deeper with every stroke. His thumb moves to my clit, applying small pressure.

"My descent began the moment I set my eyes on you." Another stroke over my pussy, and then he lifts me off the ground and carries me across the room. "And with each look, with every delicate touch, I fell further into the abyss."

He stops in front of the cushioned bench set in front of the bookshelf, letting my feet touch the soft upholstery and keeping his finger buried deep. His breath fans my hair and tickles my nape as he takes a whiff of my scent. With his other hand, he peels my shorts and panties from my body.

I whimper when his finger leaves my pussy, but mewl feeling his huge cock at my ass. With shaky hands, I grab the bookshelf before me, bracing myself against its solid form.

A kiss lands on the middle of my back. Excruciatingly slow, his lips glide up my spine, all the way to my shoulder blades. My breathing hitches with each reverent touch as I await what's coming next.

I press my forehead to the bookshelf and widen my stance. Alessandro's rough palms sweep around my ribcage and then down my stomach to my mound. Every cell in my body is humming, a tight coil ready to spring free. All I need is to have him inside me. When his cock finally slides home, I almost come at that very moment. My pussy clenches around his girth, and tremors rack my body, making it hard to stand. I let go of the bookshelf and wrap my fingers around his right wrist to guide his hand up around my throat.

"I want you to hold me here," I whisper.

If it was anyone else but him, I'd be too ashamed to even ask. Afraid they'd think I'm a basket case, damaged and fucked in the head, begging to be treated in the same manner as her abusive husband had done.

Alessandro's body stills behind me. "Why?"

"Because having your hand wrapped around my neck and knowing you would never do me harm turns me on," I say. "It makes me feel safe."

He doesn't move for a few more moments, but then his large fingers wrap around my throat. "Like this?"

His hold is too lax, just barely there. I wish it was more snug.

"I asked you a question, Ravi," he says right next to my ear.

"I need it a little tighter. Please." I pant, then bite my lip. "Do you think I'm nuts for asking?"

"Never say that again, Ravenna." The hold on my neck draws tighter, making me moan. "Better?"

A pleasant shiver races through my body. I nod.

"Good. As long as you don't ask me to hurt you, I will give you anything you want. But we should have some rules. If it gets too much, and you need my hand off, you'll tell me right away."

"Okay."

"Good girl." He kisses the shell of my ear and continues his unhurried pump.

He is so big that even with him going slowly, I still gasp for air with every stroke. His hand on my neck makes the sensation more thrilling. My legs shake, threatening to turn to jelly, and I need to hold on to the bookshelf with all my strength or risk losing my footing. When he fills me completely, I close my eyes and a steadying breath leaves my lungs.

Alessandro stalls, his right hand still at my throat, while his other hand glides upward and over my hip.

"Uncomfortable?" he asks as he gently squeezes my side.

"Just a little," I whisper. It's more intense, having him take me from behind.

"I'll make it better."

His hand slips back down, long finger sliding between my folds. He circles my clit, his movements leisurely and controlled, while his other hand matches the caresses at my neck. My breathing picks up and, with every breath, the feel of his swollen cock within me heightens.

The circling rubs around my clit get faster, and every stroke to my core just a bit more profound. His fingers on

209

my neck follow a similar rhythm, and I can't quite decide what I should focus on. I've lost all ability for rational thought.

Alessandro moves his hips, slowly rocking into me. "Are we good?"

I can't reply because I'm drowning in the sensation.

"Ravi?"

"God, yes," I choke out. "More."

He slides inside me to the hilt, and I'm ready to explode.

"It shouldn't feel so good," he rasps next to my ear. "I can't describe how incredible it is to be buried in your warmth, hearing your moans, feeling your pulse under my fingers. There isn't a comparable sensation to that, and I'm losing my mind over it, Ravi."

He pulls out and then slams back in, pinching my clit and lightly squeezing my throat at the same time. I scream, and stars burst behind my eyelids as I come.

Keeping his hand around my neck, he continues to pump while I ride the currents of weightlessness.

Ravenna's arms are wrapped around my neck as I carry her across the foyer toward the staircase.

"The front door camera," she mumbles into my neck.

"It only covers a five-foot radius around the entrance."

"How do you know?"

"I hacked the surveillance feeds."

She is silent for a few moments as if mulling over my reply, and then I hear a muffled laugh. "I thought it was the bird poop."

"What?"

"When I saw you zigzagging across the lawn. I thought you were trying to avoid bird poop or something, but you must have been taking a route that will keep you off cameras."

My lips curve up. "Clever girl."

Reaching Ravenna's bedroom, I take her inside the bathroom and lower her next to the shower stall. The light is off so I flip the switch on the wall, but nothing happens.

"Rocco shot out the light fixture," Ravenna says, her voice sounding unusually meek.

I look up at the ceiling, then scan the small space until my eyes snag on the polished brass knob on the opened door. It takes me a moment to comprehend that there is something seriously wrong with the locking mechanism. The outer part includes the turn button, but the inner handle does not. What's more, the inside knob is missing a pinhole that allows the lock to be released in case of emergency. This set provides neither privacy nor safety, and no competent tradesman would ever mount it in place.

My head snaps toward Ravenna. "The elevator."

"Yeah," she says, staring at the floor.

I bridge the distance between us and take her face in my palms. Tilting her head up, I find she's closed her eyes. "Look at me."

She just shakes her head.

"I'm so ashamed for letting him make me into this." Her voice is so tiny when she says it.

"Please, look at me."

Ravenna's eyes flutter open.

"You are a fucking warrior," I say. "You entered that battlefield without any weapons, and you fought a much stronger opponent with your bare hands."

211

"I didn't fight. The only thing I've been doing is trying to find a way to escape."

"That's what you do when you've been captured by an enemy." I bend my neck, leveling my head with hers. "You are a warrior. I want to hear you say it, Ravenna."

"I'm a warrior," she mutters.

"Damn right, you are. And don't you dare ever think otherwise." I slam my mouth to hers, sealing that declaration.

Her hands lock around my neck, pulling me closer. Without breaking our kiss, I grab her under the ass and lift to sit her on the bathroom vanity. My cock is so hard, it's close to bursting. The need to be inside her again is driving me insane. It doesn't matter that I just had her barely ten minutes ago because my body craves more.

Ravenna wraps her legs around my waist and grips the back of my T-shirt, trying to tug it over my head.

"Not here," I say into her lips. We're not doing anything in a place tainted with bad memories. I lift her off the counter and carry her into the bedroom.

When we reach the bed, Ravenna untangles her legs from around my waist and stands on the edge of the bed. Her hair is a complete mess, strands knotted and jutting in different directions. She is wearing a white top and gray shorts, which are turned inside out. I don't think she noticed when she put them back on. I love seeing her like this.

Grabbing a fistful of my T-shirt, I take it off. Ravenna's eyes flare upon seeing the ink on my chest, and the realization hits me—we've never seen each other naked. So many barriers between us, but I can easily knock this one down. I quickly shed the rest of my clothes and stand before her, letting her eyes explore to their content.

Ravenna's gaze slowly moves down my chest and abs to

stop at my fully hard cock. She bites her lower lip and traps it between her teeth as she glances back into my eyes. I need all my self-restraint not to pounce on her immediately. Reaching for the hem of her top, she pulls it over her head, revealing a lacy white bra cradling her firm breasts, the dark brown areolas visible under the intricate fabric.

"I need to see all of you," I mutter and snake my hand behind her back to unclasp her bra, then take the waistband of her shorts and slip them down her legs.

The white lace panties are next, and I take my time sliding them off, inch by slow inch. When I have her fully undressed, I step back and just stare at her perfection. My deepest fantasy comes to life. My eyes move down her delicate neck and mouthwatering breasts, then over her narrow waist and generous hips, all the way down to the tips of her toes. Even her feet are fucking perfect.

"You can't be real." I place the tip of my finger at her collarbone, inching a straight line down her front, and halt at her pussy. "Hold your breath."

I wait for her to inhale, then dip two fingers inside her pussy. Ravenna moans and grabs at my free hand, guiding it to her throat. My fingers stroke the soft skin of her neck in a leisurely gait that matches the fervent massage of her sweet pussy. Her body trembles under my touch, her sharp nails dig into the skin of my forearm. I'm pretty sure my cock is gonna blow if I don't get it in her soon, but I push that urge away. This is about her.

"Do you still dream about me?" I ask and slide my fingers even deeper inside.

"Yes." She pants as she grinds herself on my hand. "And do you dream about me?"

I slip my fingers out of her pussy and press my thumb on her clit. "Every fucking night."

Ravenna gasps and comes all over my hand.

My thumb keeps stroking her clit, prolonging her pleasure, as tremors overwhelm her frame. Only once her body sags, do I lift my hand off her pussy and scoop her up into my arms. I wish I could hold her forever, but I slowly lower her on the bed.

"You want to know a secret?" I ask as I cover her body with mine. Rising her leg by the back of her knee, I bend and fold it to the side, and finally slide my cock inside her liquid heat.

"Yes." She grabs the headboard above her head and hooks her other leg behind my back.

I start pounding into her, our gazes locked the entire time, absorbing each of her pants and moans. Safekeeping them for later.

"I dream about you even when I'm awake, Ravi."

I crush my lips to hers, thrusting into her until I come with a roar and fill her with my seed. I'm still coming down from the high, my face buried in her neck, when I hear her whisper next to my ear.

"Will you take me with you when you leave?"

An earthquake strikes inside my mind, shaking my metaphorical fortress. The thought has been nudging me for days. I want to take her with me. We could run somewhere far away, somewhere no one could find us. Until they eventually do.

It won't be just Kruger I'll need to worry about. Once I kill Rocco Pisano and the truth of who offed him eventually comes out, my name will be at the top of the Cosa Nostra hit list. Ajello won't stop until he hunts me down. If I take Ravenna with me, she'll become a target, too.

It's either her or my revenge. I can't have both. The choice before me is a double-edged sword. Can I throw away all I've worked for in the last eight years? My purpose in this life? The promises I made to me and Natalie? Can I live with that?

I close my eyes and inhale a lungful of Ravenna's scent. "I can't."

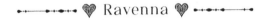

Ravenna

I stare at the ceiling above my bed, following the tiny little cracks that spread from the spot where the chandelier is attached. I've spent quite some time staring at this ceiling and this is the first time I've noticed the damage. Alessandro is lying next to me, staring at the ceiling, as well.

"I know you're planning to kill my husband before you leave," I say.

If he's surprised I've connected the dots, it doesn't show on his face. His features remain completely stoic.

"I am," he says. "The don will quickly figure out who did it and will come to ask you questions. Tell him everything, except that you knew I was going to kill Rocco."

"You think Ajello will come after you?"

"Yes."

I reach out and brush his cheek with the tips of my fingers. "What did he do? Why do you want to kill Rocco?"

Alessandro stiffens and, for several minutes, he doesn't utter a word.

"It was Friday morning, a little over eight years ago," he finally says. "I just got back from a mission and drove only a block away from my house on my way to the headquarters. I could have gone straight home and debriefed later, but I didn't want my wife to see all the blood on me."

A sinking feeling grips my stomach as I stare at his profile. His *wife*?

"She believed I worked as a security guard, while the truth was, I've been killing people for the government," he continues. "It's strange how trying to protect someone you love can get them killed. If I went directly home, she would probably still be alive. That was my last mission, and we planned on leaving that same day."

"What happened?" I choke out.

"A drunk driver, going almost twice the speed limit, ran a red light. He just left her injured on the street and fled the scene." He turns his head and meets my eyes. "Your husband."

His voice is hushed and sullen, but the words explode in my head as if he shouted them. My hand on Alessandro's cheek starts shaking. I open my mouth to say something, but no words come out. The only thing I can do is watch his face—hard lines etched in granite.

"I spent years searching for the man responsible. Rocco's father covered everything up so well that I only discovered the name of the driver a few months ago." He moves a lock of my hair that has fallen over my face, revealing my neck. "I intended to destroy Rocco Pisano's life—piece by piece— and the final step before ending it completely, I was going to make him watch while I killed his wife."

Alessandro keeps his eyes locked with mine as he moves his hand to my neck, placing the tip of his finger just below my ear.

"Eye for an eye," he whispers as he slowly slides his finger across my throat in a straight line, all the way to my other ear. "His wife for mine."

I never thought that silence could be physically oppressive, but as his eyes bore into mine, I can feel the weight of it pressing down on me from all sides. The absence of sounds is so absolute, it's almost like someone muted a movie.

Alessandro's touch vanishes from my neck. He kisses the pad of his finger and then presses it to my throat, over the spot where he meant to slice my throat.

He gets up off the bed and puts on his sweatpants, giving me a view of his bare back covered in ink. The scene is ghastly—a heap of charred skulls engulfed in flames, and atop the pile, a man hanging on a rope, his head bent as orange flames rise to lick at his legs. Above the image, scribed across his shoulder blades, a Latin script.

Oculum Pro Oculo

An eye for an eye.

I blink, trying to stop the tears from falling, but they escape anyway. How many times upon seeing me has he been reminded of what my husband took from him? So much pain and hurt.

I can't believe I asked him to take me with him. Somewhere deep inside, I knew his answer even before he voiced it, but I still hoped he'd say yes. I would gladly follow him anywhere. I'm so desperately in love with him, it doesn't matter if he loves me back. I only hoped that he would eventually.

Now, after what he just told me, I know that hope is futile. How could he ever love someone who represents so much of his despair?

Alessandro reaches for his T-shirt discarded at the foot of the bed, and as he does so, a leather string around his wrist comes undone, slipping to the floor. I noticed that bracelet the first day I met him and found it unusual. He doesn't wear any other jewelry.

He collects the leather string with a small teddy bear pendant hanging off it and heads to the door.

"Was that your wife's?" I whisper.

He stops at the threshold and, for a few pregnant moments, just stands there before replying. "Yes."

The door shuts after him with a soft click. I press my hand over my mouth, desperate to stifle a sob, but it slips out regardless of my efforts.

CHAPTER
eighteen

I LEAN MY BACK ON THE SIDE OF THE GAZEBO WITH A clear view of the second-floor window. It's after midnight, but the light in Ravenna's room is still on.

We haven't spoken since yesterday morning when I told her about Natalie. The only communication we've had was a text message she sent me earlier today, asking if I could drive her to her mom's place, and another after we returned to the mansion, saying she wouldn't be going anywhere else for the rest of the day. She sat in the back of the car on both those journeys.

I used my free time to go to the hospital and check out the security, looking for ways into Rocco Pisano's room. There weren't any. Two men are posted outside the door around the clock. All hallways have cameras, which are monitored by an off-site company with a firewall more sophisticated than I could crack, preventing me from getting into their network systems. Getting inside to kill the motherfucker isn't possible.

The only way to take him out is with a shot through the window. I scouted the building next to the hospital for a spot with direct sight to Rocco's room and found one on the top floor. It has the perfect angle to the bed. The only thing left is to get my rifle and do the deed. I could have done it today, but instead of completing my mission, I came back here to scope another window. I've been standing in the shadows, staring at the light in Ravenna's bedroom for several hours.

I miss her. I miss the small touches, like when she hooks her pinkie with mine. Her subtle teasing. The feel of having her in my arms. Last night, I almost caved and went to her bedroom. My body twitched, as if an electric current flowed through me, all because of the need to embrace her, to inhale her powdery scent, and to feel her soft black strands in my hands. I was going out of my mind and barely managed to restrain myself.

I miss *her*, even though she's there.

I told her I hate her. Several times. But the truth is, it's not her I hate. I don't think I ever truly did. I hate myself.

Because I've fallen in love with her.

The heart of the lost, lonely boy I had been loved Natalie, our feelings rooted in a shared need to survive as homeless teens. I wanted to protect her, and that slowly transformed into caring, and then love. It was the kind of love that started as a small forest stream and gradually swelled into a river. Big and steady as it follows its path. Sensible. Natural.

My feelings for Ravenna Pisano don't resemble a forest stream. They're a fucking waterfall. Unexpected. Ferocious. Passion, desire, and beautiful madness. I crave her more than a condemned man wanting his next breath.

The heart of a man who went through hell and back,

the man <u>I have become, is desperately in love</u> with a woman <u>I planned to kill.</u>

The lights in Ravenna's room turn off, casting it in darkness.

I should go get my rifle, dispose of Rocco, and leave. By this time tomorrow, I could be in Europe, away from this city filled with bad memories. Away from her.

But I don't move, just keep watching Ravenna's window for another hour before I push off and head inside the mansion. Instead of retrieving the hidden weapon from beneath the floorboards in my room, I climb the stairs.

It's pitch-black in the long hallway. I approach the last door on the left and reach for the knob. My hand stalls on the piece of ornate metal, so cold under my fingers but it still sears my flesh. I shouldn't be here. I need to turn around and leave. It's no wonder she wouldn't talk to me after everything I told her yesterday. What the fuck is wrong with me, confessing my plans to kill her? She must be scared shitless. I could have at least skipped the part about being a hitman, but it just came out, as if my subconsciousness wanted her to know. With Ravenna, I have the urge to get down on my knees and lay all the awful things I've done before her. And that scares me to death.

This has to stop. I'm ending this before the sun rises. It will take me three hours to collect my things, get to the hospital, and kill Pisano. By the time anyone notices he's dead, I will be out of the country. Yes, I'll do that. I just need to have one last look at Ravenna.

As quietly as I can, I turn the handle and step inside the moonlit room. Ravenna is lying in her bed, her back toward the door. Asleep.

Just a minute or two, I tell myself as I sit on the edge of the bed. *I'll watch her just a minute, and then I'll leave.*

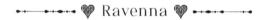 Ravenna

I've always found those few moments before coming fully awake as mystical. The boundary between dream and reality starts off as a blurry line, then it becomes more solid as night figments fade away and consciousness seeps in.

I dreamed about him again. Birds were chirping as we lay sprawled on a field of soft grass under the hot sun while he trailed his fingers through my hair.

My eyes open slowly, lids still heavy from sleep, and my vision focuses on the view through the balcony door. A sparrow is hopping along the iron railing, chirping happily. Like in my dream.

And as in my dream, someone is threading their fingers through my hair.

"I'm sorry for waking you."

I close my eyes for a second and just enjoy his touch. "It's okay."

"And I'm truly sorry for scaring you."

The mattress springs as Alessandro rises. I'm still facing the opposite direction so I can't see him, but I can hear his steps as he walks away.

"I don't think I've ever been scared of you," I whisper.

His footsteps fall silent. "Even after I confessed my intention of killing you?"

I flip over in the bed and find him standing at the door, his back toward me.

"Do you remember that day in the elevator? When it got stuck and the lights went out?"

"Yes."

"You played that numbers game with me because you knew I was having a panic attack," I say.

"So?"

"I've spent months stuck with a man who found great satisfaction in torturing me, Alessandro. Both mentally and physically. Psychological torture may not leave visible marks, but the wounds it inflicts are much worse." I pin him with my gaze. "You hated me for some reason. I didn't know why then, but I saw it in your eyes. You could have just stood by and watched me lose my shit. And still, you didn't. Even though you despised me."

Alessandro drops his head, staring at the floor. "I tried so hard to hate you. Believe me, I tried. In the end, I ended up hating myself."

My heart hurts, and I feel the squeezing in my chest. This pain is real, not some remnant in my mind. If the situation was different, I would have tried to fight for him. But I can't fight a ghost. It's clear that he loved his wife very deeply. And probably still does. That love sustained him through eight years of plotting his revenge. I can't handle the idea of being his consolation prize. Maybe, for another man, I could have lived with that. But not with Alessandro. And I can't bare knowing that he would hate himself for being with me.

There's a question that has been eating at me since he told me about his wife. I was too afraid of the answer, but I can't take it not knowing anymore.

"Did you imagine being with her, when you were with me?"

Alessandro looks over his shoulder, and our eyes connect.

"No." he steps out of the room, pulling the door shut behind him.

That soft click of the latch feels so final.

CHAPTER
nineTeen

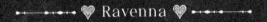

♥ Ravenna ♥

I TAKE A GLASS OF MINERAL WATER THE WAITER HANDS
me and sip, pretending to pay attention to what the
woman next to me is saying. She's a sister-in-law of one
of the Cosa Nostra enforcers, but I don't remember which
one or her name. I'm not sure why I came to this brunch.
It's some anniversary celebration Mrs. Natello organized,
and I could have easily skipped it. But I came, needing the
distraction.

If he keeps to the deal he made with the guy at the hospital, Alessandro only has three days left to kill Rocco and
leave town. Knowing that my husband will soon be dead
should bother me. Yet, I don't care one bit. If there was any
trace of compassion for Rocco that he failed to beat out of
me, it evaporated the moment Alessandro told me about his
wife, and what my husband did to her. Still, all things aside,
a man's life is in question. So, does that make me a bad person for not giving a shit what happens to Rocco now?

My eyes wander across Mrs. Natello's sunroom, taking in the vistas beyond the glass panel walls keeping us

comfortably warm and away from the frozen landscape outside. I bet, in the summer, the rolling green grass looks cheery from this location. Now, the emptiness of the lawn just draws my eye to the iron fence that surrounds the property and the ribbon of road on the other side. The ground is covered in a thin layer of snow, and the sullen skies overhead match the mood in my heart.

Turning away, my gaze falls on a group of men gathered toward the back of the room. Alessandro and a few other bodyguards stand watch. As usual, his stance is rigid but his eyes are constantly shifting, assessing the situation like a hawk. The rest of the security men are talking among themselves, not paying much attention to what's happening to the party guests.

Mrs. Natello is not very popular, so this gathering is a pretty low-level event as far as the Cosa Nostra hierarchy is concerned. There are no big shots present here. It's mostly the enforcers and their wives, but I had noticed three men who work with Rocco occasionally. They don't look like businessmen, more like hired muscle. When Rocco needs a problem to be solved on the side, without the whole of the New York Family—and especially the boss—knowing about it, he avoids using Don Ajello's soldiers.

This may be an insignificant event, but Alessandro is acting as if he's on a battlefield, waiting for the enemy to surface. He leaves nothing to chance. I love that about him. He stands by his principles, and nothing or no one will make him break them. All that intensity—what if it was directed at me? How would it feel to have him as mine? Not just in body, but his soul, as well. Maybe if we would have met in another life, I may have had a chance. In this one, we met too late. His heart was already taken.

I lift my hand, pinching the bridge of my nose. It started to tingle as if my psyche was trying to tell me something. Is today the day when he'll leave? Dear God, I'm going to miss him so much.

Alessandro turns, and for a brief moment, our eyes meet across the room. I've been avoiding eye contact with him since he left my room this morning. The pain is just too great to bear. Like now, a throbbing ache that spreads through my chest as I wonder if this will be the last look we share.

Mrs. Natello approaches, asking how we liked the appetizers. She's wearing one of the dresses I purchased last month and had my mom sell to her. The dress is worth four grand, but Mrs. Natello only paid my mom half of that.

"Ravenna, I've never seen you with your hair down, dear," she says. "What a surprise."

"I needed a change." I shrug.

She gives me an insincere smile and leans closer to me. "You know, I saw an amazing little Chanel clutch in their newest collection. It would go beautifully with my new coat."

I look at her, focusing on the small, superficial smile straining her lips. How many times has my mother sold her the clothes I've bought? She knows I've been buying those clothes, and she's never once asked why a capo's wife would resort to obtaining money in such a way. Sometimes, I think bystanders are worse than the tormentors.

"I'm sure it would." I finish my water and place the glass on the side table behind me. "Christmas sales are coming up, make sure you don't miss them."

Offering her an equally faux smile, I head across the sunroom. The amount of money I needed to run from

Rocco had been astronomical, but with him out of the picture, I have more than enough. I'm going to wait until everything settles down, then take my mom and Vitto and go someplace where Cosa Nostra doesn't have influence. I won't risk my brother falling into their hands.

I find a less crowded spot on the other side of the sunroom, beyond the tables with food and the seating areas where most of the guests have congregated, but Pietro spots me and starts in my direction. Coming to this brunch was a mistake. I'm not in the mood for socializing, but anything felt better than staying in my bedroom. Being there made me think about everything Alessandro told me. His words kept replaying in my mind, over and over. And amid the kaleidoscope of everything that happened between us, one thought kept nudging. He was with *me* when we made love.

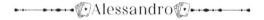

Alessandro

It's him again.

I fist my hands and force myself to stop watching Ravenna and Pietro talking on the far side of the buffet table. Not possible. It's as if my eyes are drawn to them by magnetic energy and nothing can make me look away.

Their conversation seems friendly. Pietro is one of those guys who always does things by the book, so he would never flirt with a married woman. But I've seen the way he looks at Ravenna. The moment she's free, he'll make his move, and I won't be there to stop him.

My nails dig into my palms as my fists tighten even more. By all accounts, I should be glad for her. That cultured, straightlaced motherfucker would be a good match for her. Ravenna would be happy with him. Pietro might be an uptight, sophisticated bastard, but he's more than capable of keeping her safe. Yet . . . My hands ache and rage brews inside my chest. She's mine! No one should be allowed to keep her safe but me!

I take a deep breath and start counting to ten. My decision has been made. I had to decide between my vow of revenge and her, and I chose the former. I need to let Ravenna go.

Pietro places his hand on the small of Ravenna's back, and my self-control evaporates. I stride across the room, stopping right behind Ravenna. I'm so close that her ass brushes against my thighs.

"Move," I bite out, looking down at Pietro.

He tilts his head up and raises an eyebrow. "Oh. Rocco's watchdog. I was wondering where you were."

I lean my head so I'm closer to his level. "I said, move."

Small fingers grab my hand and lightly squeeze.

"It was nice seeing you, Pietro. Say hi to your sister for me." Ravenna squeezes me again, and then quickly removes her hand from mine. "Alessandro, can you escort me to the ladies' room?"

I follow Ravenna through the French doors that open to the inside of the main house. We enter a room where the walls are covered in portraits of dogs and old people wearing froufrou clothes. Ravenna passes a couple having a discussion near the grandfather clock and enters a wide hallway leading further inside the house. Halfway down, she stops and turns to face me.

"What the fuck was that?" she whisper-yells.

I grind my teeth. "I'm just doing my job."

"I don't think there is a need for you to keep doing it, Alessandro. And we both know very well why."

Yes, I guess we do. I reach out and brush her cheek with the back of my hand. She is wearing minimal makeup today, just some eyeshadow. Her silk dress is the same emerald-green as her eyes. I don't think I'll ever be able to see that color and not be reminded of her.

Ravenna tilts her head to the side, leaning into my touch, and wraps her fingers around my wrist. "When are you leaving?"

"Tonight."

She nods, and one tear slides down her cheek, dissolving as it connects with my thumb.

"Take care of yourself, Alessandro." She steps around me, heading back down the hall.

I close my eyes, then turn around and wrap my arms around her from behind. Her scent enters my nose, and I bend, burying my face in her hair. The music and chatter out in the sunroom can be heard all the way back here, but I block out the noise and focus on the feeling of having her in my arms.

Ravenna's hand slides between our bodies and presses to my painfully hard cock. I might condition my mind to resist her, but my body never will. Every time she's near, my dick yearns to possess her. I pull her closer to me and inhale again.

"Is there an antidote for this?" I ask as I slide my palms down the front of her thighs and then up, pulling the silky fabric to her waist.

"For what?"

"You, Ravi."

A small moan leaves her lips when I pull her lace thong

to the side and cup her pussy in my palm. Drenched. I caress her folds, sliding my finger inside her warmth, then pull out my hand and bring it to my mouth and nose.

"Everything about you smells like fucking ambrosia." I lick my fingers.

The instant I taste her on my lips, the last of my self-restraint vanishes. I need to have her one more time or I'm going to lose my mind.

"Tell me to leave." I lower my hand again and, this time, I slide my finger into the depths of her pussy. "Just one word, Ravi, and I'll remove my hand."

Ravenna whimpers and widens her thighs while a shudder runs through her body. She grabs the handle on the door on our left, opening it. The room beyond the threshold looks like a study. Bookshelves, two recliners set before them, and by the far wall, a desk with some papers on top. Keeping my hand pressed to Ravenna's pussy, I tighten the hold around her waist and carry her inside the room.

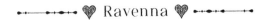

This damn dress has a zipper on the back.

I reach behind, trying to grasp the tab when Alessandro's fingers wrap around my hand, pulling it away. A kiss lands on my bare shoulder, sending small shivers through my body. Without lifting his lips off my bare skin, he takes the zipper and slowly slides it down, all the way to my ass.

"Have I told you that you are the most beautiful woman

gracing this earth?" he whispers as the silky fabric cascades down my legs.

"No," I breathe out and close my eyes.

"You are." He hooks his finger in the string of my thong, pulling it off, while his other hand strokes my ass cheek. "And I want to eat you alive."

A small yelp leaves my lips when he collects me in his arms and carries me across the room. Papers rustle under my naked ass as he deposits me on the desk and crushes his mouth to mine, sucking on my tongue as if he truly intends to eat me. I reach for the zipper on his pants, but my hands are shaking, and it takes me a few tries to open it and release his cock.

"Legs around my waist," Alessandro rasps while threading his fingers through my hair.

I lock my legs behind his back and move my ass forward, right to the edge of the desk.

"Now, take a deep breath," he says as the tip of his cock presses on my entrance. "Slowly, Ravenna."

It's almost impossible to draw in the air slowly when I feel as if I'm going to explode, but I manage. As I slowly inhale, he slides his cock inside me, inch by inch. It feels like I'm breathing him into my body, and the sensation of it nearly brings me over the edge. Only when he's fully inside do I exhale, and, for a moment, I just stare into his eyes.

I can't believe we're doing this here. There is no lock on the door, so anyone can come in and see us. Me—a married woman—being fucked by her bodyguard while her husband is in the hospital. Panic rises inside me. I grab Alessandro's wrist and quickly move his hand to my throat. As his strong fingers wrap around my neck, the panic recedes.

"Don't remove your hand," I whisper.

Alessandro nods and slams his lips to my own. His tongue fucks my mouth, hard and fast, then slow yet still demanding, until he pulls away, breathless. "Anything you need, Ravi."

He slides out slowly only to thrust into me again, his cock stretching my already pulsing pussy. It feels so good. Liberating. My eyes singe through his as he rocks into me, needing to burn his face into my memory. He stares at me with the same intensity while our breaths mix, and, suddenly, I'm overcome with the need to weep. This is a goodbye.

"Let's run away," I whisper, my voice shaking, "We'll head straight to your car and be gone, leaving everything behind."

Alessandro clenches his jaw, a pained expression crosses his face. I know what I'm asking of him. There's such turmoil in his depths as he increases his thrusts, hammering me like a madman. *Please, choose me*, I plead in my head.

"I can't." His voice comes out broken as he says it.

Shutting out the world along with my sight, my fingers slip over his short hair. As the pressure builds inside my core, my frame starts to shudder. Pleasure and pain. Seems one can't exist without the other.

"Ravenna."

My body is rejoicing while my soul weeps as Alessandro fucks me senseless. I'm shaking so much that I can barely keep my legs hooked behind his back.

"Ravenna, look at me."

I roll my head and try to grip his too-short hair. At best, my nails scrape over his scalp. "Harder. Please."

He pulls out and, with his next thrust, sends me over the edge and joins me in free fall. I whimper as I ride the high, my breathing fast and heavy. Alessandro's lips find mine, claiming them, just as he claimed me with his seed, filling me up to the brim. I don't want the world to return, so I let myself smolder in the heat of his arms a while longer.

"Ravi?"

I bite the inside of my cheek and make myself meet his eyes. Every touch we share becomes a knife in my chest, prolonging this agony. I can't do this anymore. It's killing me on the inside.

I gather myself and plead, "Can I ask you to do something for me?"

He tilts his head to the side and strokes my cheek with his hand. "Anything. You know that."

Yes. Anything, except to choose me.

"I need you to leave now, Alessandro."

His fingers still on my face.

"I'll get dressed and go back to the party," I say, willing my voice not to tremble. "I'll ask someone to drive me home in the next hour. Will that be enough time for you to get your things from the mansion?"

He drops his head, leaning his forehead to mine. "Yes."

"Okay," I choke out.

Alessandro doesn't move, just resumes stroking my cheek with his thumb, silently staring at me. That hush is shuttered by laughter outside the room, probably a few guests heading to a restroom. There is a possibility that they may walk in here, but I can't make myself care. I lift my hand and wrap my fingers around Alessandro's wrist, pulling his hand off my neck.

"I love you, Alessandro," I whisper. "Please, take care."

He shuts his eyes for a second, then takes a step back. His hand falls away from my face. I watch him as he pulls up his zipper, then turns and heads out of the room. At the door, he comes to a halt, and my heart leaps as slight hope ignites within me.

"I'm sorry, Ravenna," he says, squashing that ember to ash.

He walks out, not bothering to look back.

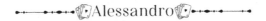

Alessandro

I stare at the sunroom through the windshield of my SUV, searching the small crowd of milling people for the green dress. I've started my car three times already, only to turn off the ignition moments later.

She told me she loves me. It almost killed me to leave her there after hearing those words. It doesn't have to be like this. Felix can easily find a hitman who could handle Pisano, and no one would be able to tie his death to me. I can call him right now, then return to the party and take Ravenna away with me.

But the beast gnawing on my soul these past eight years sinks its teeth deeper in my flesh, demanding for me to carry out Rocco's death sentence myself. It yearns for the blood I promised it so long ago, and it won't tolerate a substitution.

I've accepted my fate, but I can't make myself leave. Not yet. I need to see that Ravenna arrives home safely, and only then will I let the beast get its due.

A roar of an approaching vehicle reaches me, becoming louder as it nears. It's not a car, the exhaust noise is harsh and too high-pitched. I look toward the other end of the driveway, where a big black bike comes to a stop.

Taking my gun out of the shoulder holster, I exit the car

and hurry across the driveway while snow crunches under the soles of my feet.

"What are you doing here?" I bark as I stop in front of the biker.

Drago Popov pushes up the visor on his helmet and fixes me with his gaze. "Settling the accounts."

"We had a deal." I lift my gun and point it at his face. "Leave. Now."

"Our deal, Zanetti, only applies to Rocco Pisano. Not to the others who were involved in killing my men. And my intel says that three of them are inside at the moment."

Several more bikes approach at high speed from the rear. I turn around, my eyes snapping toward the sunroom where the guests are still having drinks. On the road beyond the iron fence surrounding the house, two bikes come to a halt. Foreboding rises inside me, then transforms into a heart-stopping panic. I'm already running across the driveway when the bikers pull out their guns and start shooting through the glass walls.

People scream, their wails mix with the sound of gunfire. In my mind, however, it all turns into a single shrilling buzz. It drills directly into my brain, to the point that it feels like my head will explode.

By the time I reach the shattered walls of the sunroom, the shooting has ceased and is replaced with the rumbling of the bikes speeding away. The air is filled with screams and yelling.

Pieces of glass are everywhere; tables and chairs lie overturned throughout the space. The bodies of two men are on the ground, twin blood pools surrounding them both. I recognize these guys right away as guns for hire I saw with Rocco on one occasion. Another goon is sprawled on the buffet table.

I frantically scan the guests huddled on the floor behind the overturned tables. There are at least thirty women here, but I can't see *her*!

White dress. Pink. Black. Black again. Yellow. But no green. Where is she? I start running around, stepping over people's hands, feet, legs. I don't give a fuck. A man approaches me, pulling on my arm. I grab him by the front of his jacket, launch him onto one of the upright seats, and continue my maniacal search. Red. Black. Gold. I stop in the middle of the room trying to calm down. And failing.

"Ravenna!" I roar at the top of my lungs.

The noise in the background of hysterical wailing and shouting comes to an abrupt halt, and dozens of eyes turn to stare at me. On the other side of the room, a partially hidden head of tangled black hair peeks its face from behind a table resting on its side.

"I'm okay," Ravenna says and stands up.

Jesus fucking Christ. She seems unharmed, but I need to assure myself. I rush toward her, not minding the people in my way. The instant I reach Ravenna, I grab her under her arms, lifting her over the table to set her in front of me. As her feet touch the ground, I run my palms down her arms and front, then turn her around, examining her back.

"Alessandro," she mumbles.

"Did any of the glass hit you?" I ask as I'm scanning the back of her head. "Let me see your legs."

"I'm fine."

I turn her to face me and kneel, going over her shins with my hands. Only after I've checked her out completely will I be able to draw a fucking breath. I lift her left foot and remove her shiny black heel. Maybe a shard has gotten inside.

"There is nothing in my shoe, Alessandro."

I shake my head and move to her other heel, taking it off as well, then glide my palm over her sole. When I'm done with my inspection, and the fact that she's unharmed finally penetrates my brain, my hands start shaking. A strange sensation washes over me, a myriad of different emotions. It feels like someone has just emptied a full magazine of high-caliber bullets right into my chest. Fear and anger. Relief. Guilt.

The walls of my stone fortress quake like never before, the thundering rumble filling my mind. *She could have died.* The thunder rolls, the sound so powerful that I'm convinced I can feel its vibrations in my bones. *I could have lost her.*

I picture Ravenna, her blood-covered body lying atop shards of glass on the floor. If I wasn't already on my knees, I'm certain I'd be now. The bloodthirsty beast yearning for retribution screams in anguish, retracting its claws as the eight-year-long hold slips. What's left of my revenge fortress shudders, its once-mighty stones falling apart before finally exploding into a cloud of fine dust.

"Alessandro?" Ravenna's hand lands on my shoulder, squeezing it lightly.

I wrap my arms around her legs and lean my forehead on her waist, pulling her to me. The next time I set my eyes on that son of a bitch Popov, I'm going to fucking annihilate him.

The sounds of crying and moaning around us finally register on me. Along with the suffering, I catch the low murmurs of Ravenna's name along with mine. It hasn't been more than five minutes since someone shot at them, and people have already started to gossip. They all can go to hell.

I feel a touch on my cheek as Ravenna takes my face between her palms and tilts my head up. "I thought you said you were leaving."

Yes, I was. Until I heard those gunshots and imagined one

hitting her. I'm taking her with me, and if ensuring she's safe means I have to let someone else kill Rocco fucking Pisano, so be it.

"We are." I rise and scoop her into my arms, pressing my mouth to hers.

Ravenna's arms lock tightly around my neck as she returns my frantic kiss, sharing my air. I squeeze her even tighter to my chest.

Gasps and shouts ring out around us, but I tune them out, completely focused on Ravenna in my arms.

"I love you, Ravi," I say into her lips. "I'm sorry it took me so long to come to my senses. If you want me to kneel down in front of you here and ask for your forgiveness, I will. Just please, come with me."

"Always." She tightens her hold around my neck. "And anywhere."

I kiss her again, turning toward the driveway. People with shocked expressions on their faces watch us as I navigate between the scattered furniture and glass, right through the shattered sunroom walls to my parked car on the driveway. They're all shaking heads and murmuring among themselves, but I don't give a fuck.

Ravenna

When we reach his car, Alessandro places me on the passenger seat and takes off his suit jacket, putting it around my shoulders.

"We should have taken your coat." He adjusts the sides of

the jacket so they cover my chest. It seems as if he's obsessed with keeping me warm.

"I'm fine." I reach out and lightly stroke his cheek.

Alessandro nods then walks around the hood, getting behind the wheel, but instead of starting the car, he leans forward and cups my face with his palm.

"Are you sure about this, Ravi?"

His eyes search mine as if he's expecting me to refute my earlier conviction. I know he needs to kill Rocco, and I don't care how many people will be after us when he does. I would go with him to the ends of the earth.

"Yes," I breathe.

Alessandro's intense attention doesn't leave me as he reaches for his phone and dials someone.

"Felix," he says when the call connects. "I need a hit-man. The target is at a hospital in New York. He's heavily guarded, so it needs to be taken care of with a sniper shot through a window. I'll send you the coordinates and a sketch of the suitable spot location I found. It has a direct line of sight to the mark."

"Are you fucking with me, Az?" a grumbly voice yells on the other side. "Last time I checked, you *are* a damn hitman with proficiency in long-range rifles, and you're already there."

Alessandro takes my chin between his fingers and leans forward, pressing his lips to mine.

"If I do it myself, someone I love will be in danger," he says into my lips.

My heart stops beating. I lift my shaking hand and place it on Alessandro's cheek.

"What happened to your plan?" I ask. "You've spent

years plotting to exact your revenge. I'm sure you dreamed of doing it personally."

"I did. But I have other dreams now." He tosses the phone onto the dash. The man on the other end of the line is still speaking, but Alessandro continues, "And all of them revolve around you, Ravi. I won't risk putting you in danger by having Ajello come after me. No retaliation is worth that."

One tear escapes my eye, but this time it's a tear of happiness, not of sorrow. I know what his revenge means to him, and now he's letting it go.

"I would have come with you regardless," I whisper.

"I would never have allowed that. What I feel for you is greater than anything I've ever felt before, Ravenna. It's like a beautiful blaze that consumes me, shining light on a darkness that has festered in my soul for so long. And I want to stay in this light forever if you'll let me."

I swallow hard and nod.

"I'm driving you back to the mansion. You'll pack your things. Just the essentials. And you'll call your mom and ask her to do the same."

"We're taking my mom and Vitto with us?"

"Yes. We will all be leaving tonight. I need to get rid of some things before we can go, and it will take me a few hours."

"Okay."

Alessandro's hand falls away from my face, and he starts the car. When he pulls out of the driveway, he looks down at my hands clasped on my lap, then places his palm on my thigh and hooks his pinkie with mine.

We're halfway to the mansion when Alessandro takes a turn, heading north. I don't comment on the change in

241

direction but keep watching his profile while stroking his palm with the tip of my finger.

A little over half an hour later, he makes a left turn, heading down the street that leads to a cemetery. We drive through the gates, and he parks the SUV curbside to a section of plots and turns to face me.

"I need to make a quick stop." He lifts my hand to his mouth and places a kiss on the middle of my palm. "Do you want to come with me?"

"Yes. But only if you want me to," I say quietly.

"I do." He nods.

We exit the car, and Alessandro takes my hand and leads me along the wide gravel path through the cemetery. I look down at our entwined fingers, feeling a bit nervous over what I'm certain we're about to face. Neither of us says a word as we follow a few narrow paths until we reach the white marble tombstone. Next to it is a young birch tree, its thin bare branches heightening the sorrow in this place. I stare at its white trunk, not daring to look directly at Alessandro for fear of seeing the regret on his face. But I can still see him out of the corner of my eye as he reaches with his free hand and strokes the surface of the stone.

The hold on my hand loosens, and his fingers slip from mine. I close my eyes for a moment, taking a deep breath. What will I see when I open them? Will he tell me he's changed his mind?

I gather the courage and lift my lids to face the truth.

Alessandro is standing next to me, undoing the knot on the leather string around his left wrist. Once finished, he places the string with the teddy bear charm atop the tombstone and takes my hand again.

"Goodbye, Natalie," he says in a rough voice, then

bends and drops a kiss to the top of my head. "Let's go, baby."

The digits on the dresser clock flip to ten-thirty, reflecting off the glass keeping out the night

There's a small backpack on the floor, barely half-full. I don't want to take anything purchased with my husband's money, so I've only packed one pair of leggings, a few tops, and some underwear. Rocco threw away everything else I brought with me to this house. Since I don't have a jacket of my own, only the expensive coats of Rocco's choosing, I put on Alessandro's suit jacket.

When I hear the sound of footsteps in the hallway, I leap from the bed and grab my phone and backpack, then dash through the door. The hallway is dark, the only light comes from the chandelier above the stair landing at the end, its glow illuminates the figure a few paces in front of me.

The bag and phone slip out of my hand, dropping to the floor with a thud as panic explodes in my chest.

"Going somewhere, bellissima?"

I freeze, unable to move as if someone glued my feet to the floor. I can't even speak.

"I got a call earlier." Rocco takes a step forward. "It was about a brunch party where my wife was apparently kissing her bodyguard. That can't be true, can it?"

I can't force words out of my mouth, the only thing I can do is just stand there and stare at him while terror floods my body. Rocco swings his arm, striking my face with such force that I end up knocked into the wall.

"You fucking slut!" Rocco roars and wraps his left hand

around my neck. "I'm going to fucking kill you! And then, I'm going to find that lying son of a bitch and skin him alive!"

"He's gone. And he's not coming back," I choke out as I finally break out of my stupor and grab his wrist, trying to dislodge his hand but failing.

You can't fight me with strength. Alessandro's voice says in my head.

I shift and duck my head under Rocco's arm, twisting my whole body in one quick movement. He loses his grip, his fingers slipping off my throat, and I run. My bedroom is close by, so I rush inside and throw my weight against the door, trying to shut it. But Rocco is right on my heels, and he kicks it open. I'm forcefully shoved back, nearly losing my balance in the process. With nowhere else left to go, I turn around to run toward the bathroom, but pain shoots through my head as I'm violently yanked from behind. I scream.

"I love it when you try to fight, bitch." Rocco laughs as he pulls on my hair.

Raising my hands, I grab his fist on my hair. His grasp hurts so much that tears burst from my eyes, but I make myself bend and rotate my body the way Alessandro showed me. Rocco yells as his wrist gets twisted but keeps his hold on my hair. Even one-handed, his size and strength are crushing my attempts to escape.

You need to go against the weak points.

I glance at Rocco's right hand, thankful that I at least don't have to worry about a blow while he's wrenching on my hair. His injured hand is still tightly wrapped in a thick layer of bandages, and he's keeping it away from his body, protecting it. I hit it with my forearm, putting as much force into my strike as I can. Rocco howls, releasing my hair, and clutches his injured hand to his chest, nearly falling forward as he does so.

Run. I need to run. The bathroom—but it's a dead end, and has no lock to keep him out. I turn around instead and step around the screaming Rocco, then dash out of my bedroom. In the hallway, I scoop up my phone and backpack and run toward the staircase.

CHAPTER
Twenty

●──•──•───•❖ Alessandro ❖•───•──•──●

THE FUCKING LIFTGATE WON'T CLOSE.

I pull it up again and move the fuel canisters to the side so I can rearrange the black body bag containing Felix's present. One of his guys delivered it last week and helped me stash it in the fridge at the back of the storage unit. I have no use for it anymore, and we'll have to make a pitstop somewhere out of the way where I can torch it.

I've already cleared out my apartment of everything that may connect my past to Rocco Pisano. When people realize Ravenna and I have left, and her husband turns up dead shortly after, I don't want anyone drawing any ties between the two events. The chances of Cosa Nostra being able to track down the hitman Felix hired are slim to none, but I'm not leaving any loose ends.

The liftgate finally locks in place. I take another look around the empty storage unit to make sure I haven't missed anything, then reach into my pocket and take out a deck of cards. The cards are wrapped in a rubber band, their edges yellow and frayed with age. It's the same old deck my old man used to teach me to play poker and one of the few things I kept from my childhood. For some reason, I never could make myself throw these away.

The ring of my phone breaks the stillness of the night. I slip the cards back into my pocket and slide behind the wheel, taking the phone off the dash. The screen flashes with Ravenna's name. She's probably wondering what's taking me so long. I can't keep a smile off my lips as I picture her standing at the window, waiting for me, so my thumb is quick to hit call answer as I press the phone to my ear.

"He's here," Ravenna's frantic whispering comes across the line.

My body stills, ice filling my veins.

Click.

The call disconnects.

"I'm coming, Ravi," I say even though she can't hear me, and peel out with my heart in my throat.

The storage unit is twenty minutes away from the Pisano mansion. I floor it, ignoring the needle as it rises to nearly 125 on a dial, and try to swallow the wave of panic swelling within me. The vehicles I pass end up being just a swipe of light—there one moment and gone the next. The closer I get, the stronger my fear becomes, as I imagine what that motherfucker could be doing to Ravenna. Knowing that the life of the woman I love depends on me keeping my cool is the only thing stopping me from losing my shit completely.

I pull up and park out of sight of the guardhouse. It's likely that Rocco gave orders to stop me if the guards see me coming, and I can't risk them alerting their boss about my arrival. I extract a set of throwing knives I keep hidden under the seat and get out of the car.

Scoping out the area, I spot one guard at the front of the

gate, an M16 hanging across his back. The other one is inside the guardhouse, watching the monitors. I creep from tree to tree until I'm close enough to throw one of my knives. It sails into the gate guy's neck, and the man falls to his knees. His buddy in the guardhouse leaps from his chair and springs outside. I launch two blades at him. The first ends up in his chest, and the other just below his Adam's apple. Stopping only long enough to slice their necks and retrieve my knives, I double back to take care of the three guys positioned outside the perimeter wall. Keeping clear of cameras along the edge of the property, I pick Rocco's guys off in quick succession by putting a bullet through each of their heads. The suppressor on my gun makes sure anyone in the mansion remains none the wiser.

The light in the entry hall is on, but no one seems to be around. I'm running to the stairs when a big crash echoes somewhere to my right. Changing direction, I race toward the east wing of the house and the cacophony of breaking glass.

"I can't wait to get my hands on you, bitch!" Rocco's yells are coming from the kitchen. "I'll kill you with my bare hands!"

I rush inside.

Rocco is in the middle of the room, a gun in his left hand but at least he isn't wielding it at the moment. All around him are shattered plates and glasses. Ravenna is at the kitchen counter, her back may be to the wall but she's facing the bastard with a kitchen knife in her right hand and a wine glass in her left. Her hair is falling over her face in a tangled mess as she stares at Rocco with a mix of fear and determination in her eyes, ready to launch the stemware at him.

Pride blooms in my chest upon seeing her, so small and terrified, yet facing her abuser and ready to fight for herself.

But I'm here now, and never again will she need to defend herself from anyone. Ravenna tilts her head up, her gaze meeting mine. Her hair slides off her face, revealing a huge red mark her left cheek.

I've heard the term blind rage several times, but I've never experienced it myself. Until this moment. It starts off as utter calmness but then fury and rancor explode like a supernova, filling every fiber of my being. I take a step forward, coming behind Rocco, and wrap my right arm around his neck while grabbing his left wrist with my free hand. My eyes lock on Ravenna's as I squeeze Rocco's limb with all my strength. The gun falls out of his hand as he thrashes within my hold, trying to free himself. I snake my other arm behind his neck, trapping his head in a rear naked choke. It's a very effective tactical move that allows me to put pressure on both sides of his neck at the same time. I can feel his labored breaths as he fights for air, his face turning a disgusting shade of purple, but no sounds penetrate my ears. A few seconds more and he's done.

Too easy. And way too fast.

For some reason, my mind goes to that old deck of cards in my pocket and my lips curve into a smile. I release my hold and let Rocco Pisano's limp body drop to the floor.

 Ravenna

The expression on Alessandro's face, as he looks down at the unconscious Rocco on the floor, is really strange. He seems controlled, but the look in his eyes is simply feral. His eyes find mine, and the ferociousness within them dissipates, replaced with worry.

"Ravi baby?" He steps toward me, then stops. "Are you okay?"

"Yes," I say. My voice trembles, and my legs are shaking, but that's from the adrenaline.

Alessandro takes another step and crouches in front of me. "I'm not going to hurt you, Ravi."

"Why would I think you'd hurt me?" I mumble in confusion. "And why are you crouching?"

"I'm trying to make myself less intimidating in your eyes, baby."

"I find you equally intimidating when you stand and . . . like that. Which is not at all."

A small smile pulls at his lips. "Would you mind dropping the knife if that's the case?"

I glance down and realize I'm still gripping a steak knife in my outstretched hand. "Oh . . . sorry," I choke out and lower my arm.

"Can I hug you? Please?" he asks as his eyes search mine.

His face is set in sharp lines, and his jaw is clenched tightly as if he's trying to contain himself. I'm momentarily confused by the way he's acting and his question, and then it dawns on me. He's afraid I'm in shock and considering him a threat, too. Silly man. I toss the knife on the floor and place my hand on his cheek.

"Yes," I say.

Alessandro leaps up, wrapping his arms around me, and lifts me.

"I'm sorry," he says into my mouth while he crushes me to his body so hard, I can barely breathe. "I should have been here."

"It's okay. I got the chance to try out those moves you taught me," I mumble and bite his lower lip.

"You won't ever need to use those moves again as long as I live, Ravi. I swear on my life." His mouth drifts along my chin to the bruise on the side of my cheek. "Are you packed?"

"Yes."

"I just need to finish something and we're leaving. Okay?"

"Okay."

"Good." He slowly lowers me to the ground, then bends and takes my face between his palms. "Wait here until I come back for you. Please."

I nod.

Alessandro drops another kiss on my lips, then heads to Rocco. He grabs my husband by the back of his suit jacket and drags him out of the kitchen. I wait by the counter for a few seconds, then dash after them.

I rush across the entry hall to the office and peek inside through the open door. Rocco is still unconscious as Alessandro puts him on one of the big baroque chairs by the wall, just under a huge oil painting. Rocco commissioned that piece shortly after our wedding. The composition is of a group of men seated at a cloth-covered table, playing cards on a pristine white surface. It reminds me of Da Vinci's *The Last Supper* in some disturbing way.

Alessandro moves the coffee table in front of Rocco and grabs another chair from the corner of the room. He then sets it on the other side of the table, facing Rocco.

"Time to wake up, Pisano," Alessandro says as he takes a seat and places his gun on the table surface.

Rocco's eyes flutter open. For a moment, he just stares at Alessandro, then leaps up off the chair, his left hand reaching for the gun.

Alessandro is faster. He snatches the weapon and sends a bullet into Rocco's thigh. "That will keep you sitting."

Rocco falls back onto the chair, screaming at the top of his lungs. Alessandro ignores his wailing and puts the gun back on the table. Calmly, he reaches into his pocket and takes out a deck of cards.

"I'm going to fucking kill you, you piece of lying shit!" my husband roars between the sobs, spit flying in front of him. His face is red, either from rage or pain.

"I know you enjoy playing for high stakes," Alessandro says as he shuffles the cards. "Since we don't have pretty rocks on hand this time, we'll play for something else. How about body parts?"

Rocco's eyes flare. He leans back in the chair, staring at Alessandro, and the surprise on his face morphs into fear.

"Let me go," Rocco blurts out. "Let me go, and I won't tell Ajello anything. But if you do me harm, and the don finds out, you're done, Zanetti."

"I don't give a fuck. You've dared to touch someone I love, so you're going to pay for that, consequences be damned."

I bite my lower lip. He decided to exact revenge after all. It's probably why he asked me to stay in the kitchen. So I wouldn't know.

"She's my wife, you motherfucker!" Rocco snaps. He obviously concluded that Alessandro is talking about me and not his late wife.

"Your soon-to-be widow, you mean?" Alessandro cocks his head to the side and starts dealing the cards. "Yes. I've been in love with your future widow from the day I stepped into your home. Now, shut up and play. Or I may decide to fuck up your other hand and then you won't be able to hold anything."

I press my trembling hand over my lips. He's doing this

for me. The last of the doubts that were still in my heart fade away, and I let myself believe that the dreams I once had and thought were burned to ashes, will come true.

Tucking the sides of Alessandro's suit jacket tightly around me, I sneak closer but hide from view behind one of the bookshelves. I wish I could run over there and kiss him, but I won't dare distract him and risk Rocco getting the gun.

I thought poker could only be played with three or more people, but it seems I was wrong. Alessandro deals two cards for each of them, face down, then places three more on the table, face up.

"I fold," Rocco sneers after he looks at his two cards.

"There is no folding in this game of mine, Pisano," Alessandro replies as he places two more up-facing cards on the table. "We'll also skip a step or two to save some time. Now, let's see what we have."

Rocco stares at the cards, then moves his gaze to the gun. I can see it in his eyes the moment he decides to reach for it. His body goes rigid as he leans slightly forward. I open my mouth to warn Alessandro, but there is no need. Alessandro's hand shoots to the right, grabbing the weapon. A gunshot pierces the air the next moment.

My husband screams and presses his hand over his bleeding shoulder.

"Does it hurt?" Alessandro asks as he lowers the gun, but Rocco just keeps wailing.

"I asked, does. It. Hurt?" Alessandro leans over the table and clasps his fingers around Rocco's bandaged hand.

The sound that leaves Rocco's lips is more animalistic than human. "Yes!"

"I'm glad. Let's continue."

I stay hidden behind the bookshelf and watch as they

play three more rounds. Each one concludes with a bullet to Rocco's body. His right bicep. Left foot. The other thigh. The pool of blood spreads all around Rocco's chair. He's barely able to sit straight. Even his sobs have lost their ardent zeal, with only a whimper sounding every now and then. The time seems to stretch into an endless span, but it's barely been five minutes.

Alessandro deals the cards again. Rocco sways in the chair and then falls forward, his head hitting the wooden surface of the table. Cards scatter around, hitting the floor one by one. Alessandro takes the gun and grabs Rocco by the hair, pulling his head up.

"Game over, motherfucker." He fires the gun, the bullet striking its mark in the center of Rocco's face.

Blood and brain matter spray out of the back, covering everything in a grisly mess.

Alessandro lets go of Rocco's head, and it falls back down onto the wooden coffee table. The last card left on the table slips down and slowly flips in the air before it lands on the puddle of blood by Alessandro's foot. The ace of hearts.

I leave my hiding spot behind the bookshelf and take a step into the room. Alessandro looks up, his body coming to an abrupt halt the moment he notices me. The front of his shirt is splattered with blood and there is some on his face and right hand, too.

"Jesus, Ravi. How long have you been standing there?"

"From the start." I take another step forward, then run to him.

When I reach him, I jump into his arms, knowing without a doubt he will catch me. And he does. I wrap my arms around his head, fingers frantically skimming the short hair, and slam my mouth to his.

"I love you," I whisper into his lips.

He squeezes me to his chest so tight, that I find it hard to breathe.

"I don't think love is a strong enough term to describe what I feel for you, Ravi," he says between the kisses. "I wish I could find the words to describe it. It's like a beautiful flame engulfing my heart, which has transformed into full-blown burning madness. Everything else is insignificant to its light."

"Then let's burn together," I utter and scrape my nails on the skin of his neck.

A low rumbling sound leaves Alessandro's mouth as he carries me across the room and places me on the big desk in the center of the room. He strips his suit jacket from my shoulders, then proceeds with tearing off the rest of my clothes until I'm sitting on the desk completely naked.

"So beautiful." He places his hand around my neck, stroking the skin there with his thumb, and I feel myself getting wet instantly. "And finally, only mine."

He keeps his palm on my throat while his other hand travels down my front, the tip of his finger tracing a straight line down my chest and stomach, then slides it into my pussy. A gasp leaves my lips when he curls his finger inside me.

"How does it feel to be only mine, Ravenna?" he asks while the hold on my neck tightens slightly.

I take a deep breath and lean forward, marveling at the feel of his hand pressing into my neck. "Like I'm finally free."

Alessandro's dark-blue depths peek into mine as he removes his finger from my pussy and lifts his hand to his mouth. His gaze doesn't waver as he licks my juices off his flesh.

"Each time I taste you, your nectar is sweeter," he says, staring at me like a hungry beast preparing to pounce. "I'm finding it really hard to decide whether I want to have you with my cock first, or with my mouth."

A shiver passes through my body. I place my hands on the collar of his bloody shirt and pull. The top two buttons fall to the floor while his hand again slips to my pussy, teasing at my entrance. I pull on his shirt again, ripping off another button, and revealing more of his inked chest. In response, the hold on my neck tightens just a fraction as the tip of his finger slides into me.

It's strange to go so slowly when thus far, our every encounter has been an explosive burst. Still, I find myself enjoying the look of restraint on Alessandro's face. I see the barely controlled frenzy in his eyes, and I know that he's struggling not to impale me with his cock right away.

Another button falls, and his finger slides a bit deeper.

"You seem to enjoy torturing me, Ravi," he rasps.

A small smile pulls at my lips. "I see you're playing along."

His finger slides in fully, making me gasp. My hands are trembling as I undo the last two buttons and move to the zipper on his pants.

"I need you to go faster, Ravi baby," he says as he presses his thumb over my clit. "Or I'm going to lose it."

"That's something I would very much love to witness," I say as I push his pants down his hips.

A growl leaves Alessandro's lips. His finger vanishes from my pussy in an instant, and his hand releases my neck. I let out a frustrated cry, which quickly transforms into a squeal as he grabs around my waist and turns me around.

"Bend your legs, baby, and kneel on the desk," he says while I dangle in the air.

I might be short, but I'm certainly not scrawny, and the way he's holding me like I'm a doll makes me so wet, it's embarrassing. But I nod and do as he says as he slowly lowers me to the desk's top.

"Lean forward and widen your legs so I have a better view of that sweet pussy."

I lower my chest and press my forehead to the wooden surface, an electric current running up my spine where Alessandro's palm travels up my back.

"Look how well we fit," he whispers as his hand comes around my neck. "Deep breath, Ravi."

I grab the edge of the desk and inhale, and Alessandro slides inside. His cock fills me, stretching me almost to the point where I can't take it anymore. My moans morph into screams of ecstasy when he starts slowly rocking his hips.

It's blasphemy. I'm kneeling on my dead husband's desk, getting beautifully fucked by the man who killed him. Only steps away from the still-warm body of our foe.

I don't care. God help me, but I don't care.

My body starts to shake, and I'm getting closer to the precipice each time Alessandro slams into me. The pressure builds under his steady rhythm until I feel myself becoming weightless and explode.

"The camera . . ." I say as Alessandro carries me toward the stairwell.

"Doesn't matter. No one is left alive to watch the video feed."

I tighten my arms around his neck and kiss him on his stubbled jaw. "So, what happened to the security guys at the guardhouse?"

He stops in the middle of the stairway and looks at me.

"They posed a threat to you, so they have been neutralized. I won't apologize for that."

A man of few words indeed. With that declaration, he resumes climbing the stairs.

Once we reach my bedroom, Alessandro sets me down on the bed, then walks to the foot of it and kneels on the floor.

"What are you doing?" I blink at him in confusion.

"Downstairs, that was me losing control." He wraps his hand around my ankle and lifts my foot to his mouth, placing a kiss on my sole. "Close your eyes, Ravi baby."

I let my eyes flutter shut and concentrate on his lips trailing soft kisses up my lower leg.

"And what is this?" I whisper.

"This . . ." He moves to my other leg, kissing the arch of my foot there, too. "This is me worshipping you."

Alessandro's palms slowly glide up my legs, inch by inch, followed by his lips trailing small kisses along the path—one on my right leg then on the left, the pattern repeating. When he reaches my inner thighs, I feel the mattress dip as he climbs onto the bed.

"Keep your eyes closed," he says in his rough voice, "and no peeking."

A kiss lands on my lower belly while his palms stroke the inside of my thighs.

I bite my lower lip and fist the bed sheet with my fingers. His hands glide up toward my pussy, while his mouth moves down at the same time. Kiss and stroke. Kiss and stroke. I wonder what will reach my core first—his hands or his mouth, and the sweet anticipation is just heightening my arousal.

His lips press to my clit at the same instant as his fingers come to my entrance. "Deep breath," he instructs.

I don't even need to do it consciously because his mouth

closes around my clit just as his finger enters me, and I gasp for air. Wetness seeps down between my butt cheeks as his warm tongue licks at my bud, his strokes hard but slow. His finger slides deeper, little by little. My already sensitive pussy aches with need, wanting more, but he is relentless. Such a sweet torture. Unhurried, methodical laps of his tongue, and then another finger plunges inside. My legs shake and my core clenches. I let go of the sheet and grab his hair instead, pulling his head more toward me.

Alessandro's lips press to my clit, and he starts sucking on it. Shivers shoot up my spine, all the way to the base of my skull. I arch my back and moan as the pressure in my core builds.

"Please," I pant. "I'll go mad."

"You won't," he mumbles into my pussy and resumes licking my clit, while his rough fingers slide in and out of me, sinking just a tiny bit deeper each time.

"Alessandro!" I yell, losing my composure.

He thrust his fingers in completely and sucks at my clit so hard that I burst into a million pieces the very next moment.

I'm still shaking from the aftershocks when he licks my pussy one last time and lifts his head.

"I'm not done, Ravi baby."

"What?" I choke out.

Placing a quick kiss on my pussy, he stands up and starts removing his clothes.

"Did you think that my mouth would be enough?" he crawls over my body and places his elbows on each side of my head, dipping his head toward me and ensnaring me in his dark-blue pools. "I could never get enough of you."

His gaze keeps mine as he slides his cock inside my molten core. I shudder.

"Sensitive?" he asks.

"A little."

Wrapping his arm around me, he rolls us until I'm on top of him. I rotate my hips slowly, loving the way it feels to have him under me like this. His cock is huge, filling me to the brim, and each little move ignites every one of my nerve endings. I revel as his hand travels up my stomach and chest to wrap around my neck.

"I'm so sorry," he says suddenly, his voice sounding broken.

"What for?"

Alessandro doesn't reply, only watches me with a strange look in his eyes. I lean a bit forward, and Alessandro lifts and places his other hand on my cheek.

"I love you, Ravenna. More than anything or anyone else I've ever loved," he whispers. "Please, remember that."

I don't understand why he sounds so . . . sad. Rocco is gone. We're finally free.

"What's going on?"

"Nothing, baby." His lips curve up into a small smile. "I just wanted you to know. That's all."

I keep riding him, marveling at the feel of his body under mine, while he keeps staring at my face, that sad smile ghosting his lips the entire time.

CHAPTER
Twenty-one

I PULL THE BLANKET UP TO COVER RAVENNA'S NAKED shoulder and sit on the edge of the bed, staring at the phone in my hand. Several scenarios were running through my head as I was lying next to Ravenna earlier, her head tucked into the crook of my neck. None of them were great, and each option seemed worse than the last. The moment I offed Pisano, I knew there were only two outcomes to this situation. Either I turn myself in—forfeiting my own life, or we run but, eventually, Ravenna will come to harm because of what I've done.

I find the name I'm looking for in my contacts list and dial. It's well after midnight, but he'll answer. No one calls the don at this time unless it's an emergency.

"What happened?" Salvatore Ajello's voice comes through the line.

"Rocco Pisano is dead," I say.

"Did the Serbs get him?"

"No. I did."

I've been working directly for the don for years, and he

gets me well enough to know that I wouldn't kill anyone without a reason. Especially a capo. But it doesn't change the fact that I did so without his approval. I went against the don and betrayed the Family. The punishment for that is death. And since he probably already knows what happened at the brunch party, including me and Ravenna kissing in front of everyone, he'll be coming after both of us.

Ajello remains silent, making panic rise in my chest. To keep Ravi safe, I wouldn't bat an eye over killing him, too. But I'm not sure I'll ever get that chance.

"Please." I close my eyes and squeeze the phone in my hand. "My life is yours. Just . . . let Ravenna go."

"Did he deserve it?" he asks.

"He deserved much more than what I served up."

Another pause. It probably lasts mere seconds, but it feels like eons to me.

"Are you at Rocco's house?" Ajello asks.

"Yes."

"The body?"

"In his office."

"All right. Listen to me very carefully, Zanetti. You have four hours to clean up your shit, then take your woman and be gone by five. Do you understand?"

He's letting us go?

"Do you understand, Zanetti?"

"Why?" I ask.

"You saved my wife's life. Now, I'm gifting you yours, so we're even. If I'll ever see you in my city again, you're dead."

"We'll be gone in four hours."

"Good. Make sure you cover your tracks, because if anyone connects you to this fucking mess, I'm giving my men the green light to come after both of you."

He disconnects the call, leaving me no doubt he means it.

I set down my phone and stare at it while the wheels in my brain begin to spin. A minute later, I dial another number.

"I need another body," I say as soon as Felix answers the call.

"What?! Are you insane? Do you know what time—"

"Stop talking, Felix. This is an emergency."

"Life and death?"

"Yes. I need a female body, black hair, twenties. Delivery location is New York, I'll send you the address."

"Fine. I'll have something for you next week."

"I need it delivered in three hours, Felix. Not a minute longer. And I need a car."

I cut the call and run out of the room to get my laptop and the blueprints for the mansion.

Planning a house fire that appears as if it was a gas leak and erasing all evidence of my involvement in about two hours is nearly impossible, but I don't have a choice. Even if the gas leak doesn't hold up, it won't matter as long as they believe that Rocco, Ravenna, and I died in the blaze.

I check the blueprints spread out on the floor next to the bed one more time, then glance at Ravenna. She's still soundly asleep.

"I'll make this work, Ravi."

Grabbing my laptop, I open up the video surveillance software and pull up the archived data files, finding the recording from the gate camera that shows my car when I left earlier today. The time log is for just after four in the afternoon. I edit the half-a-minute clip, switching it with a dummy video of the closed gate. Then, I skip ahead to when I snuck in and killed the two security guys at the guardhouse. I alter that part as well, along with a few frames where cameras caught me offing the rest of the guards.

It takes me almost two hours to edit every compromising frame. Since I already had several saved clips from various times in the day, it was a matter of finding suitable ones and manipulating the log entries before splicing the feeds, resulting in a clean continuous recording that shows me and Ravenna arriving at the mansion midafternoon, and then Rocco showing up at half past ten. With that done, I override all cameras between the front door and the gate to display a still image for the next two hours.

The first phase is done. Time to head downstairs to set up the stage for phase two.

The low rumble of the engines fills the night as I'm taking out the empty fuel canisters through the front door. A few seconds later, two black SUVs round the bend in the driveway and come to a stop near the front steps. The driver's door of the leading car opens and a man in his late forties exits. My body bag buddy from last week.

"Another delivery from Felix Allen," he says and walks up to open the vehicle's cargo area. "Female. Black hair. Died of natural causes. I couldn't get one in early twenties on short notice, so you got someone in their late thirties. Sorry."

"It'll work." I nod. There won't be much left of the body to identify anyway. If there is, I'll have Felix do his magic and alter the DNA test results to show a match.

"Tell Felix he owes me," the man says and throws me the car keys.

"There are two bodies by the gate and three more along the perimeter wall." I take out five diamonds from my pocket and hand them over. "Can you dispose of them for me?"

"Sure."

I watch as he pulls away in the other vehicle, then take the body bag out of the car and throw it over my shoulder.

Rocco and the body of the male from my SUV are already arranged in the kitchen. It might not be the ideal location, but the natural gas furnace is right underneath, so the kitchen will suffer the biggest damage when the heater explodes. I add the female's body to the scene, collect the body bag, and take it back out to the vehicle Felix's guy delivered. I shove the empty jerry cans into the cargo space, then transfer the stuff out of mine to the replacement SUV. When everything is done, I start the vehicle and turn on the heat, then head back inside the mansion to get Ravenna.

Ravenna

"Ravi."

I open my eyes and squint at Alessandro. He's crouching next to the bed and, although he looks tired, his eyes are sparking in the dim light.

"It's time to go, baby." He reaches out and brushes my cheek with the back of his hand. "I'll take your bag to the car."

"What's going on?"

A smile pulls at his lips as he leans forward to drop a quick kiss on mine. "In order for us to get away, we need to die first."

He collects his laptop and some papers off the floor and leaves the room.

As I'm descending the stairwell ten minutes later, I'm hit with a strong smell of gasoline. The odor is so overwhelming that my eyes begin to water and a sudden cough seizes my throat. I bury my face in the crook of my elbow and run across the entry hall as fast as I can to get outside.

Alessandro is standing by an unfamiliar black vehicle, holding the driver's door open for me. He has a gas mask around his neck, and in his other hand, he's holding a bottle with a rag sticking out of it.

"Drive to the gate and wait for me," he says. "I'll be there shortly."

"What are you going to do?"

"Looks like the guys who installed the new furnace for Rocco may have fucked up. There's a serious gas leak."

"When did it happen?"

"In about twenty minutes." He pulls the gas mask over his face and heads inside the mansion.

The last time I drove was a year ago when I borrowed the car from Melania to take my mom to see a doctor, so I need to concentrate on the controls. Creeping up to the gate, I decide to stop just at the bend in the road, which allows me to see both the estate entrance and the mansion's front doors. When I turn around to look through the rear window, Alessandro is nowhere to be seen. The bottle with the rag that he had in his hand is left on the driveway where the SUV had been.

I spend the next twenty minutes switching my gaze between the clock on the dash and the back window, waiting for Alessandro to come out. My patience is running thin and I'm considering going back to look for him when the front door opens and Alessandro steps out.

He casually strolls to the middle of the driveway, then stops and removes his face mask. My phone starts to ring. I answer the call while keeping my eyes on Alessandro, who is holding his phone to his ear.

"Cover your ears, Ravi baby," his voice comes through the line.

"Okay," I whisper and watch as he puts away his phone and bends to collect the Molotov cocktail off the ground.

My heart begins to gallop as he turns to face the house and takes something out of his pants pocket. I'm too far away to see what it was, but the tendril of flame that seems to spark from his hand lets me know that it's his Zippo lighter. He brings the bottle over the flame, lights the rag, and launches it at one of the house windows on the ground floor, breaking the glass.

Alessandro is already running toward the car when a thunderous boom reverberates through the air. As if I'm watching a scene from a Hollywood film, my eyes are glued to his huge form emerging from a cloud of smoke, while the flames at his back are rising toward the night sky, casting an orange glow on everything within the vicinity.

I yank on the door handle and get out of the car, wanting nothing more than to make sure he's okay, but I don't get a chance because the instant Alessandro reaches me, he pulls me into his arms and slams his mouth to mine.

"Would it be weird if I ask you to marry me the same night you became a widow?" he mumbles into my mouth.

"I don't know. Would it?" I laugh.

"Who cares? We're officially dead anyway." He leans away and fixes me with his gaze. "Will you marry me, Ravi baby?"

I take his lower lip between my teeth and bite it. "Yes."

267

epilogue

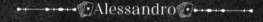

Alessandro

Two years later, a village near Le Puy-en-Velay, France.

BEEP.

My hand stills halfway to the toaster.

It's one of the alarms, signaling a perimeter breach. I have motion detectors everywhere, set up to create four concentric circles of security around our property. When triggered, it means someone has crossed one of the sensor boundary lines and is getting nearer.

I look toward the back deck where my wife is setting up for breakfast, whistling something to herself. Her mother and brother said they'd drop by later, but it's too early to be them.

Beep. Beep.

Two beeps mean the intruders have reached the second boundary. Based on how fast they are moving, it must be a vehicle.

"Ravi," I call as I slide open the drawer and take out my gun. "I need you to go upstairs, baby."

Ravenna stops what she's doing and looks over her shoulder. "Is something wrong?"

"Looks like we have some uninvited guests."

Having a fence around the property as well as cameras may be useful security measures, but I would never set these up around our home. My wife won't ever again feel like a prisoner whose every step is being watched. And anyone who wishes her harm would need to go through me first to reach her.

Ravenna leaves the plates on the table and heads inside the kitchen. Her long hair cascades like a shimmering black curtain down her back and bounces up a little with every step she takes. She rounds the breakfast bar separating the living area from the kitchen and comes to stand next to me.

Beep. Beep. Beep.

"Please," I say and nod toward the stairs leading to the loft.

She just smiles at me and reaches into the large decorative bowl on the counter, from which she takes out one of my other guns and cocks it.

"No," I growl.

Beep. Beep. Beep. Beep.

Fuck. They've crossed the last perimeter boundary.

"Ravenna."

She tilts her head to the side and places her palm on my cheek. "You'll never have to tread through the enemy lines alone, Alessandro. You taught me well." She lifts onto her toes and kisses my lips. "I'll be okay."

I never should have told her about my missions. Or trained her to shoot.

A car horn blares outside. The person behind the wheel doesn't seem to be satisfied with one honk and keeps hitting the thing in quick succession like a maniac. It's a combination of short and long honks, the pattern repeating in cycles.

"Perfect," I mumble and kiss my wife, then throw the gun back into a drawer. "You can put that away, baby."

"Someone you know?"

"Unfortunately."

I step through the front door and glare at the newcomer. There is only one person who'd come to my home and use his car horn as Morse code to relay a message. The message?

It's me, hi.

"Really, Belov?" I cross my hands over my chest.

"What? You're not a fan of pop-rock?" The blond man jumps out of his car and narrows his eyes at me. "How long has it been? Ten years? Man, you're old."

"Alessandro." Ravenna peeks from behind me. "Are you going to introduce your friend?"

"Yes, *Alessandro*. Won't you introduce us?" Belov smirks.

"That's Sergei Belov, baby. The guy who almost blew me up during a mission. Twice." I say, then look back at my ex-comrade. "What are you doing here?"

"We came for a visit."

"Who's 'we'?" I grumble.

The passenger door to Sergei's car opens and Felix Allen steps out. "It's business, not a social call. We're here for a return favor in lieu of payment for the services I've rendered."

"What services?" I ask.

Felix adjusts his glasses and reaches into his pocket, taking out a folded piece of paper. He clears his throat, then begins to read aloud.

"Obtaining several sets of top-of-the-line counterfeit documents. Hacking into federal, state, and local governments databases, and accessing-slash-deleting-slash-modifying various

records and information, hacking into law enforcement systems and appropriating confidential information"—he pauses and looks up at me before taking a deep breath and exhaling—loudly—as he proceeds—*"thirteen times. Locating and appropriating black market long-range weapons, falsifying or eliminating serial numbers, as needed. Setting up two offshore bank accounts and purchasing . . ."*

I can't help but roll my eyes at the drama queen, then wrap my arm around Ravenna's waist, placing my palms on her belly protectively. She's four months pregnant, but the bump is still barely noticeable. Meanwhile, Felix continues listing all the stuff he did for me over the years.

"That's the guy who helped you get out of Z.E.R.O.?" Ravenna whispers.

"Yup." I drop a kiss on the top of her head while Felix keeps yammering.

". . . blackmail, calling in favors from Yakuza, as well as two Camorra factions. Arranging the disposal of corpses on a regular basis, hiring then firing a very expensive hitman . . ."

"But he looks so . . . grandfatherly." She laughs. "If I saw him at a crosswalk, I would offer to help him across the street."

"He would probably bite off your hand. And him looking like a grumpy old man only makes him more dangerous."

". . . acquiring a body of unique characteristics, as well as incurring a storage expense until a set of delivery instructions were received, procuring another body under an extremely short timeline, and the cost of an orchid bouquet."

Felix puts the paper away and places his hands on his hips.

"Storage expense for a body?" I ask.

"Yes." He nods. "You requested a six-foot-seven specimen. I had to buy a larger fridge."

"And the bouquet?"

"My doctor said I needed to cut down on sugar intake. Guadalupe found the body when she was searching for my ice cream stash so I had to apologize for causing her distress."

I look at the heavens and shake my head. "What do you want?"

"I need you to accompany Sergei on a tiny private mission for me." He shrugs and brushes the nonexistent dust off his suit jacket. "Nothing too significant. Three days, maybe four, max."

"What kind of mission?"

"A rescue mission. A short trip to Mexico and back. It'll be a piece of cake, Az. I swear."

"I see. If it's an absolutely meaningless one, why can't Belov handle it himself?"

"The location is kinda guarded," the old man mumbles, avoiding my gaze.

"How many men?" I ask.

Felix shrugs but doesn't reply.

"A hundred and three," Sergei throws in and smiles. "It's my buddy Mendoza's compound. Hopefully, he won't realize it's me when we storm it."

"And your brother is okay with you invading his partner's location?"

"Not really." Sergei cringes. "Let's keep this on the down-low. Roman will lose his shit if he finds out."

Charming. "And who are we rescuing?"

"Kai Mazur," Felix says.

"Yeah." I snort. "Not happening."

"You owe me!"

"That man is seriously fucked-up, Felix. He will probably think we came to take him out and will try to kill us first."

"You always see the worst in people," Sergei pipes up. "Kai is a decent guy."

"*Kai is a decent guy?* If I remember correctly, you two tried to kill each other at least five times."

"A decent, fucked up guy?" he grins.

I pinch the bridge of my nose, barely able to believe this shit I'm hearing. It's true. Crazy people just gravitate to each other.

"Come on, Az," Sergei says. "We can't abandon him."

"All right, damn it."

A crunch to my right.

I snap my rifle toward the source of the sound, seeing that it's only a rodent scurrying amid the fallen leaves.

The air is heavy with humidity, making it hard to breathe, especially in full-gear tactical outfits and night vision equipment. I reposition, focusing my scope back on the wooden gate where two men are standing guard.

"That lunatic couldn't let himself get caught in a cooler climate, could he?" I grumble.

"I'm sure he'll be more considerate next time," Sergei says as he keeps twisting the wires on his self-made bomb.

"How the fuck did he get captured?"

"No idea. Felix thought Kai was dead until his name came up in a message he intercepted over one of the unofficial channels. Can you believe that old bastard still has a back door to Kruger's comms? Anyway, looks like the Mexicans had him for quite some time. Mendoza's son-in-law got arrested in the US last month, so they've offered up a swap—Kai for sonny-boy."

"How long is *some time*?"

Sergei finishes with the bomb and sets it down on the ground. "Three years."

"Three years? Jesus fucking Christ. Are you sure he's alive?"

"They would never kill him. Too valuable of a bargaining chip," he says and reaches for his sniper rifle. "But what state we'll find him in, that's the million-dollar question. Let's get closer."

We move closer to the gate and take cover behind a big bush. I keep the guards in my scope while Sergei takes out a small tablet device from his backpack and flips it open. "By the way, I saw the recording of your funeral. Beautiful service."

"Thank you."

"Do they still believe it was a gas leak?"

"Those who need to, yes." I nod toward the compound in front of us. "How many bombs did you set?"

"Twelve along the outside of the walls. Thirty-seven inside. Couldn't do any at the gate since it's guarded twenty-four seven." He hovers his finger over one of the keys on the keypad and takes the bomb he just made in his free hand. "Man, I love this shit."

He throws the bomb toward the gate. The thing lands between the two guards and explodes. A second later, a deafening boom fills the air as all the explosive devices Sergei had set detonate simultaneously. The ground shakes as if an earthquake has struck under our feet, sending dirt, wood, and building debris sky-high. I'm just waiting for the hellmouth to open and swallow us whole.

"You sure that's enough, Belov?" I ask sarcastically while a cloud of dust and smoke rises above the fifty thousand square feet of Mendoza's compound.

"It'll have to do," Sergei says. "Couldn't get more C4 on short notice."

It takes almost twenty minutes for the dust to settle enough for us to actually be able to see anything. The explosions knocked out the electricity and the entire football field-size compound falls into darkness, with the only light coming from a dozen or so fires that have sprung up in the area. The scene really does look like hell now.

"Now," I say and pull my bandanna over my mouth and nose, then head toward the gate.

Screams and cries echo all around as we walk among the demolished structures. An occasional gunshot adds to the cacophony as we off the survivors on our path. Everything, except for the huge hangar in the middle of the compound, lies in ruins. Several men are positioned at the entrance, their guns raised as they frantically search for incoming threats. I take out five as I approach on the right, while Sergei disposes of four more coming up from the other side.

"Back," he says and heads around the hangar as I continue walking toward the front entrance.

Three more guards jump out when I reach the hangar door, but I quickly take care of them and step inside.

It's obviously a storage facility, likely drugs since that's Mendoza's business, with crates piled on top of each other on all sides, almost reaching the ceiling. I turn right between two rows of containers, searching for hostiles. Several gunshots sound on the other side of the building as Sergei sweeps his flank. I reach the end of the row and turn into the next one.

I'm nearing the middle of the hangar when I hear Sergei's voice in my earpiece.

"Holy Mother Mary, Jesus, and Joseph," he chokes out. "East corner. Get your ass over here. Now, Az."

I turn left and hurry toward Sergei. He's crouching, holding a fluorescent light stick over something on the ground. I shift my NVDs up and approach, getting a closer look. The sight that greets me leaves me at a loss for words.

A man, barely skin and bones, is lying curled on the ground. His pants are torn and dirty, and what's left of his T-shirt is hanging like a rag over his chest. Every inch of the visible skin is covered with a layer of dried blood. His face is turned toward us, but if it wasn't for a shock of long matted hair, I never would have recognized him. The last time I saw Kai, he was about the same weight as me, but now he looks like a fucking skeleton.

"Is he alive?" I ask.

"Kind of. See if you can find anything to break that." Sergei nods toward the thick metal chain shackled around Kai's right leg and bolted to the wall.

I run toward the hangar entrance to get a bolt cutter and other tools I saw on a table close to the door, and hurry back. The skin around Kai's manacled ankle is raw. It's as if the crazy motherfucker tried to chafe his foot off to free himself.

"Hold him down," I say. "I don't want him going berserk thinking I'm an enemy."

"He's barely breathing, Az. I don't think he's capable of anything else."

I take a step forward and place the head of the bolt cutter around the chain, getting ready to make the cut, when a heel of a bare foot connects with my chin.

"Jesus fuck!" I snap. "I told you to hold him down, damn it!"

Sergei gets down on Kai, straddling him over the chest and grabbing his wrists. Kai lets out an animalistic roar and headbutts Belov so hard, Sergei's head snaps back.

"Shit." I reach into my jacket and take out a small plastic box with a syringe inside.

Felix got us the tranquilizer in case we'd have trouble overpowering Kai, but once I saw the state he was in, I didn't think it was necessary. The crazy bastard lives to prove people wrong. I uncap the needle and plunge the thing into Kai's thigh. He keeps thrashing around for several more seconds, trying to get a hit on Sergei's head before his body finally sags. Kai's eyes are vacant, silently staring off into the distance, but I notice his lips moving. I crouch next to him and bend low, trying to hear what he's saying, but the words don't make any sense.

"Are there tigers in Mexico?" I look at Sergei.

"Nope. Why?"

"I think he's delirious," I say. "He's calling for 'his tiger cub.'"

The End

Dear Reader

Thanks so much for reading Alessandro's and Ravenna's story! I hope you'll consider leaving a review, letting the other readers know what you thought of Burned Dreams. Even if it's just one short sentence, it makes a huge difference. Reviews help authors find new readers, and help other readers find new books to love!

The next book in the series is **Silent Lies,** which follows Sienna (Asya's sister) and Drago. This is a grumpy-sunshine, arranged marriage, age-gap story. I truly hope you'll like this couple because I enjoyed writing their story sooo much. They might seem like the absolute opposite at first glance, but I think this possessive, OTT, jealous man is the perfect match for Sienna.

NEXT IN THE SERIES

Drago & Sienna

There is only one punishment
For spies and liars,
A slow and painful death.

And my sweet, angelic wife,
Who bewitched everyone in my home,
From my men - even to my dogs,
Is the worst traitor of all.

I want to hate her,
But instead, I'm yearning to hear,
Every silent lie that leaves her irresistible lips.

SILENT
Lies
NEVA ALTAJ

About the author

Neva Altaj writes steamy contemporary mafia romance about damaged antiheroes and strong heroines who fall for them. She has a soft spot for crazy jealous, possessive alphas who are willing to burn the world to the ground for their woman. Her stories are full of heat and unexpected turns, and a happily ever after is guaranteed every time.

Neva loves to hear from her readers,
so feel free to reach out:

Website: www.neva-altaj.com
Facebook: www.facebook.com/neva.altaj
TikTok: www.tiktok.com/@author_neva_altaj
Instagram: www.instagram.com/neva_altaj
Amazon Author Page: www.amazon.com/Neva-Altaj
Goodreads: www.goodreads.com/Neva_Altaj

Made in the USA
Columbia, SC
29 July 2023

21028174R00161